The Moonlight Dreamers

The Moonlight Dreamers

SIOBHAN CURHAM

WALKER
BOOKS

This is a work of fiction. Names, characters, places and incidents are either the product of the author's imagination or, if real, used fictitiously. All statements, activities, stunts, descriptions, information and material of any other kind contained herein are included for entertainment purposes only and should not be relied on for accuracy or replicated as they may result in injury.

First published 2016 by Walker Books Ltd
87 Vauxhall Walk, London SE11 5HJ

2 4 6 8 10 9 7 5 3 1

Text © 2016 Siobhan Curham
Cover illustration © 2016 Kate Forrester

This book has been typeset in Berolina

Printed and bound in Great Britain by Clays Ltd, St Ives plc

British Library Cataloguing in Publication Data:
a catalogue record for this book is available from the British Library

ISBN 978-1-4063-6582-5

www.walker.co.uk

For Sara Starbuck, with infinite love and gratitude

"Yes: I am a dreamer. For a dreamer is one who can only find his way by moonlight, and his punishment is that he sees the dawn before the rest of the world." – Oscar Wilde

Chapter One

On the night it all began, a full moon hung over Brick Lane, casting everything in a pearly glow. The official reason Amber had come up to the roof garden was to sulk, but as soon as she caught sight of the moon her frown softened. It was so huge and appeared to be so close that she couldn't help reaching out, as if hoping to touch it. As she looked at her hand silhouetted against the pale light, a question popped into her head. *How many words has my hand written during the sixteen years I've been alive?* Amber was always being struck by random questions like this. She considered it a curse because they popped up at the most inappropriate moments – like that time during a history exam when there'd been a question about the last time Henry VIII visited the Tower of London. *What places have I already visited for the last time?* Amber immediately found herself asking, followed swiftly by: *What will be the last place I ever visit?* She'd then wasted about ten minutes of precious exam time mentally compiling lists of all the places she wished she'd visited for the last time – *school, crowded supermarkets on a Saturday, the dentist* – and some of the places she'd prefer to die – *on a chaise longue in Paris, smoking a long, thin cigar; riding a fairground carousel with the wind in her hair; tucked up in a four-poster bed listening to Billie Holiday.*

Amber dropped her hand into her lap and took a deep breath. The cool night air smelled of car fumes, fried onions and coriander. Way down below, the kitchens of the Indian restaurants that backed on to her house were a hive of activity. But Amber didn't mind the clattering of pans or the chefs yelling their orders in Bengali. She was so used to the nightly commotion that it felt soothing.

Then she heard her dad's voice cutting through the noise and instantly tensed. She could only catch odd words but she knew he was talking about her.

"Doesn't understand … responsibility … my career…"

Amber sighed. All Gerald ever thought about was his stupid career. Then came the gentle lilt of her other dad, Daniel. She couldn't make out a single word he was saying but she could guess. He would be smoothing things over, trying to make Gerald see that sometimes their daughter needed their time and attention – *like when she was taking part in a national debate for school!* But yes, of course, Gerald's career was of vital importance. And yes, of course, no one else could really understand the pressures facing an internationally renowned artist. Daniel was like the relaxation music played in health spas, but in human form. Amber loved him more than anything or anyone else in the entire world, and she was infinitely grateful that at least one of her dads cared, but sometimes she wished he wasn't quite so soothing. Sometimes – lots of times – she wished he would stand up to Gerald.

She heard a door closing downstairs. Gerald was probably retreating to his studio to lick his wounds. When he'd told her at dinner that he wouldn't be able to go to her debate because he'd been invited to a gallery opening in Prague, she'd accused him of being a self-centred despot. Despot had been her word of the day from Dictionary.com. It was like some spooky kind of word karma – as if Dictionary.com had known that Gerald was going to be particularly obnoxious that day. He'd actually choked on his salmon when she said it, his face flushing crimson. Then he'd flung down his knife and fork and started yelling. Gerald always yelled when he knew he was in the wrong – it was one of his worst traits. Usually Amber would yell right back but tonight she'd felt too close to tears, so she'd chosen to sulk on the roof garden instead.

It had been a totally rubbish day. That morning, for some bizarre reason (like she'd been up too late blogging the night before to remember to set it), her alarm hadn't gone off, so she hadn't had time to sculpt her hair into its trademark quiff. This meant she'd gone to school feeling as awkward and exposed as if she'd been wearing just her underwear – her most faded and frayed underwear. And school had been worse than ever – and not just because of her hair. In maths,

Mr Frasier (a definite despot if ever Amber saw one) had set a "surprise algebra test". Amber's first instinct had been to question his use of the word surprise. Surely surprises were meant to be good things – fun things – like "surprise parties" or "surprise winners". Shouldn't he have called it a "shock-horror algebra test" instead? But Amber had learned from past experience that Mr Frasier didn't take too kindly to having his teaching methods questioned, so she silently turned over her paper and was immediately plunged into alphabetic hell. This was what she hated most about algebra – the way it stole her beloved letters and twisted them into things that made her head ache. Maths was supposed to be about numbers – it should leave letters to writers who created beautiful things with them, not ruin them in nonsensical equations. At lunchtime, her head still aching from the test, she'd taken refuge in the library. But to her horror, almost as soon as she'd sat down, the library was invaded by the OMGs. The OMGs was Amber's name for the so-called cool girls in her year, the ones who starved themselves until their heads looked too big for their bodies and wore so much make-up their skin looked as if it had been painted on from a tin. The ones who said "OMG" practically every other word. They never normally set foot in the library at break. In their world, the library was a total no-go area because you couldn't smoke there, or talk loudly about boys. But today for some bizarre reason – maybe because they knew Amber was having such a crappy day and they wanted to make it even worse – they descended in a haze of celebrity-brand perfume and fake laughter.

"Is it true that you, like, dress in men's clothes when you're not in school?" an OMG called Chloe asked, coming to perch on the edge of Amber's desk.

Amber ignored her and carried on reading. This didn't deter Chloe, who draped herself across the desk as if she were modelling for a lingerie shoot. "Is it because your dads are, like…"

All of the OMGs fell silent at this point. Amber wanted to wail. They'd known for years now that her dads were gay. Why was it still an issue?

"My dads are like what?" she asked, still not looking up, even though the words in her book had all blurred into one.

"Gay," Chloe said, defiantly, as if she was telling Amber something she didn't already know.

"Why would my dads being gay make me want to wear suits?" Amber asked, immediately kicking herself for getting sucked into The Most Pointless Conversation in History.

"Well, has it, like, made you gay too?"

At this, Amber leaned forward in her seat and stared Chloe straight in the eyes. "I'm guessing by that logic that your mum and dad must be completely imbecilic then."

"What's that supposed to mean?" Chloe asked, her glossy mouth gaping open.

Amber hadn't hung around long enough to see her work it out.

Now she felt hot tears welling in her eyes. She blinked

them away and looked down at the book in her lap. She was not going to cry. No way. Today had been bad enough already. She opened her book. The only thing that could lift her from a gloom like this was a game of What Would Oscar Say? This was a game Amber had invented a couple of years ago, when she first discovered her writing hero, Oscar Wilde. Any time she was feeling down or angry or confused she would leaf through a book of his quotes and randomly pick one. His dry wit and sarcasm never let her down. Amber began flicking through the pages. She was sick of being on her own all the time. She was sick of feeling like the odd one out. She craved excitement and adventure. She needed to change her life. But how? She stopped flicking and looked down at the page. Her eyes were drawn to a quote:

"Yes: I am a dreamer. For a dreamer is one who can only find his way by moonlight, and his punishment is that he sees the dawn before the rest of the world."

Amber let the words wash over her. This was how letters should be arranged, in a way that actually made people stop and think, that made them feel better about themselves. She shouldn't feel bad about being different. She should feel proud. She shouldn't feel bad about dreaming of something better. Amber looked up at the moon. It seemed to be glowing brighter than ever, as if it was shining just on her.

Amber felt a strange sensation, as if the moon was waiting

for her to realize something. She leaned back and gazed into the darkness. So what if she wasn't like any of the other girls at school? So what if her dad was a self-centred despot? She was a dreamer – a moonlight dreamer. Just like Oscar Wilde. Amber put down her book and went over to the edge of the roof garden. Below, a stream of people was winding its way towards the food trucks in the courtyard of the Old Truman Brewery. To her right, the lights of Brick Lane stretched out like a jewelled scarf. For the first time all day, Amber felt a prickle of hope. She was in the heart of London, surrounded by millions of people. Surely there must be other people like her out there somewhere. Other people who didn't fit in, or want to fit in. Other people who craved excitement and adventure. Other moonlight dreamers.

Chapter Two

Maali hurried along Brick Lane towards TAJ's Store, mentally reciting the list of groceries her mum had asked her to get. *Gram flour, paprika, two bunches of coriander and ... what was the other thing?* Her mind went blank for a second. *Ah yes, coconuts.* Maali grinned as she thought of what it was for. Her mum's coconut burfi was the finest in all of London – probably the UK. People came from all over to buy sweets from their Indian confectionery store, and the melt-in-the-mouth burfi was the best seller by far.

Maali checked for traffic, then crossed the narrow road. The cobbled pavement on the other side was glimmering from the earlier rain. Although it was almost eight o'clock at night, everything seemed unusually bright. Maali glanced up and saw a huge full moon overhead. She reached into her coat pocket for her phone. She'd never seen the moon so big. She stopped beside the mosque. The moonlight was causing the mirror-tiled minaret to glisten like a magician's wand. It was breathtaking. Maali clicked on the camera and adjusted the zoom until she had the perfect shot. But just as she took the picture, a group of City businessmen barged past, jolting her arm.

"Hey!" Maali looked at the men crossly, then quickly looked away. She could tell from their flushed faces and bloodshot eyes that they'd been drinking.

"Whassup?" one of them asked, leering down at her.

"I was trying to take a picture," Maali muttered, stuffing her phone back into her pocket.

"And?" the man challenged. His breath was hot and reeked of sour alcohol.

"Don't piss her off, Dave," another man said with a snigger. "She might issue a fatwa."

Maali glared at him. *Actually, I'm not Muslim, I'm Hindu,* she wanted to yell. But what was the point? In his ignorant mind they were probably the same. She lowered her gaze and hurried off. The men's coarse laughter echoed after her. As she approached TAJ's she ran through her list again. *Gram flour, paprika, two bunches of coriander* ... then stopped. Further along the Lane, stomping its feet on the pavement outside the Truman Brewery, was a unicorn! Maali blinked to check she wasn't seeing things, but the unicorn was still there. Its coat was snowy white and a long, cone-shaped horn protruded from the centre of its forehead. She had to get a picture of it – and this time no one was going to stop her.

As she raced towards the brewery, Maali couldn't stop grinning. This was what she loved about living on Brick

Lane – you never knew what surprise you'd come across next. Of course, it hadn't always been like this. When she was little it had been dull and dreary – endless curry houses and leather jacket shops and grotty clothes factories tucked away in the basements and backstreets. But then the artists had moved into Shoreditch, and almost overnight they'd transformed the rundown brewery and surrounding neighbourhood into a magical world where almost anything could happen: random fashion shoots, impromptu gigs, graffiti art that was so beautiful it ought to have been hanging in a gallery. And now, a unicorn.

Of course it wasn't really a unicorn. As Maali got closer she saw that it was a white horse with a fake horn attached to its head. But it still looked incredible. A teenage boy was holding the horse's reins while beside him a trendy-looking woman with purple hair was talking to a trendy-looking man with blue hair. As Maali drew level with them she got her phone out. She would pretend to send a text and quickly take a picture instead. She glanced at the horse. Close up, it was huge. The horse bowed its head and looked at her for a second, then snorted. Curls of steam spiralled from its nostrils into the cold night air. Maali grinned as she thought of what her brother, Namir, would say when she told him there'd been a unicorn on their street. Namir was only seven and he was mad about fantasy stories. She had to get a picture or he'd never believe her.

"All right?"

Maali jumped. The boy holding the horse was speaking to her. She felt her face start to burn in that annoying way it did whenever a boy so much as looked at her.

"Hi," she muttered.

"The things I have to do," the boy said, shaking his head. Maali had just enough time to notice that he was grinning and his brown eyes were twinkling before she looked back at the ground.

"What are you doing?" she muttered, curiosity outweighing her shyness.

"I'm making sure Snowy doesn't bolt while these eejits decide which is his best side." He lowered his voice. "They're from the Chill Bar. They're doing a promotional video for a new cocktail, the Velvet Unicorn." He shook his head again, but his eyes were smiling.

"But where" – Maali stared up at the horse – "where's he from?"

"The City Farm, round the corner," the boy replied. "That's where I work, isn't it, Snowy?" He scratched the horse under the chin. It gave him an affectionate nuzzle. Maali smiled. It still looked magical, standing there in the moonlight.

"Would it be OK if I took a picture?" she asked shyly. "For my little brother, I mean. He loves unicorns."

The boy grinned. "Of course."

"Right, Adam, we've decided to take the horse into the courtyard," the woman said, turning to face them. Her purple hair was cut into a razor-sharp bob and her eyes were heavily lined in black. She was the kind of woman who made Maali long for the power of invisibility – the kind of woman who could freeze you to the spot with just one stare.

"Ash," the boy replied.

The woman frowned. "What?"

"My name's Ash – short for Ashley."

"Oh." She looked and sounded completely uninterested. "Can you just bring him through for us?"

"Sure, but…" Ash looked at Maali. "What's your name?" he whispered.

"Maali," she whispered back.

"Maali would just like to take a quick picture first."

The woman raised one of her thin, pencilled-on eyebrows. "Who?"

"Maali." Ash nodded at Maali.

The woman looked her up and down and then looked away, as if summing her up and discarding her all in one second. "Well, I don't think we've really got time for—"

"Go on," Ash said, smiling at Maali, and he stepped back, out of the way.

Maali flicked to the camera on her phone and crouched down. She knew instinctively that the "unicorn" would look even more impressive photographed from below.

"We really do need to get a move on," the woman said.

Maali centred the shot.

"Come on!" the woman said, barging past and knocking Maali's arm.

The picture was a blur.

Ash shrugged helplessly and tightened his hold on the reins. "Well, it was nice meeting you," he said.

"Yes. You too," Maali muttered. She managed to maintain eye contact for a second before looking down at Ash's feet. He was wearing scuffed black boots, the kind that bikers and rock stars wear.

"You should come and see us at the farm some time. Old Snowy here seems to have taken quite a shine to you!"

Maali looked up to see the horse gazing down at her. "Yes." She searched for something else to say but all the words in her brain had decided to hide.

"See you around, then," Ash said.

"Yes. See you."

Ash made a clicking sound with his tongue and led the horse away.

Maali stood watching them until the *clip-clop* of Snowy's feet faded into the distance.

This was what Maali loved the most about life: one moment you could be popping out to get some groceries and the next, somehow everything had changed. She wished she could bottle this tingling feeling and apply it like a perfume any time she wanted. With a sigh, she turned and headed back to TAJ's Store. *Gram flour, paprika, two bunches of coriander and coconuts. . .*

Chapter Three

"Tonight I'm going to read a brand-new poem. It's called 'The Day My Womb Died'."

As Sky watched the woman at the microphone she felt as if her stomach had turned to lead.

"It's based on my life with my ex-husband," the woman continued. Her hair was dyed a carrot-orange and in the heat of the basement her eyeliner had smudged into big black rings. If a fashion editor had to name her look they'd probably call it the Punk Rock Panda. Sky gripped her mug of ginger tea. Coming to the Poetry Café was supposed to have been a lifeline, wrenching her day from the jaws of disaster. On the tube to Covent Garden she'd imagined a night of poetic inspiration, the air filled with thought-provoking metaphor and soothing verse. So far there had been a ranty poem about war that had gone on for twenty-two minutes, a cringily erotic poem from a woman who looked old enough to be her grandma, and now this. Sky took a deep breath. Maybe the poem wouldn't be as bad as the title…

"To have and not to hold," the Punk Rock Panda began. "Our marriage left me cold."

Sky closed her eyes.

"In sickness and in health.
You slept with her in utmost stealth."

Sky bit her lip to keep from groaning. Then she opened her eyes and glanced around the room. There were only four other people there. She hadn't minded this too much at first – she was still buzzing from the fact that she was here, in the Poetry Café, in the heart of London, all by herself at the age of sixteen. It should have been brilliant. It should have been one of the best, most exciting nights of her life. It should have taken her mind off the fact that, right at this moment, her dad was playing happy families with his dumb new girlfriend and her even dumber daughter. But instead…

"Till death us do part.
The only death around here is my heart
And my womb – as dead as a tomb."

Sky watched as the woman wrestled the microphone from the stand and took a step towards the audience. There was no point, really – the room was so small, if she took another step she'd be sitting in their laps. The ranty war poem man in the front row recoiled.

"I divorce you! I divorce you! I divorce you!" the woman screamed at the audience.

Sky felt the sudden and completely overwhelming urge to laugh. It started in the pit of her stomach and worked its way into her chest. She mustn't laugh! She didn't want anyone to ask her age and, besides, the woman looked terrifying. Sky bit her tongue, but the laughter was massing at the back of her throat now, threatening to explode at any moment. *Think of something sad!* she told herself. So she thought of her mum. And the words "cancer", "malignant" and "inoperable". As always, it did the trick. Her laughter shrank like a burst balloon and Sky leaned back in her chair.

"OK, well – er – thank you, Sister Dignity," the host said, swiftly taking the mic from the woman and placing it back on the stand. "Now, would anyone else like to read?" She looked into the audience and her eyes met Sky's. *Oh no*, Sky thought, but then to her complete surprise, she heard herself say, "Yes, please."

Everyone turned to stare at her. Somehow, Sky got to her feet and, somehow, she made it to the microphone. She'd never read her poems in public before. Ever. The only person in the world she'd ever read them to was her dad – in the snug privacy of their houseboat. Now here she was, in the poetry capital of the capital, about to read some of her work to a basement full of strangers. OK, a handful of strangers. But still…

Clenching her hands together, Sky plucked up the

courage to look at the audience. The Punk Rock Panda was quietly sobbing in the back corner. The man in the front row was gazing into his lap. Only the snowy-haired lady was looking at her – giving her an encouraging grin. Sky smiled back weakly and took a deep breath.

"Ladies and gentlemen," the host announced into the microphone, "please welcome…" She broke off and looked at Sky. "What's your name?" she whispered.

Sky's mouth was suddenly so dry it felt as if it were coated with flour. "Oh, er…" For a moment her mind was paralyzed with fear, then adrenalin kicked in. "Halo," she said. Halo was the pen name she used when she posted her poems online. It was also the nickname her dad had given her mum. As soon as she thought of her mum she felt the usual warm sensation around her like an aura. *Are you there?* The warmth grew. Sky smiled and felt herself relax. "I'd like to read a poem called 'Do They Have Daisies in Heaven?'"

The room fell silent. Sky took a deep breath.

"When I was little, we made daisy chains,
out in the woods where sunlight fell like glitter…"

And as she read her poem the strangest thing happened. It felt just like it did when she was writing. Everything else fell away – all the stress about her dad and his new girlfriend and her stupid daughter, and the fact that she was reading in public. None of that mattered any more; all that mattered were the words. All that *existed* were the words. And then, before she knew it, she'd reached the end.

"I wish I'd made a chain so long it still bound us together. Do they have daisies in heaven?"

There was a moment's silence in which Sky hurtled back to reality, no longer immersed in the private woodland world of her poem. The man in the front row brought his chunky hands together and clapped. Really loudly. Then he let out a cheer. And then all the others were clapping too – even the Punk Rock Panda at the back. Although there were only four of them, the applause echoed right through Sky, making every cell in her body dance.

"Thank you," she whispered into the microphone. "Thank you."

Her body was still humming from the applause as she made her way back to the station twenty minutes later. She'd given her first ever poetry performance – in the Poetry Café in Covent Garden! Sky felt inspired, empowered, alive. She also felt starving! She noticed a tiny shop to her right. The steamy window was lined with shelves of pizza. She slipped inside and bought a huge slice of margherita. The cheese was bright yellow and rubbery, but Sky didn't care. It smelled delicious. As she left the shop and carried on walking she heard the sound of a guitar. She let the melody carry her right past the entrance to the station. A busker had set up on the edge of Leicester Square. He was tall and thin and wore a scuffed leather jacket, faded jeans and cowboy boots. He looked as if he'd stepped straight out of an eighties rock video. Everyone was rushing by him, to and from the cinemas, restaurants and bars, but Sky felt compelled to stop and watch. Something about the attentive way he played his guitar and the heartfelt tone of his voice was captivating. As the song built to a crescendo, Sky wanted to throw her head back and sing along. Instead, she took another bite of pizza and looked up at the sky. A huge, silvery moon shone down on the square like a spotlight. Words started to pop into her mind. *Glimmering. Luminous. Shimmering. Lunar. Lovely. Opalescent. Pearly. Giant. Glitterball.* She knew that if she waited long enough, those words would organize themselves into a poem. But she didn't want to miss the end of the song, so she took another bite of pizza and filed the words away to the back of her mind for later. Sky had always felt sorry for buskers when they didn't have an audience, but as she watched the man crooning each word as if he were singing to a lover, she realized something really important for the very first time: as long as you were doing what you loved, it didn't really matter how many people were listening.

DO THEY HAVE DAISIES IN HEAVEN?
BY SKY CASSIDY

When I was little, we made daisy chains,
out in the woods where sunlight fell like glitter.
"I crown you Princess Wood Nymph!" you cried
as you placed your delicate chain on my head.
"And I crown you Queen Petal-Face Buttercup!"
    I said
as I placed my chain around your lily-white neck.
That afternoon, the world was one big fairytale,
our lives an endless happily ever after.
Little did I know it was the beginning of the end,
our own "once upon a nightmare".
I wish I'd never stopped picking those daisies.
I wish I'd made a chain so long it still bound us
    together.
Do they have daisies in heaven?

Chapter Four

If tonight had a hashtag, Rose thought to herself, it would be #OMG for sure, for the cringey way her mom, Savannah, was acting like a little girl, giggling and tossing her long blonde hair, and the mega-cringey way her mom's stupid new boyfriend, Liam, was acting like he was Rose's new best friend. If she had to give Liam a hashtag it would be #loser.

She pushed her plate away and studied her nails, and the black polish chipped at the edges. Savannah had told her to repaint them for dinner. Rose had point-blank refused. It was bad enough she'd had to come to this stupid dinner – Liam's stupid daughter, Sky, hadn't even bothered to turn up!

"So, tell me, Rose, what do you want to do when you get out of school?"

He was Irish as well. An Irish yoga teacher. #OMG right there. Weren't Irishmen supposed to be construction workers? Or banjo-playing folk musicians? What the hell was he doing being a yoga teacher?

"She wants to go into modelling, just like her mom," Savannah said, her southern drawl as soft as honey. At least, that's how the gushing magazine interviewers always described it.

"Really?" Liam looked at Rose. His eyes were bright blue. Too bright. She didn't like the way they pierced right through you.

Rose shrugged. "I guess."

"What do you mean, you guess?" Her mom's face switched into one of her you'd-better-not-be-messing stares. If she hadn't just had a Botox refresher it would have been a full-on frown.

Rose returned it with an I-don't-care stare of her own.

"I mean, I *guess* I want to be a model."

"Ah, sure, you're still very young," Liam said with a smile. "There's plenty of time to decide."

I'm not very young, I'm sixteen! Rose wanted to yell at him, her list of anti-Liam hashtags growing by the second. "Whatever," she muttered instead.

Why couldn't Savannah see what was going on? Liam had no money. He lived on a boat, for chrissakes! He was some broke Irish hippy who was looking for a meal ticket. Why couldn't Savannah see that he was only interested in her money? Why couldn't she stay single for more than a day? Why did Rose's dad have to leave them? Why did he have to go back to America with his stupid girlfriend? Why? Why? Why?

"I think I might go do some homework," Rose mumbled, dangerously close to tears.

"But you've barely touched your dinner," Liam said.

"She's got a casting at the weekend, haven't you, darling," Savannah said.

Liam looked blank. "A casting?"

Savannah nodded, her emerald green eyes wide with pride. "Yes, for an ad campaign for H&M. It's her first official casting, it could be her big break." She smiled at Rose, the same dazzling smile that had launched a hundred lipsticks and lit up the covers of a thousand magazines.

Rose looked away. She felt a strange mixture of anger and adrenalin building inside of her. It made her want to run out of the house and keep on running. For ever.

"But…" Liam said.

Rose and Savannah looked at him.

He shook his head. "Nothing."

"Please may I be excused?" Rose muttered.

"OK," Savannah said with a sigh. "But first we have something to tell you. Liam and I – well – we've decided that…" She paused and looked at Liam. He reached across and took hold of her hand. "Liam's moving in." Savannah's smile was so wide now it was practically splitting her face in two.

"What?" Rose's head filled with confusion. They'd only been together for a few months. Why was he moving in? And how could Savannah tell her like this, with him sitting right in front of her? "But…" Rose searched for some reason why this couldn't happen, some kind of small print. She turned to

Liam. "What about your houseboat? What about Sky?"

"Sky's moving in too," Savannah said joyfully, like she was announcing that Santa had just been.

"I'll probably let the boat out, to earn a bit of money," Liam added with a grin. He looked like the cat who'd just got the cream – or the cat who'd just got the Hampstead mansion.

Rose was so angry she could barely breathe. "How much money do you get from letting out a boat?" she asked.

"Well, I'm not sure yet," Liam said.

"How much did you pay for this place, Mom?" Rose turned to her, angry tears stinging the corners of her eyes.

"That's completely irrelevant, Rose." Savannah's voice was tight now too. They were suddenly playing a game of emotional chess. "This isn't about money, sweetie – it's about love."

Checkmate.

Rose knew that if she tried to speak, a sob would burst out, so she got to her feet instead. She ran from the room, along the echoey hall, through the huge front door and down the steps. She ran until she got to the Heath. She didn't care that it was dark and she'd been told countless times not to go there at night. She just kept on running until her legs were heavy and her lungs felt as if they'd caught on fire. She hated everyone and everything, but she especially hated adults and the way they could destroy your life with just one sentence. Her dad had done it when he'd told her he needed to be with Rachel. And now her mom had done it with "Liam's moving in." Liam and his stupid hippy daughter with her stupid hippy name and curly hair and floaty dresses.

Finally, Rose collapsed on the grass. It was still wet from the rain, but she didn't care. She didn't care about anything any more. She lay down and closed her eyes. Her heart was pounding so hard it felt as if her ribcage might explode. Her entire life sucked! What was she going to do?

She opened her eyes and gasped. A full moon was suspended in the sky. She'd never seen one so huge. It reminded her of the nursery rhyme her dad used to sing to her: "Hey diddle diddle, the cat and the fiddle, the cow jumped over the moon." In her book of rhymes, the picture of the moon had been as huge as the one above her now and it had a smiley face. Rose would snuggle into her dad as he read to the end of the rhyme: "The little dog laughed, to see such fun, and the dish ran away with the spoon." She'd always giggled at the illustration of a dish and spoon running away together on spindly legs. Now though, she started to cry. Why did life have to be so hard? She looked back at the moon, the tears in her eyes making it blur even bigger. *Please, please, let something good happen*, she begged.

EPIPHANIES

Regular readers of this blog will know that I've been fed up with my life for aaaaaaaaaages. (If you aren't a regular reader of this blog then you might want to read my recent posts, "I'm a Teenager – Not a Celebrity Clone", "Where are our Heroines?" and "Is My Life Over Before It's Even Begun?" to get up to date.)

But this week, I had what Dictionary.com would call an "epiphany". Well, actually, I had two epiphanies:

Number one: Some people will always disappoint you.

Number two: Your dreams are like guiding stars. They help you get out of the most boring and unhappy situations. All you have to do is follow them.

Here are this week's Wilde Words from my hero, Oscar Wilde. Use them wisely:

"Yes: I am a dreamer. For a dreamer is one who can only find his way by moonlight, and his punishment is that he sees the dawn before the rest of the world."

Amber

Chapter Five

It was Saturday morning and Daniel was cooking blueberry pancakes. Blueberry pancakes were Amber's all-time favourite breakfast and Daniel always made them when he knew she needed cheering up. Gerald had gone to Prague. He'd missed Amber's debate and he'd missed her tying the opposition in verbal knots. But Amber didn't care – Daniel had been there, and he'd looked so proud when she delivered her final, killer line, it had almost made her heart burst.

"Maple syrup?" Daniel asked as Amber took a seat at the kitchen table.

"Please." She poured herself a glass of juice.

"Are you working all day today?" Daniel asked, rooting around in the cupboard for the syrup.

"Yep. Till five."

Every Saturday, Amber worked in a vintage store called Retro-a-go-go on Brick Lane. It was a treasure trove of old clothes, books and records and it was one of her favourite places in the entire world.

"I was wondering if you'd like to go out somewhere afterwards."

Daniel came over and placed the bottle of maple syrup on the table in front of her. He wore his usual Saturday morning outfit of pyjama bottoms and hooded sweatshirt. Although he'd just turned forty, with his chiselled bone structure and thick gold hair he still looked young. Unlike Gerald, Amber thought unkindly. Gerald was almost twenty years older than Daniel, with receding white hair and a growing paunch. She often wondered if Daniel ever regretted being with Gerald, and more recently, in her lowest moments, she had taken to fantasizing that one day he'd tell her he'd had enough of Gerald's diva strops too and that he and Amber were moving out. Her last fantasy had a new twist – Daniel telling her that he was her biological father and she never had to see Gerald again.

"We could see a movie," Daniel continued. "The new Woody Allen's on at the Curzon."

That was another clue in the list of evidence Amber had been compiling as proof that Daniel was her biological dad – they both loved movies. Gerald wouldn't even set foot in a cinema. "Why would I settle for cheap celluloid imitation when I can experience the blood and guts of theatre?" he would cry whenever they invited him to join them.

"That would be great," Amber said now with a grin.

Her stomach gave an appreciative rumble as Daniel brought over a plate of pancakes. Thin ribbons of steam curled off the edges and a pool of melted butter had formed in the centre.

"Are you sure you're OK?" Daniel asked, sitting down at the other side of the table. "About Gerald – you know..." His green eyes filled with concern. Daniel's eyes were another piece of evidence, as she had green eyes too. They'd said they'd never tell her which of them was her biological dad; they said she didn't need to know because they both loved her as their own. But it didn't matter – the evidence was undeniable.

"I'm fine," Amber said breezily, and she almost meant it. She still felt a faint dull ache when she thought of Gerald missing her moment of glory, but it was nothing she hadn't dealt with before, and anyway, today was a work day *and* it was the day she would put her plan into action. Amber smiled as she thought of the cards in her bag. It had taken her all week to get the wording right, but finally she was happy with it.

"That's good," Daniel said with a relieved grin, and they both dug into their pancakes.

Outside it was one of those golden autumn days, when the world looked as if it had been painted in oils. As Amber walked along Hanbury Street, the bright sunshine perfectly matched her mood. Ever since she'd had the idea for the Moonlight Dreamers she'd felt a weight lifting. The tension of feeling that she was stuck in the wrong place eased just knowing that she might finally have found an escape. But who would she ask to join her? Determined to be selective, she'd printed only a handful of cards. As Amber turned on to Brick Lane, a road sweeper trundled past with his cart. Every week, Friday night swept in, bringing with it a wave of clubbers and party-goers, and swept out leaving a flotsam and jetsam of beer bottles, chip wrappers and cigarette butts. "Flotsam and jetsam" was one of Amber's favourite phrases – it sounded like the name of a comedy duo. She was wondering where the words had originally come from, when the door to the flat above the Indian sweet shop burst open and a girl came rushing out. She was wearing a silky kaftan over silky trousers covered in beautiful swirls of deep green and blue. It reminded Amber of a peacock's feathers. Was the girl going to the mosque? Were Muslim girls allowed in a mosque? She'd only ever seen men and boys coming out of the one on Brick Lane. A flurry of questions about life as a Muslim girl started crowding Amber's mind.

Then, suddenly, the girl stopped and crouched down by the kerb. Amber slowed her pace to watch. The girl took a phone from her pocket and took a picture of whatever was on the ground in front of her. Amber drew level and had to bite her lip to stop herself gasping in surprise. The girl was taking a picture of a dead pigeon. Thankfully, its pale grey body was intact. In fact, it looked as if it was just sleeping.

"Oh – I—" the girl stammered as she noticed Amber. "I was just – it just looked so…"

"Peaceful," Amber murmured, gazing down at the bird.

"Yes." The girl stuffed her phone into her pocket and got to her feet. She had pale brown skin and huge dark eyes, as shiny as conkers.

"Here, take this," Amber said, holding out one of the cards.

The girl stared at her for a moment before taking it. "What is it?" she asked.

"You'll see," Amber called over her shoulder as she strode off down the street.

Chapter Six

Embarrassment rooted Maali to the spot. What must she have looked like? Like a weirdo who went around taking pictures of dead things, that's what. Her face began to burn. Sometimes she wished she didn't get such strong urges to take photos. But it was a reflex, and the thought of being able to capture a picture of death, and death looking so, well, so *peaceful*, had been too tempting. What must the girl have thought of her? Maali sighed. The girl had looked really cool, with her quiffed black hair and her bright green eyes. It wasn't the kind of cool that made Maali feel intimidated; it was the kind she admired. She loved what she'd been wearing too: a pinstriped suit, complete with a silver pocket watch on a chain and polished brogues. Maali imagined taking a photo of her leaning against a brick wall, looking at the pocket watch. Huh, some chance of that happening. Why, oh why, did the girl have to find her hunched over taking pictures of a dead pigeon? But she'd said she thought the pigeon looked peaceful too, and had given her a card. Maali snapped out of her embarrassed trance and looked down at it.

Maali reread the card to make sure her eyes weren't playing tricks on her. Usually when girls gave out cards on Brick Lane they were for clothes sales. She had never seen anything like this before. What did it mean? And what did the quote mean? *Was* she a Moonlight Dreamer?

She *was* sick of being told how to look, or at least she was sick of people judging her for how she looked. And she definitely got fed up with being told what to do all the time.

She wasn't sure what an "imbecile" was, but she definitely had moments when she felt as if her class was full of fakes. Did she dream of freedom and adventure, though? She certainly loved to daydream. In fact, if it weren't for her daydreams, she would probably find the endless routine of school, working in the shop and helping take care of Namir pretty dull. But was she a Moonlight Dreamer?

She studied the quote and, as she tried to picture herself "finding her way by moonlight", thought back to the night earlier that week when there'd been the huge full moon, which had cast everything in its magical glow. Then she thought of the "unicorn" and twinkly eyed Ash, and she got that tingly feeling again. She looked along Brick Lane. In the pale morning light it looked so drab and tired, as if the street itself were suffering from a hangover. *Was* she a Moonlight Dreamer? Even though she still didn't quite know what the quote meant, she had the sneaking suspicion that she was.

Sky raised the axe above her head and brought it crashing down onto the log. The wood fractured into splintery lumps. Normally it took a few attempts to get a log to split, but this morning, raw fury seemed to have given her a Goliath-like strength. Her dad wanted to move in with *that woman*. He wanted to rent out their boat – *their home* – and move into her soulless show-house in Hampstead. How could he? Sky brought the axe down again and pieces of wood went flying all over the grassy canal bank.

"Jesus, has someone been putting steroids in your porridge?"

Sky refused to turn round at the sound of Liam's voice. How could he joke at a time like this?

"I bet you won't miss all the wood-chopping once we've moved," he carried on, clearly completely oblivious to her pain.

"How do you know what I'm not going to miss?" She turned on him, eyes blazing with anger. "For your information, I'm not going to miss anything because I'm not going to leave. If you want to live with that brain-dead idiot, go ahead, but I'm staying here."

They stood on the bank of the canal staring at each other. Sky had never spoken to her father like this before. He was so mellow and easy-going, it had been impossible to get mad at him – until he met *that woman*. Since he'd become Savannah Ferndale's personal yoga trainer he'd lost the ability to think straight. OK, she was incredibly beautiful, but he'd had incredibly beautiful and well-known clients before. What made Savannah so special? It was like she'd cast a spell on him.

"I'm not leaving you here," Liam said, finally breaking the silence.

Sky looked at him hopefully. Was he starting to see how crazy his plan was?

"It'll be good for you, being part of a family again."

"What?" Sky stared at him. Was he out of his mind? "They

aren't my family. You're my family. You and Mum."

Her dad flinched. He took a deep breath and ran his hand through his wild blond hair. "Your mam's dead, Sky," he said quietly. "She's been dead five years – we need to move on."

Sky was engulfed by a sudden wave of sorrow. She'd learned long ago that when you lost a person, you didn't just lose them on the day they died, you lost them every day all over again in moments like this.

"I don't want to move on," she stammered. "Not if it means moving in with *them*."

Liam took a step towards her. His eyes were glassy with tears. "I want you to have a proper home," he whispered.

"I do have a proper home." She pointed to the boat. "This is my proper home – *our* proper home."

"It's a boat," he said. "A boat that's about to get feckin' freezing all through the winter. I don't want you living somewhere like this. I want you living somewhere you don't have to chop wood or clean out the toilet. I want you to live somewhere with – with…" he looked all around, as if searching for the right word … "radiators."

"Somewhere with *radiators*?" Sky echoed incredulously.

"Oh, jeez, you know I'm no good with words." He looked at her hopefully. "I want you to be safe and warm."

"And what about my happiness?" Sky muttered sullenly.

He stared at her for a moment. "What about *my* happiness?" he finally replied.

Sky frowned. "What do you mean?"

He took a deep breath. "I mean, it's been five years since your mam died and all that time my whole focus has been on you. Keeping you fed and schooled. Taking you all around the world. Teaching you about life. And you know what, I was happy to carry on like that. I didn't plan on falling in love, I—"

"You love her?"

"Sure, of course I do! I wouldn't be moving us in with her if I didn't."

"But…" For once, Sky couldn't think of anything to say. He loved *that woman*. A little voice inside her cried, *what about me? Don't you love me?* But she smothered it. It was true – he hadn't had any serious girlfriends since her mum died. He'd thrown himself into being a dedicated dad – into being her mum *and* dad. If she said anything now it would look as if she didn't want him to be happy, and she did. Just not with *that woman*. "OK," she whispered, looking down.

He stepped closer. "OK?"

"OK – but can we keep the boat too?" Sky looked at him imploringly.

Her dad was grinning from ear to ear. He grabbed her hands and pulled her into a hug. "Yes, we can keep the boat," he said. "Thank you. I love you."

"I love you too," Sky replied. But for the first time in her life, that love felt tinged with something else. Something sour and dangerously close to resentment.

THE MOON
BY SKY CASSIDY

Sometimes, I think the moon is a goddess,
watching us with her wise silver face,
sighing when we cry,
smiling when we sleep.

Sometimes, I think the moon is a giant glitter ball
spinning and glimmering
so we can dance
and sing.

Sometimes, I think the moon is a spotlight,
painting the earth silver
so we can find beauty
and avoid pain.

Chapter Seven

All the way to the model casting Rose had wanted to run away. On the tube she'd wanted to take the wrong line deliberately and now, walking down Long Acre, she felt the overwhelming urge to dart into one of the brightly lit clothes shops and not come out. But the prospect of her mom throwing one of her diva meltdowns forced her to continue, counting down the store numbers as she went, until she arrived at number 223. Rose was about to press the buzzer when the door flew open and a tall, thin girl came flying out. She was clutching a portfolio and she looked upset. A middle-aged woman followed, looking even more upset. Rose guessed that she was the girl's mom. There was no way she would have let her mom come with her today, no matter how much she begged. For a start, it was painfully embarrassing to go any place with her mom, but going to a casting with her would be the pits. Everyone in the modelling world treated her mom like she was the Queen, Mother Teresa and the Virgin Mary all rolled into one. The constant butt-kissing and grovelling made Rose want to vomit. And besides, if they knew whose daughter she was they'd probably give her the job on the spot. There was no way she wanted to get cast for a job just because of her mom; she wanted to get work on her own merits or not at all.

Rose took a deep breath and stepped inside. The door opened on to a steep flight of stairs. She climbed them two at a time up to a reception area. About ten other girls were sitting on chairs around the edge of the room, all glossy hair and gleaming teeth. It was the most glamorous waiting room ever. A prissy-looking woman with half-moon glasses was sitting behind the reception desk. She eyed Rose up and down.

"Yes?" she said.

"I'm here for the casting," Rose muttered.

The woman looked down at a clipboard on the desk in front of her. "Name?"

"Rose Levine."

"Right." The woman ticked something and handed a form to Rose. "Fill this out while you're waiting, please."

Rose took the form and sat down. She could feel the eyes of the other models burning into her, checking to see if she was serious competition for the job. Like she cared about the stupid job! Rose stared at the form. The first section was pretty straightforward: name and agency. Her agency was Panache – her mom's. Rose felt sticky with embarrassment – would they want to represent her if she wasn't Savannah Ferndale's daughter?

A large, glamorous woman in five-inch heels came striding into the room. "Rainbow Jones?" she called, looking around. The girl sitting opposite Rose got to her feet. She was so thin her collarbones were protruding like a coat hanger. Rose watched her follow the plump woman into the casting room. There was something about the difference in their physiques that made her prickle with anger. Rose put her form down and rummaged in her bag for her secret chocolate stash. Her mom banned any kind of candy from the house, so buying chocolate had become Rose's private act of rebellion. She ripped open the wrapper. The girl sitting next to her gasped and actually shifted away in her seat, as if just watching Rose eat it would make her gain weight. Rose sighed and looked back at her form. The next section was for her personal statistics. Rose squirmed as she thought of her mom measuring her that morning and the way she'd sighed with disappointment when she'd measured her waist. Rose had left the scrap of paper with the figures on her bedside cabinet. Why should it matter anyway? Her mom had made her wear a ridiculously tight black dress. "So they can see your body shape as soon as you walk into the room," she'd explained. "The whole idea is to make their job as easy as possible." Surely they'd be able to know whether she was thin enough from looking at her?

Rose broke off another piece of chocolate and popped it into her mouth. It was orange-flavoured, her current favourite. She closed her eyes and let the blend of sweet citrus and bitter cocoa melt on her tongue. The door to the casting room opened and Rainbow came out. Her shoulders were hunched over and she looked dangerously close to tears. The large woman followed her, looking down at her clipboard.

"Rose Levine," she called. As Rose got to her feet, the woman looked at the chocolate and scowled. "Come on through," she said curtly. As Rose walked past Rainbow, she offered her the rest of the chocolate. "Enjoy," she whispered, with a wink. Rainbow stared at her for a moment, then grabbed the bar. "Thank you," she muttered with a weak smile.

The casting room was small. Rose had imagined it would be a huge studio, but it was no bigger than the kitchen at home. Four people were sitting behind a desk, two men and two women.

"This is Rose Levine," the clipboard woman said.

Rose hovered by the door.

"Well, come and stand on the mark then," one of the men said.

Rose looked at him blankly for a moment, then spotted a cross made from tape in the centre of the floor. She went and stood on it.

"Your form?" the woman said, reaching out her hand.

"Oh, you haven't completed it," a pointy-faced woman said.

Rose shook her head.

"Why not?"

"I didn't know what to write," Rose muttered.

"You didn't know what to write?" one of the men echoed in hushed tones, as if she'd just told them there was a bomb planted beneath the table.

"No."

Pointy-face woman leaned forward and stared hard at Rose. "You don't know your own statistics?"

"No." Rose bit on her lower lip to stop herself from adding, "I have better things to do with my brain."

The casting panel exchanged glances, then Pointy-Face looked back at the form. "And you're represented by Panache?" The disbelief in her voice was palpable.

"Yes."

"She does have very good bone structure," one of the men said, looking Rose up and down.

"Yes, and I like her neckline," the other man said, "but the attitude…" He broke off, shaking his head.

"Yes, the attitude is all wrong," Pointy-Face said smugly.

"What's up with my attitude?" Rose stared at her.

"I beg your pardon?" Pointy-Face frowned.

"This is a casting," one of the men said sternly.

"So?"

"So, we'll ask the questions, if you don't mind."

Rose's heart was racing from embarrassment and indignation. "Well, actually, I do mind."

"OK. That's enough," the man said. He turned to look at the woman with the clipboard, who was staring at

Rose, mortified. "Next, please, Constance."

Rose felt outraged. She hadn't wanted to come to this stupid thing in the first place. There was no way she was going to leave feeling even worse than when she'd arrived. "What's wrong with my attitude?" she snapped.

Pointy-Face let out a fake laugh. "That question is what's wrong with your attitude, young lady. Please leave; we have a lot of other people to see today. People who actually take their job seriously."

Rose's entire body flushed with anger. "You mean they do exactly what you tell them? Well, if being a brain-dead sheep is what you want, then I'm glad I've got a bad attitude."

"OK, let's go," said Constance, placing her hand on Rose's elbow. Rose shook it off.

"Don't worry – I'm going."

It wasn't until she was back outside and walking down the windswept street that Rose's anger began to fade. And, surprisingly, in its place came something very close to relief. For what felt like her entire life, her mom had been guiding her towards following in her modelling footsteps. And Rose had blindly obeyed because she hadn't really known what else she could do. She still didn't know, but what she did know with a dazzling clarity was that she definitely did not want to be a model.

Chapter Eight

Amber rummaged through the tray of vintage brooches with a sigh. Her Moonlight Dreamers recruitment campaign wasn't going according to plan. She'd handed out three cards since she started work and something had gone wrong each time. The first girl she'd given one to had seemed really promising. She'd bought a 1920s bangle and a walking cane with a brass handle in the shape of an owl. This was Moonlight Dreamer behaviour if ever Amber saw it, but when she'd given her the card with her change, the girl had looked at it quickly and then returned it, with a swift, "no, thanks".

The next girl had taken the card but as soon as she left the shop, Amber saw her throw it in the bin. Then, just before lunch, a Japanese girl had come in. She'd spent ages looking through the tray of brooches and she and Amber had had a great conversation about Victorian fashion. Amber had given her a card feeling totally confident that this would be a perfect fit. But then the girl had told her that she was only in London on holiday and she was flying back to Japan the next day. Amber was back to square one. She very much doubted the Indian girl would want anything to do with being a Moonlight Dreamer – and even if she did, would she be allowed? *What do Muslim girls do in their spare time?* Amber wondered. She shoved the question to the back of her mind. All she wanted was a couple of friends, a couple of kindred spirits to help her live the life of her dreams. Was it really so hard to find them? She took out her pocket watch and flicked it open. Four-thirty. In about fifteen minutes Gracie would be back from the market and it would be harder for Amber to approach anyone else. Gracie was the owner of Retro-a-go-go – a flamboyant woman who'd moved to Brick Lane back when it had been a Jewish neighbourhood. "I've seen 'em all come and go," was her favourite phrase, followed closely by, "Blimey, darl, it comes to something when the kind of frock I used to wear dancing gets called vintage!"

Amber was just about to tidy up the back room when the bell above the door jangled and a girl walked in. She had long, curly blonde hair and was wearing harem pants, with a pair of floral Doc Marten boots and a scuffed biker's jacket. It was a fashion fusion Amber instantly approved of. The girl looked about the right age too.

"Oh, hello," she said, noticing Amber's gaze.

"Hello." Amber mustered up her most welcoming smile. This might be her last chance of the day. She mustn't blow it. "Are you here on holiday?"

The girl looked at her questioningly. "What, on Brick Lane?"

Amber blushed. "No. I mean in London."

"Oh. No. I live here. Well, on the canal, down by Victoria Park."

"That's great!" Amber could barely contain her glee. She took a deep breath and told herself to play it cool.

But all of a sudden the girl looked really sad. "Well, I do at the moment. But I think I'm going to be moving soon."

If the girl said she was about to emigrate to Japan, Amber thought she might scream. "Where to?" she asked.

"Hampstead," the girl muttered.

"But that's great!" Amber exclaimed. "I mean, Hampstead's lovely and – so near."

The girl looked at her curiously, as if suddenly realizing how weird this conversation was becoming.

Amber cleared her throat. "Is there anything you're looking for in particular?"

The girl nodded. "I'm looking for a comfort-buy," she said.

"Ah, I see." Amber nodded thoughtfully. She knew all about comfort-buys. She reached down under the counter and pulled out a battered shoebox. "How about one of these?"

The girl came over and looked into the box. Her curly hair cascaded over her shoulders.

"I love reading these vintage postcards when I'm feeling down," Amber explained. "It's like eavesdropping on a historical conversation. Or one side of the conversation, anyway. Listen." She pulled a card from the box and began to read. *"Dearest Florence, I trust that this card finds you in the pink. Things are becoming quite trying here. The Hun certainly seem intent on causing maximum damage. But I got the smokes you sent me and they have put a spring in my step. Thank you. With all my love, Ernie."* Amber handed it to the girl. "It was sent during the First World War – from the trenches. Isn't it amazing to hold it and to think of where it's been?" Amber felt a sudden pang of alarm as she watched the girl. What if she didn't get it? What if she thought she was a freak like everyone at school did? But the girl carried on studying the card.

"What do you think 'in the pink' means?" she finally asked.

Amber gave an internal sigh of relief. "It means to be healthy. Pink skin rather than pale, I guess."

"That's so cool." The girl looked at Amber. "Do you think he made it back from the trenches?"

"I hope so."

The girl nodded. "Me too. Can I buy it?"

"Of course." Amber reached under the counter for a paper bag.

"I think I'll get a couple of others too," the girl said, rifling through the box.

Amber smiled. "Sure." And as she put the postcard into the paper bag she slipped her last Moonlight Dreamers card in with it.

Chapter Nine

Maali added some condensed milk to the pan. She could hear her mum chatting and laughing with a customer in the shop. She loved the sound of her mum laughing – it was like birdsong. Her dad called her his hummingbird. Maali sighed. How cool must it be to have someone call you their hummingbird? A vision of Ash popped into her head. *"You are my hummingbird, Maali," he whispered, before leading the unicorn away. Then he stopped and looked back over his shoulder at her. "I was thinking, maybe you and I could go on a date sometime."* Maali closed her eyes and pictured his twinkly smile. *"A date?" she whispered. "Yes," he replied. "We could go to Highgate Cemetery and take photos of all the graves."* Maali sighed. *"That would be great."*

"What would be great, pet?"

Maali jumped. Her mum was standing in the doorway of the shop kitchen, smiling at her.

"Oh, I was just…" Maali broke off, embarrassed.

"Daydreaming again?" Her mum came over and looked into the pan. "Hmm, I can see that."

"I'm sorry." Maali quickly added some more condensed milk and a creamy sweet smell filled the air.

"What were you dreaming about this time?" Her mum took some cardamom from the shelf and sprinkled it into the pan.

"Oh, just about somewhere I can go to take some photos." Maali bowed her head to avoid her mum's gaze. There was absolutely no way she could tell her the whole story – that she was dreaming about a boy, and a non-Hindu boy at that!

"You and your photos!" Her mum gave her a hug. "How about you go do your noon prayers and do some daydreaming about God?"

Maali laughed. She passed the wooden spoon to her mum and went out into the narrow hallway and up the steep stairs that led to their flat above the shop. Maali went past the shut door of her parents' bedroom and the open door of Namir's room, with his latest Lego construction taking up most of the floor. Finally, she reached the narrow stairs at the very end of the hall. Her bedroom was her favourite place in the whole building. Tucked right up in the attic, away from the hustle and bustle of Brick Lane, it was also the perfect place to come to pray. There was something about being up so high and the tranquillity of the room that made her feel somehow closer to the gods and goddesses.

Maali knelt beneath the skylight, in front of her shrine. Although they had a family shrine in the living room, Maali had created her own, more personal one here, on top of an old mango crate. She'd covered the crate with a cornflower-blue scarf and placed a figurine of the goddess Lakshmi in the centre. Lakshmi was the goddess of love, prosperity and beauty, and Maali's favourite of all the Hindu gods. In front of Lakshmi she'd placed an apple as an offering, with a small silver bell on one side of it and a wooden elephant incense holder on the other. She'd also strung some fairy lights around the edge of the box. She didn't need to turn them on, though: the autumn sunshine streaming through the skylight was casting a pale golden glow.

Maali tipped her head back and felt the gentle warmth on her face. Then she lit the incense and rang the bell. She began her prayers as she always did, saying thank you to all the gods and goddesses. "Thank you for my family and our home and my mum's sweets. Thank you for the fact that I don't have any science homework this weekend – although obviously I'm not thankful that Mrs Cooper has the flu – well, only for the no-homework part. Please help her recover soon." Maali paused before turning her attention to the statue of Lakshmi.

"Thank you for all the beauty in the world, Lakshmi. And thank you for helping me to capture it in my photos. And thank you for the magical things that happen in my life and – thank you for my daydreams." Maali frowned at the statue. "Is it wrong to be a daydreamer, Lakshmi? I know some people would say that it is, but I'm not sure."

Maali waited for a moment. Sometimes, Lakshmi would

whisper an answer inside her head. At least it felt as though it was Lakshmi. She always said something way wiser than anything Maali could ever come up with. But this time all she could think about was the card she'd been given that morning by the girl with the cool hair. *Are you a Moonlight Dreamer?* The words echoed in her mind. Maali finished her prayers and flipped open her laptop. Then she dug the postcard from her pocket and clicked open her email.

Rose walked into the pub and did a quick scan. As was usual for a Saturday afternoon in Camden, it was full of tourists and day-trippers, the wooden floor beneath their stools and tables cluttered with shopping bags. She breathed in the warm smell of alcohol and relaxed a little. In her jacket pocket her phone vibrated with a text message. Rose ignored it. It was bound to be her mom again, wanting to know how the casting had gone. Rose was nowhere near ready for that particular showdown. She pulled her lipstick from her bag and gave her lips a quick slick of Ruby Tuesday. Although she'd been drinking for months now and had never been ID'd, she still felt a frisson of fear every time she walked into a bar. She liked it, though – it added to the thrill, and lately she'd been craving thrills.

"Yo, Rosie!"

Rose instantly cringed. OK, this wasn't good. She was pretty sure she'd never read in *Cosmo* that cringing at the sound of your boyfriend's voice was a sign of true love.

"Over here."

Matt was standing at the bar, waving and holding a twenty-pound note in his hand. He was one of those guys who would be more aptly described as beautiful rather than handsome; with high cheekbones tapering into a perfectly chiselled chin and huge dark-grey eyes fringed with long lashes. As usual, he was wearing coloured chinos (today they were a deep plum), and as usual, half of his Calvin Klein boxers were on display. Rose never could get her head around that particular trend. Whenever she saw a guy with his boxers on show she felt the overwhelming urge to give him a wedgie.

"Hey!" She made herself smile as she walked over.

"He-ey!" Matt looked her up and down, his eyes lingering on her skin-tight dress. "You look great."

Rose pulled her jacket around her. She didn't feel great. She felt ridiculous. If she hadn't been avoiding her mom she would have gone straight home after the casting and got changed.

"What do you want to drink, babe?" Matt nodded to the array of drinks behind the bar.

Rose cringed again. Matt had the really annoying habit of talking just like the East End gangsters in the movies he loved to watch – even though he was a chino-wearing public school boy from Chelsea whose parents owned a huge chunk of Cumbria.

"JD and coke," Rose muttered. "Where are we sitting?"

"Through there." Matt nodded towards the back of the pub.

"Cool. I'll go through and say hi to the others."

"Hold on." Matt grabbed hold of her arm. "How about saying hi to me first?"

"I did say hi to you…" Rose looked at him blankly for a second. "Oh." She cringed yet again. This was definitely not a good sign. She could just imagine the advice columnists at *Cosmo* yelling, "Girlfriend, you're so not into him!" She stood on tiptoes and kissed Matt quickly on the cheek. "There you go," she said in a singsong voice as if she was talking to a toddler.

"Come here," he said, pulling her towards him. He smelled of aftershave and beer. Before Rose could back away, his mouth was pressing down on hers, hard, and as she felt his tongue trying to part her lips she wanted to retch. She shouldn't have come here, straight from the casting; she wasn't in the right frame of mind. In the eighteen months since her dad had left she'd been cocooned in a weird kind of numbness. But what had happened at the casting had ripped part of her cocoon away, leaving her feeling raw and exposed. Rose pulled away from Matt and bumped into a man behind her.

"Here, watch what you're doing, love," the man slurred. His face was red and shiny.

"What's wrong with you?" Matt muttered.

"Nothing. I – I'm not feeling so good."

"What? Again?"

Rose felt dangerously close to tears. This was crazy. What the hell was wrong with her?

"You know what, I'm gonna go get some fresh air." She

looked at him. He looked back at her blankly. The *Cosmo* columnist in her head fired a quiz question at her: When you tell your boyfriend you aren't feeling well and need some fresh air, does he (a) Look concerned and come with you, or (b) Look pissed off and turn away?

"OK." Matt sighed, turning back to the bar.

Rose made her way outside, her eyes filling with hot tears. Damn. Damn. Damn. Why did she have to go to that dumb casting? She had to get a grip. She hated feeling this weak. Rose marched off in the direction of the canal. She needed to go for a good long walk and get her head straight. But when she got to the bridge and looked down at the row of colourful houseboats lining the bank, she was filled with dread. Next week Liam and his dumb-ass daughter would be moving in, and what little peace and privacy she had would be totally wrecked.

Rose looked around frantically. Her nerves were jangling now like she'd downed ten espressos. She marched over the bridge, past the tattoo shop and the T-shirt shop and the Gothic jewellery store. Every one had a different rock song blaring out. A car drove past with hip-hop pounding from the stereo. Stay calm, she told herself. Just keep your head down and keep on walking. Then she heard a soft and gentle voice, with a foreign lilt.

"Excusez-moi. . . Excusez-moi."

Rose stopped and turned round. A young woman was standing in a shop doorway. Her shiny raven hair was piled on top of her head and her brown almond-shaped eyes twinkled. She wore a fifties-style floral dress with a pink polka-dot apron. She had the most beautiful, welcoming smile Rose had ever seen.

"Would you like to try?" the woman asked, holding out a plate.

"Who, me?" Rose felt so disoriented that she needed to check.

"Yes. If you like?"

Rose focused on the plate. It contained bite-sized chunks of what appeared to be cake. But it was like no cake Rose had ever seen before. The sponge was a beautiful shade of lilac and the icing was a delicate pale pink. Rose's stomach grumbled. The only thing she'd eaten all day were the couple of squares of chocolate at the casting. She was suddenly starving. "Yes. Please."

The young woman smiled and held the plate towards her. Rose took a piece of cake and put it in her mouth. "Oh – my – God!" she mumbled, as the flavour melted onto her tongue. "What *is* that?"

"You like?" the woman asked hopefully.

Rose nodded as the last sugary traces of frosting dissolved in her mouth. "I love!" she exclaimed. "But what flavour is it? I've never tasted anything like that before."

"It is lavender and plum," the woman replied. "My new invention."

"You invented it?" Rose looked at her in surprise. What a cool thing to do.

"*Oui* – yes – I am a patissier. I invent new recipes all the time." The woman smiled shyly, the tips of her cheeks flushing pink. "You want to come in and try some more?"

Rose nodded and followed the woman into the shop.

"Wow," Rose whispered as she looked around.

She seemed to have stepped from grungy Camden High Street into a Disney film set. The shop was a palette of pastel colours, from the primrose-yellow walls to the eggshell-blue floorboards. Although it was tiny, every inch of space was used to full effect. A row of small, round tables covered in pink gingham lined the wall to Rose's right. On the left was a glass cabinet containing trays of cupcakes in every colour of the rainbow.

"This is awesome!" Rose said, still drinking in the details – the old-fashioned coat and hat stand, the shelf of well-worn recipe books, the painted sign on the back wall saying "*Everything changes when you dare to dream.*"

"*Merci.* Thank you," the woman said, smiling at Rose. "Please, won't you take a seat?" She nodded at one of the tables.

Rose sat down.

"Can I get you something to drink?"

"Yes, please." Rose scanned the chalkboard on the wall behind the counter. "Could I get a hot chocolate, please – with cream and marshmallows?"

"Of course. And to eat?"

As Rose started reading the list of cakes she literally started to drool. The combinations were fantastical – like something Willie Wonka might have conjured up: Chocolate and Cherry Cola, Coconut and Lime, Coffee Bean Surprise, Lemon and Raspberry, Orange and Salted Caramel…

"Do you need some time to decide?" the woman asked.

Rose nodded as she continued to read: Honey Popcorn, Irish Coffee, Pear and Chocolate…

"No problem. I make your drink. I'm Francesca, by the way."

Rose smiled. "I'm Rose." Every time she breathed in, another delicious aroma flooded her nostrils. Cinnamon, chocolate, vanilla, strawberry… The warmth of the shop started seeping into her bones. All of a sudden she felt very, very tired.

"Well, in that case, you must have one of my favourite creations – the Rose Red."

Rose looked at her and laughed. "I guess I must."

Sky glanced up from her book and over at her dad. It was about the hundredth time she'd done this since she'd started trying to read, as if she wanted to imprint the image on her brain while she still could. Liam was sitting cross-legged in his usual spot, at the end of the bench seat closest to the front of the boat. He was reading from his battered copy of *The Bhagavad Gita*. Every so often he would smile – a quiet, calm smile. He was smiling now. Sky felt a twinge of pain so sharp it almost made her gasp. What would happen once they'd moved into that huge house? Would she even see her dad? She'd only been there once, briefly, about a month ago, to meet Savannah and

Rose. It had felt more like a museum than a home, with its five floors of echoey rooms, and pieces of furniture so delicate and beautiful they looked as if they should be in display cases. Their entire houseboat could fit inside the hallway, and it was so tatty in contrast. But Sky wouldn't have swapped it for anything because it was home. It was where she and Liam had come when her mum had died. It had been their refuge and their fresh start. It had healed them, just as Liam had said it would, living so close to the water and the wildlife. Mother Nature had rocked their sorrow away.

Sky looked at the logs glowing and crackling in the stove and the thick rug they'd bought in Nepal draped over the window to keep out the draft. She took in the piles of books on the floor and the shrine to Buddha beneath the porthole and her dad's guitar, Bess, propped against the fold-up table. That guitar had been everywhere with them – India, Peru, Thailand, Ireland – but it was so battered and worn, she couldn't imagine Savannah allowing it over her pristine doorstep. She couldn't imagine Savannah allowing *any* of their things over her pristine doorstep.

"Here, Sky, listen to this: 'It is better to live your own destiny imperfectly than to live an imitation of somebody else's life with perfection.'"

Sky felt that twinge of pain again. Would Liam still read quotes to her when they were living in Savannah's house? Or would he start reading them to Savannah instead? She didn't seem like the kind of person who'd be remotely interested in the books her dad liked to read. She grimaced as a nightmarish image popped into her mind: Savannah reclining on a chaise longue as she made Liam read quotes to her about celebrity weddings from *HELLO!* magazine.

"What do you reckon?" Liam said.

"It's lovely," Sky replied flatly.

"You remember that." Liam looked at her seriously. "Better to live your own life imperfectly than live it by some eejit's idea of perfection."

That's what I'm trying to do, Sky felt like saying. *You're the one who wants me to change everything.* Feeling dangerously close to tears, she leaned down and picked up her bag. She'd feel better after reading her vintage postcards. First the one from Ernie. She let her fingertips trace the faded scrawl. It felt so weird to think it had been written in a First World War trench. She imagined gunfire and smoke, and his hand trembling as it had written the words "in the pink".

"What's that you've got?" Liam asked.

"Some old postcards. I bought them at a vintage shop in Brick Lane this afternoon. They're really cool. Here – take a look." Sky passed the card to Liam. She picked up the next one. It had a picture of a full moon on the front. It looked really new. She turned it over. "Oh!"

"What's up?"

"Nothing." Sky frowned as she studied it. The other side was printed, as if it were an advert. *Are you a Moonlight Dreamer?* she began to read.

From: lakshmigirl@googlepost.com

To: wildeatheart@googlepost.com

Date: Sat 17th October 12:40

Subject: Moonlight Dreamers

Hello,

You gave me a postcard today and it asked some questions. Here are my answers:

Yes, I am a girl aged between 14 and 16.

Yes, I'm sick of being told how to look, what to do and where to go.

Yes, I do feel trapped in a world of fakes – especially when I'm at school. And I wasn't sure what an imbecile was at first, but I thought it sounded great so I looked it up, and yes, my world is full of them too.

And yes, I do dream of a world of freedom and adventure – and romance.

I really liked the quote on the card. At first I wasn't sure what it meant, but then I thought about how I feel when I dream – and I dream a lot, trust me! – and I think that the writer is actually being ironic when he or she says that seeing the dawn before the rest of the world is a punishment. Isn't there a saying "to see the light", and doesn't it mean to understand something? As in, one day I hope people will see the light and realize that what you wear is not who you are. I think dreaming helps us to make sense of stuff and work things out. And I think that's a really good thing. Maybe the writer should have put the word punishment in speech marks to make it clear that they were joking. Anyway, I really like the quote, so I think I must be a Moonlight Dreamer. What happens now? Do you let me know for sure?

Yours sincerely,

Lakshmi Girl

From: lakshmigirl@googlepost.com

To: wildeatheart@googlepost.com

Date: Sat 17th October 12:41

Subject: Re: Moonlight Dreamers

PS: If this is some weird kind of advert for a clothes sale, please don't email me back. Thank you.

Chapter Ten

Amber looked at her inbox. She blinked and looked again. It was still there. An actual email about the Moonlight Dreamers. Nervousness fluttered in her stomach. Now that someone else had typed those words, her dream had gone from drifting like a dandelion seed inside her head to something real. It had taken root in someone else. This was both exciting and nerve-wracking. Who was it from? It must have been the vintage postcard girl. Amber looked at the time the email had been sent, and frowned. It was too early to have been the vintage postcard girl; she hadn't come into the shop by then. So it must have been the dead pigeon girl. Amber reread the email. She really liked the girl's interpretation of the quote. She also thought that Wilde was being his usual sarcastic self when he said that to see dawn before everyone else was a punishment. She read to the end and frowned. What *did* happen now? She'd been so focused on getting someone interested in her idea that she hadn't really given the rest of it much thought.

"Amber, honey!" Daniel called from downstairs. "I'm

just popping out to get the Sunday papers before I go to the airport."

"OK!" Amber called back, her stomach instinctively tightening. He was going to the airport to collect Gerald, which meant that there were only a few hours of peace and quiet left. She refocused on the computer screen. *"What happens now?"* What did she want to happen now? What had she been hoping for when she'd come up with the idea in the first place? She got up from her desk and went over to her favourite thinking place – her bed. Amber considered her bed to be one of her greatest achievements – a monumental feat in comfort creation – from the feather-soft patchwork quilt to the warm-as-toast woven blankets and the huge family of cushions, each one lovingly hand-picked from Spitalfields Market. Before she lay down, she flicked through her record collection for her Ray Charles LP. When she'd asked for a vintage record player last Christmas, Daniel had laughed his head off. "Are you sure you wouldn't prefer an iPod?" he'd asked. But Amber genuinely preferred old things – it didn't matter whether they were furniture, music or clothes. Second-hand things had an air of mystery about them, a secret history, and they were one of a kind. Much as Amber hated to admit it, this was the one and only area in which she saw eye-to-eye with Gerald. "We are living in the era of cheaply produced tat," he liked to say. "Reigned over by Ronald Bloody McDonald!"

As Amber gently placed the needle upon the vinyl, the

record crackled into life. She threw herself onto her bed and snuggled into her nest of cushions. *What happens now?* She closed her eyes. A vision of her and a group of girls popped into her head. It was dark and they were seated in a circle, hunching forward as if confiding their deepest secrets. Amber imagined the kind of conversation they would have – a deep conversation. A meaningful conversation. Nothing like the kind of trivial chat the other girls had at school, which consisted mainly of bitching about celebrities and one another. The Moonlight Dreamers would talk about their dreams and how they were going to achieve them – how they were going to *help* one another achieve them. That was it! Amber opened her eyes and gazed at the ceiling. She slowly began to smile.

Sky wasn't really sure which was worse – the fact that she'd been dragged across London to spend Sunday "bonding" with *that woman* and her daughter or the fact that they'd come to the Tate Modern. She stared blankly at the "work of art" in front of her. It was called "The Goat". It was actually an ironing board someone had spray-painted silver. That was it – and yet it was on display in one of the top art galleries in London. It seemed symbolic somehow of the whole stupid sham of an outing. With every second of so-called bonding Sky hated Savannah more. She hated the way she was so self-aware the whole time, constantly looking around to see if anyone had noticed her – therefore ensuring that everyone did. She hated the way Savannah giggled at every word her dad said, like some kind of lovestruck teenager. She hated the way she dressed like a teenager, in her high-cropped hoodie and low slung jeans. And she hated her stupid American accent and the way every sentence she uttered ended with an uplift that made it sound as if she was constantly asking questions.

"Wow," Savannah said breathlessly as she came to stand beside Sky. "Isn't it awesome?"

Sky stared at her. Surely she couldn't be talking about the ironing board? But Savannah was gazing straight at it, batting her stupid long eyelashes. Maybe she was being sarcastic.

"It just blows my mind how some people have that kind of creative vision, you know?" She looked at Sky, wide-eyed. "I mean, to look at an ironing board and to see – to see" – she squinted at the title card – "a goat."

"Oh, for chrissakes," Rose muttered behind them.

Sky turned round to face her. There was no denying that Rose was stunningly beautiful. She had Savannah's high cheekbones and huge green eyes. But unlike Savannah, Rose looked more natural. Her skin was dewy rather than spray-tanned, and her face was make-up free. She looked even more pissed off than Sky felt.

"This place is a joke," she muttered, before wandering off.

"Rose!" Savannah sighed.

"All right, girls, step away from the ironing board." Liam came bounding towards them, grinning broadly. Sky shook her head in despair. How could he be so happy? How could he not see what a stupid idea this was?

"Jesus, Mary and Joseph!" Liam frowned as he studied the exhibit card. "The feckin' goat! Are they having a laugh? The Emperor's New Clothes, more like."

Sky couldn't help a small, smug grin. Her dad could see what a joke the exhibit was straightaway. He didn't think it showed great creative vision, he thought it was a pile of crap. Proof that he and Savannah were terribly suited, right there. He'd just been blinded by her looks. As soon as he realized what an idiot she was, he'd be out of there in a shot.

"I think it's cool," Savannah said, causing Sky to cheer internally. "I mean, to have that kind of vision. To see the artistic potential in an ironing board." She looked at Sky and grinned. "I have to tell you, any time I lay eyes on an ironing board all I see is boredom and pain!"

Sky looked at Liam for his reaction. But instead of laughing, or saying Savannah was being ridiculous, he smiled and slung his arm round her shoulders. "Well, you know, I'd never really thought about it like that before."

Oh, please! Sky stomped off before they started necking right in front of her. Rose was standing by the door to the next room, staring at the floor. Sky looked the other way as she tried to sneak past her.

"This is bullshit, isn't it?" Rose said.

"What?"

"This is bullshit." Rose shrugged her shoulders. She was

wearing a scuffed leather jacket and jeans. She looked a lot more normal than when Sky had last seen her and Rose had been dressed as if she'd just sashayed off a catwalk.

"What is?" Sky asked.

"This place," Rose replied. "I mean – a silver ironing board!"

Sky laughed and felt herself relax. She hadn't realized how tense she'd been. Just then, a group of German tourists entered the room, clad in brightly coloured coats and clutching their phones.

"Watch this," Rose whispered as she gazed back to the floor. "Oh. My. God!" she exclaimed loudly.

"What is it?" Sky followed Rose's gaze. She was looking straight at an air-conditioning vent.

"This is like, incredible. I have to get a picture of it!" Rose pulled out her phone, crouched down in front of the vent and took a photo. One of the Germans walked over. The others looked for a second, then joined him.

Rose looked at Sky and winked. "Have you ever seen anything quite so beautiful and so – so—"

"Artistic?" Sky offered, playing along.

"Yes, exactly. I thought the ironing board was good but this – this is amazing!" Rose took photo after photo of the air vent. "It's called 'The Beaver'," she called to the Germans. They nodded and pulled their own phones out, jostling to take a picture of the air vent.

Sky bit her lip to keep from laughing. Then she heard the clip of Savannah's heels behind her.

"What's going on?" Savannah asked. "Honey, what are you doing? It's an air vent!"

Rose stood up. Sky expected her to be grinning but she looked furious. "I know – and that's an ironing board, Mother. A freakin' ironing board!"

Savannah's face froze. "Rose! That's enough." Then she turned to Liam. "I'm so sorry, honey, she's having a few issues at the moment…"

"My only issue is being forced to come here!" Rose yelled.

The group of Germans fell silent. Then one of them took a picture of Savannah.

"Now look what you've done," Savannah hissed at Rose. She fished in her bag for a huge pair of dark glasses. "Now they've recognized me we'll have to go."

"Don't worry!" Rose yelled. "I'm gone."

Sky cringed as Liam placed his hand protectively on Savannah's shoulder. For the first time since she'd come into her life, she felt really sorry for Rose.

Chapter Eleven

"I'm bored!"

If there was one phrase Maali dreaded her brother saying it was this – especially when she was the one looking after him. Her mum was down in the shop. Her dad was at a meeting. It was only lunchtime. There were two long hours before her dad would be back. Two long hours of "I'm bored!" if Maali didn't think of something to do.

"Why don't you watch *Harry Potter*?"

"I've watched it."

"Why don't you watch it again?"

"I've watched it again. I want to do something else."

Maali looked at her laptop and sighed. She'd really been hoping to do some photo editing.

"I want to go out," Namir said, tugging at her sleeve.

"Out?" Maali looked at the photo of the pigeon. She'd been dying to try it with a sepia filter.

"Yes. Can we go to the park?"

Maali thought of the rusty climbing frames and ramshackle swings at the local park and her heart sank.

There was no way she wanted to go there. It was bad enough having to babysit; having to babysit in a cold, grotty park was the worst possible way to spend a Sunday.

"It's raining," she said, desperately clutching at any straw she could find.

"No, it's not!" Namir bounded over to the window and pulled back the curtain. A shaft of sunlight poured in. "Come on, let's go!" he said, heading to the door.

Sighing, Maali shut down her laptop. Then she had an idea – an idea that sent a tingle down her spine. "I know. Why don't we go to the farm instead?"

Namir's dark brown eyes grew wide as saucers. "The City Farm?"

"Yes. We can see all the animals." *And maybe Ash, too*, her inner voice added in a knowing tone, causing Maali to blush.

Namir started hopping from one foot to the other, the way he always did when he was excited. "Can we see the sheep?"

"Yes, of course." Something weird was happening inside Maali's ribcage – something fluttery and pounding all at the same time.

"Yes!" Namir shouted. He ran over to Maali and hugged her tightly. "Love you, Hermione."

Maali looked down at him and laughed. "Love you too, Harry Potter. Now go and get your coat."

The fluttering in Maali's chest reached fever pitch as the farm loomed into view. Ash probably wouldn't even be there, she told herself. *But what if he was?* Maali pulled her hat down against the cold breeze. Why was she being like this? It was crazy. They'd only met once and for a couple of minutes. Why couldn't she stop thinking about him? *It's love at first sight*, her inner voice whispered. *You've read about it in books and poems, and now it's actually happened*. Maali stopped, overcome by a sudden wave of fear. It was one thing to daydream about Ash, but to go to the farm, looking for him – it suddenly felt a little too real. On the other side of the road a group of kids were running out of the council flats, laughing loudly.

"Come on." Namir tugged at her hand.

"I don't know if—"

Namir tugged again. "Look! Look! There's a camel!"

"What?! Where?" Maali followed Namir's gaze over to the farm.

"There! In the field."

Two llamas were grazing on a threadbare patch of grass by the entrance to the farm. "They're not camels, they're llamas," Maali corrected with a laugh, and she started walking along the road. She couldn't let Namir down now. And besides, it was Sunday. Ash probably wouldn't be working.

The farm was surprisingly busy given how cold it was. As soon as they got through the gate, Namir ran over to the pig enclosure, oinking loudly. Maali glanced over at the stable. A teenage boy with ginger hair was raking up a pile of dirty straw. Maali felt a strange blend of disappointment and relief.

"Maali! Maali! Look!" Namir cried.

Maali turned round.

"The pig's having lunch."

A huge pig was snuffling about excitedly as one of the farm staff tipped a bucket of scraps onto the floor in front of it.

"Yuck! It's eating potato peelings!" Namir yelled before dissolving into a fit of giggles.

But Maali wasn't looking at the pig any more. She was looking at the boy feeding it. And he was looking at her.

"Hello again," Ash said with a twinkly eyed smile.

Maali opened her mouth to answer, but no words came out.

Rose stepped inside the house and slammed the door behind her. The noise echoed around the empty hall, causing the dewdrop-shaped jewels on the chandelier to quiver. For a second, she wished she had a baseball bat so she could smash every last one of them. She hated this damn house almost as much as she hated her mom – and she hated her mom a lot right now. How dare she embarrass her like that? And in front of Sky and Liam too. Rose's blood had turned to liquid rage; her whole body was burning up. She pictured the three of them playing happy families right now as they had lunch together in some fancy restaurant and talked about how weird she was.

"I think she's suffering from some kind of anger-management issues," she imagined Savannah saying to Liam and Sky. That's what she'd accused her of last night. That, and being "selfish and ungrateful". The worst thing was, after spending a couple of hours drinking hot chocolate and eating all kinds of delicious creations in Francesca's shop yesterday, Rose had come home feeling more positive than she had in ages. She'd planned how she was going to tell her mom what had happened at the casting – she'd worked out her damage limitation plan. But she hadn't figured on the modelling grapevine. It turned out that the casting manager had told Panache Agency all about her "attitude problem", and they in turn had told her mom – who was waiting with both barrels loaded the minute she walked through the door. Rose had managed to keep her cool last night, but today was the limit. She'd never felt so humiliated in her life.

She slung off her coat and stomped up the stairs. She marched into her bedroom and over to the window. Hampstead Heath was spread out below her like a green velvet blanket. It was an OK view, she guessed, but she wanted to be back in New York, looking at the rich green of Central Park and the yellow taxicabs buzzing round it like wasps. She didn't want to be in this dumb place where nobody understood her. She took out her phone and called her dad. With every long purr of the ring tone she became increasingly tense. "Just pick up already!" she muttered. Then, after what seemed like for ever, there was a click and she went through to voicemail.

"Hi! Sorry, I'm not able to take your call right now," she heard her dad say in his clipped British accent. "But you know what to do. Beep. Message. Thank you."

Rose terminated the call and threw her phone onto her bed. It was so unfair. Why was he over there while she was here? He was the British one, not her. When her parents had split they'd wanted to put an ocean between themselves, but couldn't they at least have arranged for her to be where she felt most at home? She sat down on the end of her bed and put her head in her hands. She'd never felt emptier or more alone. Her Beyoncé ring tone snapped her from her gloom. She grabbed her phone and looked at the screen, hoping to see *Dad calling*, but it was Matt. For once Rose didn't cringe. After the crappy morning she'd had, she needed to talk to someone, and she didn't much care who.

"Hey," she said softly into the phone.

"Hey." His voice was soft too. She'd obviously been forgiven for running out on him yesterday. "Where you at?"

Rose didn't even cringe at his fake American accent. "My bedroom."

"Really? What you doing?"

Rose ignored the suddenly interested tone. "Nothing much. Where are you?"

"Still in bed."

"Really? It's, like, almost two."

"I know. A gang of us went to The Island last night. It was sick."

The Island was the latest hot club in town – a renovated warehouse in East London with a Treasure Island theme.

Rose had thought it was a bit Disneyland when she'd first gone a few weeks ago, but now she felt a twinge of envy. If only she'd been out getting trashed and dancing herself into oblivion last night instead of getting the hairdryer treatment from her mom.

"Wanna come over?" Matt said.

"What, to yours?"

"Yeah. My parents won't be getting back from skiing till really late."

The last time she'd been to Matt's things had gotten kind of heavy. He'd wanted to go all the way. She'd got to second base and ended up faking a headache – cheesiest excuse ever. She couldn't bear the thought of going through that again. "I can't. I'm grounded." It wasn't exactly a lie: she was pretty sure as soon as her mom got home that would be the first thing she said.

"Oh man! I really want to see you." There was an urgency in his voice now. If they'd been in the same room it would have unsettled her, but the fact that he was so far away made her tingle instead. After the morning she'd had, it was good to feel needed.

"I know," Matt murmured, "why don't you send me a picture?"

"A what?" But she knew what he meant.

"A picture – of you."

"But you have pictures of me."

"But not … private pictures."

"Oh." Rose sat still as she tried to figure out her next move.

"We've been going out for four weeks now," Matt whispered. "I need *something*." The intensity in his voice was making her feel really weird. A mixture of nerves and adrenalin. She liked this sudden power over him. It made her feel strong again.

"OK," she whispered into the phone. "I'll see what I can do."

THINGS I **HATE**!

- Selfish people
- People who don't think about other people's feelings ever – not even their own children's
- Parents who would rather go away than watch their daughter – or son – take part in something really major – like, say, a national debating final
- Parents who go away and then, as soon as they're back, start droning on about themselves instead of asking how their daughter is and how she did in her debating final (if she had taken part in a debating final)
- Parents who can't take criticism and have to go off and sulk in their room if anyone dares to point out that they might be in the wrong
- Parents who like playing opera loudly – just to annoy you
- Parents who are ridiculously melodramatic all the time and make you want to fling yourself off the nearest clifftop whenever they come in the room!!

Here are this week's Wilde Words, from my hero, Oscar Wilde. Oh, so true!

> *"Some cause happiness wherever they go;*
> *others whenever they go."*

Amber

Chapter Twelve

Maali turned on the fairy lights around her shrine. She lit the incense. She rang the bell. She stared at the Lakshmi figurine. Lakshmi smiled back serenely.

"Why couldn't I have said something?" Maali whispered. "Why did I have to stand there staring at him like a – like a – starey thing?"

Nice to see you, Ash had said.

Maali had nodded and then she'd turned and walked away. She'd spent the rest of the time at the farm studiously avoiding the pig enclosure and kicking herself for being such an idiot. It wouldn't have been so bad if seeing Ash in the cold light of day had brought her to her senses, but if anything he looked even nicer. His hair was ruffled in the breeze and he was wearing a khaki T-shirt with NO MORE WAR printed on it. Maali blushed as she remembered the way the muscles in his arms rippled as he tipped the bucket of feed onto the floor.

"What's wrong with me?" she asked Lakshmi imploringly. "How am I ever going to meet my soulmate if I can't even talk to a boy?"

Lakshmi looked so poised, so wise. Surely she would be able to help. Maali shut her eyes. "Please, please, please," she prayed, "help me find the courage to talk to boys. To talk to a boy. To talk to Ash."

Amber stared at her email from Dictionary.com. Usually their word of the day seemed uncannily appropriate to her mood, but not today. Today she needed a heavy black cloud made from letters. Something like "morose" or "melancholy" or "moribund". She most definitely did not need "hurdy-gurdy". Hurdy-gurdy was way too happy. It conjured up images of jolly, smiling people dancing a jig, not of a death-row prisoner the night before their execution.

Amber always started feeling like a death-row prisoner by Sunday evening as she started counting down the hours to school. It was hard to believe she'd once loved it. That was back during the pre-secondary school years, which was so long ago it felt practically prehistoric. In primary school no one cared that she had two dads. No one cared that she was different. Back then everyone was different and they all got along fine. It was as if, as soon as they started secondary school, kids were reprogrammed to want to be exactly the same – and hate anyone who was even slightly different. Amber was about to dig out her most mournful Billie Holiday album and fling herself face down on her bed when there was a knock on the door.

"Can I come in?" Gerald called.

Amber sighed. It was all so predictable. When he'd forgotten to ask how her debate was, she hadn't said a word. Daniel must have told him to say something. He'd probably written him a script.

"Yes," Amber muttered.

"Amber?" Gerald called again.

"I said yes!" she yelled.

"All right, all right, no need to announce it to the whole of Londinium." Gerald strode into the room. He was wearing his paisley dressing gown and brown leather slippers. His cropped white hair was still damp from the shower. "So," he said as he glanced about the room. "So..."

"So, what?" Amber said, staring up at him from her desk. Surely he hadn't forgotten what he was there for already?

He looked at her. "What? Ah, yes. Your debate. How did it go?"

"Brilliantly, thank you."

"Yes. Daniel said you did very well." He smiled at her.

Against her better judgement, Amber felt a speck of warmth inside her chest.

"I was wondering..."

The speck grew to the size of a pea. "Yes?"

"I met an art student at the gallery opening, a young man called Sven. He said he'd like to interview me for his blog. Apparently my work inspired him to take up painting." Gerald broke off for a moment, taking a dramatic pause for full effect. "Anyway, he'd like to interview me on Skype, and as you know, I don't know the first thing about the blasted worldwide internet thing, so I was wondering if you might help me."

The warmth Amber had been feeling was abruptly extinguished by a cold stab of hurt. So he hadn't come up to ask about her debate at all. "No," she said tightly.

Gerald's jaw dropped in shock. "Pardon?"

Amber turned back to her computer. "I said no. I won't help you. Now, if you don't mind, I have homework to do."

"You won't help me? Well – I – I—" he spluttered. "Why not?"

"When do you ever help me? With anything?" she asked as she turned back to look at him.

Gerald's face was journeying through a spectrum of reds and purples. "When do I ever help you?" His voice climbed an entire octave in the space of a sentence. "When do I ever *help* you?"

"Yes. When?" She stared at him defiantly, but inside she was starting to feel really sick.

"I thought it would be nice – I – oh, I give up!" He flung his hands in the air and turned to go.

"How can you give up something you never even started?" Amber's heart was pounding now.

"What's that supposed to mean? What have I never even started?"

"Being a proper parent."

Suddenly there was a terrible silence.

Gerald stared at her, his eyes full of rage. "I don't know

why I—" He shook his head. "I don't need to listen to this," he muttered and walked out of the room.

Amber sat at her desk, motionless. What was he going to say? "I don't know why I – *bothered having you*," her inner voice filled in the blank. Her eyes filled with tears.

"Well, I give up on you too," she muttered at the closed door. Just then, the email notification sounded on her computer. As she read the subject line, her hurt faded: **Yes – I am a Moonlight Dreamer**. Amber clicked the email open. It was a poem. A shiver of excitement ran up her spine as she began to read.

MOONLIGHT DREAMER

BY SKY CASSIDY

Glittering
glimmering
you light the loom
as I weave my dreams.

Glistening
shimmering
you fill the air
as I dance my dreams.

Waxing
waning

you paint the page
as I write my dreams.

For I am a Moonlight Dreamer
a dreamer by moonlight
still awake when dawn breaks
your spell.

Chapter Thirteen

Sky looked at her inbox expectantly. She wasn't exactly sure why. It wasn't as if she was going to get a reply straightaway, but she couldn't help feeling intrigued. It must have been the girl in the vintage store who gave her the Moonlight Dreamers card. How else would it have got in the bag? Yes, she most certainly did want freedom and adventure and, yes, she was definitely sick of being told what to do – well, being told that she had to move in with *that woman*, anyway. And the quote about being a moonlight dreamer had been awesome.

Sky had almost emailed back immediately, but then she started wondering whether the girl in the shop had put it there after all. Maybe it had been mixed in with the vintage postcards and Sky hadn't noticed. But after the terrible morning in the art gallery and an even more terrible lunch with Liam and Savannah – where Savannah had been all over Liam like an adoring fangirl – Sky felt desperate for something, anything, to distract her from the disaster area that her life was fast becoming. So she'd written her response in a poem. That way, if it wasn't from the girl and was some kind of trick, she wouldn't have given too much away. Now she just had to wait and see.

Sky snuggled down into her bunk. The nights were definitely getting colder, but she didn't mind – she'd always liked winters on the boat. Liam was wrong – she didn't care about radiators, their log burner was far cosier. Over lunch, Savannah had asked them to move in this Tuesday. She'd done her stupid doe-eyed expression at Liam and said that Rose needed a calming male influence. And, of course, never being able to resist someone in need, Liam had agreed, looking at Sky only as an afterthought. She felt sick to the pit of her stomach as she thought of the prospect of only two more nights on the boat. How could her dad think that their moving in would help Rose? It was obvious she didn't want them there.

Sky felt for the amethyst pendant around her neck and held it tight. The pendant had belonged to her mum and Sky had worn it every single day since her mother died. "Why did you have to leave us?" she whispered into the darkness, tears burning at her eyes. But then her email notification pinged. Sky scrambled for her phone and clicked on the inbox.

From: wildeatheart@googlepost.com

To: halopoet@hotmail.co.uk; lakshmigirl@googlepost.com

Date: Sun 18th October 22:40

Subject: Moonlight Dreamers Meeting

Hello,

Thank you so much for responding to my appeal. I am happy
to confirm that you both definitely sound like Moonlight
Dreamers. And I am even happier to discover that I am not
alone. Are you free this Tuesday evening at 6.30? I will be
in the 1001 Café in the Truman Brewery (upstairs at the
back, at the table with the Moroccan lamp and the leather
chairs with holes in the arms – it's not as bad as it sounds,
I promise!). If you would like to find out more about being a
Moonlight Dreamer, meet me there.

Best wishes,

Amber

PS: This is not an elaborate clothes sale promotion. I'm just
a teenage girl who wants to find the confidence to live her
dreams. I hope you are too…

Sky reread the email, feeling a mixture of curiosity and
relief. Amber had to be the girl from the vintage store – that
must be why she said it wasn't a clothes promotion. Sky
switched off her phone and snuggled down into her bunk.
She wasn't sure what to make of the email, but it did sound

exciting. And anyway, Tuesday was the day she and her dad would be moving into Savannah's place, so a reason to go out that evening had to be a good thing.

Maali glanced at the figurine of Lakshmi before rereading the final sentence of the email:

> PS: This is not an elaborate clothes sale promotion. I'm just a teenage girl who wants to find the confidence to live her dreams. I hope you are too...

Could her prayer have been answered? Only a couple of hours earlier she'd begged Lakshmi to help her find the confidence to talk to Ash, and now she'd received this email from the girl with the super-cool hair. It couldn't be a coincidence, surely? Maali smiled at the little statuette. "Thank you," she whispered. Lakshmi smiled back.

"What do you mean, they're moving in early?" Rose glared at Savannah across the breakfast bar.

"Exactly that. I've asked them to move in this Tuesday." Savannah stared back at her.

"And I don't get any say in it?" Rose slammed her slice of pizza down on her plate.

"Are you kidding?" her mom asked. "After the way you've been behaving lately? As I was saying to Liam and Sky at lunch, you've had things your own way for too long. It'll do you good to have to share things as part of a family."

"You said that? To them?" Rose felt sick. She pushed her plate away.

"And why are you eating that crap?" Savannah glared at the pizza. "How are you ever going to get down to model weight if you live off junk food?"

"I don't want to get down to model weight," Rose snapped. "I don't want to be a model!"

Savannah's eyes widened, her long and perfectly mascaraed eyelashes emphasizing her shock. Rose could see something else in her eyes too. Savannah looked genuinely hurt. "But – but – what are you going to do instead?"

Rose took a deep breath. "I want to be a patissier."

"A what?"

"A patissier. I want to make cakes."

Savannah laughed. "You want to make cakes? But that's…"

"What?" Rose stared at her defiantly.

"That's crazy."

"Why?"

Savannah looked around the kitchen. "Because … you're my daughter," she answered lamely.

Rose frowned. "What's that supposed to mean? It's *my* life. Just because you're my mom doesn't mean you can control what I do."

"Oh, really?" Savannah's face flushed.

Self-doubt began to bubble up inside Rose. She shoved it down and got to her feet. "Really!" she said and walked out.

When she got to her bedroom she saw the notification light flashing on her cellphone. She had three new messages from Matt. She felt a stab of dread as she thought of the photo she'd sent him earlier – a selfie in her underwear, though with the lighting so low he'd barely be able to see anything. She clicked on his messages:

Sick! :-)

Can u send me another? Lose the bra next time ;) xxx

Where r u?!

Rose heard footsteps on the stairs.

"Things are going to change once Liam's here," Savannah said, barging through the door.

"Mom, get out of my room!"

"I'm serious. I will not have you back-chatting me like that when he and Sky move in."

Rose's phone pinged. Another text from Matt.

You're so hot it's driving me crazy xxx pls send another pic!

"I mean it, Rose. I don't want you embarrassing me again, do you understand?" Savannah was pouting as if she was doing a cosmetics shoot.

Rose's eyes smarted with hot, angry tears. *What about all*

the times you've embarrassed me? she wanted to yell. Her whole life she'd had people telling her how lucky she was to have the party-animal model Savannah Ferndale as a mom – "she must be so much fun" they'd say. But they didn't know the downside of having one of the world's most famous, "fun-loving" models for a mom. They didn't know how painful it was to have to compete against an army of hangers-on to get your mom's attention. They weren't there all those nights Rose had lain in bed, listening to a party raging downstairs and longing for her mom to send everyone home so she could read her a story. They didn't know how excruciating it was when her mom turned up to a parents' evening at school, drunk on champagne from yet another launch, or seen the other side of Savannah – the insecure, selfish side who believed in her own hype and needed everything her own way. Rose turned away and hugged her pillow. Her phone beeped.

I want to see you nkd!

"Do you understand?" Savannah said again. Her phone rang and her face instantly lit up. "Antonio!" she cried, taking the call. "Yes, I'd love to. You wouldn't believe the day I've had… Oh, you know, teenage dramas!"

Rose listened as Savannah's voice and footsteps faded along the hall. Antonio was Savannah's manager. He was also her butt-kisser-in-chief. Rose was certain there had to be a clause in his contract telling him to agree with everything Savannah said and call her "darling" at the end of every sentence. Rose grimaced and rolled over. She looked back at Matt's texts. Downstairs, she heard her mum laughing loudly – about her, probably. Well, she'd show her. Savannah might be able to boss Antonio and her other clingers-on around, but there was no way she was telling her what to do any more. Rose pulled off her sweatshirt and unclipped her bra.

Chapter Fourteen

Tuesdays were usually the low point of Amber's week. Any day that had double science followed by PE was bound to be grim, but the fact that it was still three days away from the weekend turned it into a living hell. But this Tuesday Amber didn't care that in science they were studying the periodic table – another complete waste of the alphabet, as far as she was concerned. And she didn't care that in PE her sadistic teacher made them play hockey in the freezing rain. She didn't even care that when she got back to her locker she found FREAK written on the door in scarlet lipstick, because tonight was the night of the first Moonlight Dreamers meeting so, hopefully, she would finally stop feeling so alone.

Sky looked around her new bedroom in disbelief. It was practically bigger than their entire boat. Of course, she hated everything about it, but if she had to pick one thing that she didn't hate quite so much, it would be the huge bay window. Sky perched on the edge of her double bed and looked outside. A young mum was pushing a pram up the hill. She was dressed in a tracksuit and trainers, but you could tell from the gleam of her skin and the sharp cut of her hair that she was wealthy. She didn't look happy, though. Rose leaned forward. There was no denying it: the window was a perfect spot for people-watching.

Outside was a huge sycamore tree, its branches almost bare now, apart from the few yellowing leaves that were stubbornly clinging on. The tree was so close that if Sky leaned out she'd be able to touch the top branches. She hadn't been this close to the top of a tree since she and her dad used to climb them when she was younger. She lay down on her side and looked at the branches bobbing in the breeze. It was as if the tree was waving at her. This made her feel less sad – until she heard the sound of her dad and Savannah laughing downstairs. It was lunchtime and, following a morning's yoga together, they were both drinking green juice and eating a vile-looking beetroot salad that Savannah's nutritionist had prepared for them. Sky had passed on lunch – she didn't have an appetite, not even for normal food. Ever since she'd woken up that morning she'd felt sick with dread.

Rose was at school and wouldn't be home till five. Liam had home-schooled Sky since she was twelve, but she guessed there wouldn't be any lessons today. She looked at her belongings by the door: all of her worldly goods crammed into two suitcases, next to a vintage trunk full of her mum's stuff. Sky wondered what kind of mood Rose would be in when she got home. Somehow she didn't think she'd be throwing them a welcome party. She sighed. At least she had the Moonlight Dreamers meeting to escape to. She looked back at the tree and tried to pretend she was in a tree-house in the middle of a forest – miles and miles away from Savannah and her stupid, fake laugh.

As Maali walked home from school along Brick Lane she felt little bursts of nervousness and excitement going off inside her like fireworks. There were only three hours until the Moonlight Dreamers meeting. For about the hundredth time that day, she wondered what it would be like. And for about the hundredth time, she contemplated not going. As she walked past the Truman Brewery and the spot where the unicorn had stood, her face flushed as she thought of Ash. It always happened – it was like some weird kind of biological reaction, like the way you sneeze when you sniff pepper. She still couldn't believe she'd acted like such an idiot that day at the farm. She realized that she had to go to the Moonlight Dreamers meeting. No matter how awkward it might be, if it gave her the confidence to talk to Ash it would all be worth it.

Rose paused before putting her key in the door. The second she stepped inside the house nothing would be the same. She'd be stepping into a life where she had even less of a say over what happened. But what was the alternative? A cold, sharp breeze whistled up the hill and under her coat. She took a deep breath and walked in. The first thing she saw was a tatty old rucksack and a pair of men's walking boots next to the door mat. Rose listened for any sounds of life, but the house was silent. Then she heard Liam's voice coming from the living room.

"We think it's for the best," he said quietly.

"For who?" she heard Sky say, in a much louder voice.

"For you. It'll do you good to be back in a school. It'll do you good to mix with more youngsters."

So, Sky was home-schooled. Rose gave a wry smile; that explained a lot.

"I don't need to mix with more youngsters," Sky said, her voice getting higher.

"Yes, you do. Sure, Rose goes to school, and it hasn't done her any harm."

Sky gave a dry little laugh. Rose bristled.

"Hi, honey!"

Rose jumped as Savannah came running down the stairs, barefoot, in a super-short leopard-print dress.

"They've arrived!" Savannah exclaimed, gesturing towards the living room and grinning like crazy. "Come say hi." She shot Rose a glance that said *and don't mess up*.

Rose dumped her school bag on the floor and trudged into the living room. Liam was standing in the bay window and Sky was perched on the arm of the sofa, scowling at the floor. She was wearing a skater dress, woolly tights and DM boots. If it wasn't for the fake sunflower in her hair she wouldn't look too bad.

"Hey, Rose," Liam said with a grin. "How was school?"

How was school? What did he think she was, five? "Great," Rose muttered.

"Sky might be joining you there soon," Liam said, smiling at Savannah. Savannah went over and took his hand.

"Oh, really?" Rose frowned. "How are you going to afford the fees?"

"Rose!" Savannah snapped.

"He won't need to because I won't be going," Sky said, staring right at Rose.

"OK, how about we talk about this later – after dinner?" Liam said, looking at Savannah. She smiled at him and nodded.

"I won't be here for dinner," Sky said.

"What?" Liam stared at her.

Rose watched them curiously. This was proving to be a lot more entertaining than she'd imagined.

"I'm going out," Sky said, getting to her feet.

"But where?" Liam looked at her helplessly.

"We thought it might be nice if you girls hung out together tonight," Savannah said to at Sky. "Give you a chance to get to know each other."

Sky gave a bitter laugh. "Yeah, well, I'm sorry, it'll have to be another night."

"Now, hang on a minute." Rose had never heard super-hippy Liam sound stressed.

"I have to go out." Sky looked desperate. Rose wondered

what she had planned. Maybe she was meeting a guy. She pictured some hippy dude waiting for Sky somewhere, dressed in a floral shirt and playing a mandolin. Then she thought of Matt and her own friends and the gig they were supposed to be going to in Camden tonight.

"How about if I go with her?" Rose suggested, looking from Liam to Savannah. Then she gave Sky a pointed look, trying to convey the fact that she had no interest in going out with her, just in finding a way of getting them both off the hook.

"Oh, well, I don't know," Savannah said doubtfully, looking at Liam.

"I think it's a grand idea," Liam said hopefully.

Sky looked questioningly at Rose, then shrugged her shoulders. "OK."

"Great!" Liam said. "Where are you going?"

"To an event at the Poetry Library," Sky muttered.

Rose shuddered. She seriously hoped Sky wasn't actually expecting her to go with her.

"The Poetry Library?" Savannah asked, looking blank.

"Yes, on the Southbank," Sky replied curtly, without looking at her. She glanced at Rose. "I'll just get my bag."

"Yeah, and I've got to get changed," Rose said.

They both left the living room and made their way upstairs. Rose wondered when she ought to tell Sky that she wasn't really going with her. Probably best to wait until they'd left the house. "I'll see you back in the hall," she said, going into her room before Sky could reply.

As soon as she sat down on her bed, her phone beeped.

Been looking at ur pic all day :-) Seb says we can stay at his tonight after the gig. He'll be staying at Natasha's so we'll have the place to ourselves ;)

Rose stared at the text. The winky-faced emoticon seemed to be leering at her. A ball of panic welled up inside her. Why had she sent Matt that photo? Now it was going to be even harder to fend him off. She scrolled back to the picture and cringed. She'd been so angry at the time, she hadn't been thinking straight. She'd seen enough photos of her mom to know exactly what to do – lean forwards slightly, pout – not that her mom had ever done topless shots, but her campaign for Victoria's Secret had left so little to the imagination that she might as well have. Rose looked at the picture of herself, pouting and half-naked, and her skin began to crawl. She had to get Matt to delete it. *What's the big deal?* her inner voice said, the mean inner voice that always piped up whenever Rose felt cornered. But for once it didn't do anything to soothe her growing unease. She jumped as her phone went off again.

Don't worry – I've got protection ;) xx

Eew! Rose dropped the phone like it was a hot coal. What was she going to do? How was she going to get out of this one? It had been a horrendous day. There was no way she wanted to spend the night fighting Matt off and there was no way she was going to stay at Sebastian's house. But that meant… Rose groaned. That meant spending the evening with Sky at the freakin' Poetry Library.

Sky sat down on her bed and stared at the tree. The wind was blowing its branches so close they were practically tapping on the window. "Damn!" she said out loud. "Damn! Damn! Damn!"

Why did Rose want to tag along on her night out? And how was she going to explain where she was actually going? She didn't really know herself! Now she would look like even more of an idiot. But at least she was able to go out; that was something. She waited for a while before going back downstairs. When she got into the hallway there was no sign of Rose, and for a moment Sky contemplated making a run for it. But then she heard Rose's footsteps. She'd got changed into tight black jeans, a man's plaid shirt and biker boots. She'd also let her hair down, and the honey-coloured ends were tumbling in loose curls over her shoulders. The only make-up she was wearing was a slick of bright red lipstick. If she didn't look so sullen she would have looked breathtakingly beautiful.

"Let's get out of here," Rose muttered as she marched past Sky.

Chapter Fifteen

Despite the fact that she lived only round the corner, Amber got to Café 1001 a whole hour early. She had to be sure that she'd get the table at the back and, anyway, being at home was no good for her already jangling nerves. Gerald was having a total hissy fit because she wouldn't help him with his Skype interview, stomping around the house like a red-faced rhinoceros, muttering and sighing loudly. Amber didn't know what his problem was; Daniel had already said that he'd help him. She settled back into her leather armchair and attempted to relax. It was all going to be fine, wasn't it? She decided to play a quick game of What Would Oscar Say? and flicked through the pages of her book until her eyes settled on a quote:

"Success is a science; if you have the conditions, you get the result."

Amber smiled and looked around the café; it was half filled with skinny hipsters hunched over their laptops and flat whites. The usual soundtrack of Brazilian dance music was playing, and the faint chinking of cutlery was coming from the counter downstairs. The conditions were definitely right for the first ever Moonlight Dreamers meeting, so Oscar seemed to think that it would be a success – and who was Amber to argue?

Rose frowned as she followed Sky down the station steps. "I thought we were going to the Southbank."

Sky shook her head. A train was just pulling into the platform – a train bound for East London.

"But you said…" Rose followed Sky onto the train. It was crowded with weary-looking commuters and both girls had to stand right by the door – way too close to each other for Rose's liking. Sky obviously felt the same; she started gazing around the carriage in every direction apart from Rose's.

"I thought the Poetry Library was on the Southbank," Rose muttered.

"It is," Sky muttered back.

"But…"

"I'm not going there." Sky looked down.

"Oh. So where are we going?"

"Shoreditch."

"Shoreditch?" Rose's mind started working overtime. She liked Shoreditch. With its arty vibe and quirky coffee shops, it reminded her a bit of Brooklyn – but the thought of going there with Sky, who clearly would rather have been watching paint dry than be with her, wasn't appealing at all. And then she had a terrible thought. "You're not going on a date, are you?"

Finally, Sky made eye contact. "What?"

"A date. Tonight. You're not dragging me along on a date, are you?"

"I'm not *dragging* you along on a date, or anywhere else," Sky hissed.

A few of the surrounding commuters looked at them. Rose leaned a little closer and lowered her voice. "If it wasn't for me, you wouldn't even be allowed out tonight."

"Oh, really?"

"So where are we going?"

Sky gave a sigh. She looked really embarrassed. "To a meeting."

"A meeting?" Rose had not anticipated this answer. "What? Like an AA meeting?"

"No!" Sky practically yelled, causing more commuters to look over at them. This was the thing Rose hated most about commuter zombies – they were so starved of anything interesting in their lives, the slightest sign of activity on the tube caused them to practically orgasm.

"OK, chill. I was only asking. It would be kind of nice to know where I'm going to be spending this evening."

Sky's face flushed bright red. "It's a surprise," she said, in the least enthusiastic voice Rose had ever heard.

Maali lifted the hatch in the counter and slipped out into the front of the shop.

"Don't be too late, pet," her mum said, straightening a tray of pistachio burfi.

"I won't," Maali said, a guilty queasiness stirring in her stomach. This was the first time she'd ever lied to her mum, and it didn't feel good. She'd told her she was meeting some girls from school to do their science homework. Maali felt a stab of panic. What if there were girls from her school at the meeting?

Maali wasn't exactly unpopular. It was more that she was invisible. Ever since she'd started secondary school she'd trained herself to be a chameleon, blending into the background to avoid drawing attention to herself. Her two best friends, Praya and Preethi, had also developed this ability, and between them they'd managed to avoid becoming targets for the scary kids, but the threat was always there. Maali almost did a U-turn back up to the flat, but then she thought of the girl who'd given her the postcard. Amber. She hadn't seemed at all like those scary girls. And anyway, this was too important. She had to take the risk: the entire future of her romantic life was at stake.

"Er, excuse me, aren't you forgetting something?" her mum said, just as she reached the shop door.

Maali froze. "What?"

Her mum smiled and opened her arms.

Maali laughed with relief. Her mum didn't let any of them go anywhere without a hug. She went over and hugged her tightly. "Here you are," her mum said as she let go, handing her a white confectionery box. "Some burfi, to help you girls with your homework."

Maali felt another stab of guilt as she took the box. "Thanks, Mum." Lying was really horrible. She said a quick prayer to Lakshmi in her head, asking for forgiveness, and vowed that as soon as she'd found the confidence to talk to boys she would never lie to her mum again.

Amber took a sip of her camomile tea and glanced at her pocket watch. It was 6.29. One more minute until the others were due to arrive, unless of course they were late – or not coming at all. Amber checked her emails for the millionth time. No new mail. She breathed a sigh of relief. But they might not bother letting her know that they weren't coming. They might have forgotten all about it. They might—

"Hello."

Amber looked up from her phone to see the dead pigeon girl standing on the other side of the table. Her hands were clasped in front of her and she looked about as nervous as Amber felt.

"Hello!" Amber shot to her feet and held out her hand. Why was she holding out her hand? That was the kind of thing Gerald did. She quickly withdrew it, just as the girl held hers out. "Oh, er, sorry." Amber grabbed her hand and gave it a shake. "Sit down. Make yourself comfortable." What was wrong with her? Why was she talking and acting like such an idiot?

The girl sat, or rather, perched, on the edge of the armchair opposite Amber's, as if she might flee at any moment. There was a second's silence, which seemed to stretch into an hour.

"I'm Maali," the girl said.

"Oh yes, sorry, I'm Amber."

"Nice to meet you."

"Nice to meet you too."

"Well, to meet you again."

Amber nodded. "Yes, of course. The pigeon."

Maali shifted awkwardly and looked into her lap.

"I like dead things too." Amber's face flushed as soon as the words left her mouth. What was wrong with her!

"Do you?"

"Yes. I mean, I don't like them, as in, have an obsession with them or anything."

"No, me neither."

"I just don't think we talk or think about death enough – you know, as a society."

Maali looked at her.

"Of course, it might be different for you – in your – your culture." Oh great, Amber thought, now you sound like you're obsessed with death *and* a racist.

Thankfully Maali only nodded thoughtfully. "In Hinduism we believe in reincarnation."

"You're Hindu?"

"Yes." A look of defensiveness flickered into Maali's huge

brown eyes, like she was expecting Amber to say something negative.

"Cool. Yeah, I guess the thought of reincarnation must help. It must be reassuring to believe that you'll be coming back, you know, after you die."

Amber's inner voice began to wail. This was why she had no proper friends; she was absolutely rubbish at conversation. Most girls talked about their latest make-up purchase or what they'd watched on YouTube, but not her. She launched straight into an in-depth discussion about death – after a firm and hearty handshake.

"It helps a bit, I guess." Maali settled back in her chair. "But it still makes my head hurt when I try to imagine not actually being here any more – as me."

The tension in Amber's chest began to ease a little. "Me too," she said with a smile. "Can I get you something to drink?"

"Oh, yes, please, that would be great, could I—"

"Er, hello."

Amber looked up to see the poet girl from the shop standing right behind Maali. She looked really stressed. Another girl was standing behind her – the kind who instantly put Amber on her guard. Thin and beautiful, with a bright scarlet rosebud of a mouth. She reminded Amber of the OMGs at school. Amber looked at Sky questioningly.

"I hope you don't mind but I've brought…" Sky glanced at the girl behind her. "This is … Rose."

"Hi," Maali chirped. "I'm Maali."

"Hello," Sky said. She looked back at Amber anxiously.

"Hi, no, that's fine. The more the merrier. I'm Amber."

Rose raised one of her perfectly plucked eyebrows. Amber was completely unprepared for this nightmarish turn of events. She'd assumed that by making it invite-only, she'd be able to control who came.

"So, what exactly is this all about? What are you guys doing here?" Rose said, staring at Amber.

She was American. Amber wasn't sure whether this made things better or worse. She searched for something to say, but it felt as if her tongue was tied up in a tight knot. What if this girl laughed at her? What if she called her a freak? Then, randomly, one of Amber's favourite Oscar Wilde quotes popped into her head: *"Be yourself, everyone else is already taken."* She took a deep breath.

"We're here for the first meeting of the Moonlight Dreamers," she said, way more confidently than she actually felt.

Chapter Sixteen

"The Moonlight Dreamers?" What the heck were the Moonlight Dreamers? Rose stared at Sky. But Sky kept her gaze fixed firmly on Amber.

"Yes," Amber said. "It's a group for teenage girls who are sick of being told who to be and how to look, and who want to find the confidence to live their dreams. It's supposed to be secret." She looked at Sky pointedly. Sky's face flushed.

Rose's brain started working overtime. Far from dragging her to a dullsville poetry event, Sky had brought her to the meeting of some kind of secret society. She hated to admit it, but it sounded pretty cool. Amber looked pretty cool too. Rose loved the way she'd styled her hair into a quiff and the whole men's suit thing looked awesome.

"Cool," Rose said, barging past Sky and sitting down next to the shy-looking Asian kid.

"Really?" Amber looked at her like she didn't quite believe her. "I mean, you do understand that you mustn't tell anyone about what goes on here tonight."

Rose nodded and settled back into her armchair. "Sure.

I won't say a word." This night out with Sky was shaping up to be way more interesting than she ever could have imagined.

Sky sat down next to Amber, not knowing what to think. She'd been certain that Rose would make fun of the whole thing and had been hoping that she would leave, but from the way Rose was staring at Amber, the very opposite was happening; she seemed engrossed. Sky shifted back in her squishy armchair but didn't take off her coat, just in case Rose did or said something embarrassing and they needed to make an emergency exit.

"So," Amber said, reaching under the table and pulling out a battered leather briefcase, "I wrote some rules to give us some kind of guidelines, but please feel free to add your own." She took out some leaflets and handed them out. "I'll go and get some drinks while you have a read. What would you like?"

"Diet Coke, please." Sky fumbled in her bag for her purse.

"It's OK, they're on me," Amber said with a tense smile.

"I'll have a cappuccino," said Rose, taking off her jacket.

"Could I have an orange juice, please?" Maali asked, sitting bolt upright on the edge of her chair. She reminded Sky of a little bird about to fly away at any moment.

As Sky took a leaflet Maali smiled at her, and a pair of dimples appeared either side of her mouth, making her look even sweeter. They settled back and began to read.

MOONLIGHT DREAMERS ~ THE RULES

1. *The Moonlight Dreamers is a secret society – members must never speak a word of its existence, or of what happens at the meetings, to others.*

2. *Meetings will begin with members reciting the "Moonlight" quote from Oscar Wilde.*

3. *This quote is the Moonlight Dreamers' motto and must be memorized by members – and NEVER forgotten.*

4. *All members must vow to support the other Moonlight Dreamers in the pursuit of their dreams – always.*

5. *Moonlight Dreamers are proud of being different. They would rather die than be the same as everyone else. Being the same as everyone else is a crime against originality; the human equivalent of magnolia paint.*

Sky shivered with excitement as she read the words. It was all so mysterious and poetic. But then she thought of Rose reading the leaflet. She didn't seem like the kind of girl who wanted to be mysterious or poetic – or different. She glanced across the table. Rose was studying the leaflet, her face etched into a frown. Sky's heart sank. Amber headed over to them with a tray of drinks. "So?" she said as she placed the tray down. "What do you think?" She looked at Sky anxiously.

"I really like it," Sky said defiantly, wanting to get in

before Rose could say anything to ruin it.

"Me too!" Maali exclaimed, her brown eyes gleaming with excitement. "Especially the last bit."

They all looked at Rose, who was still staring at the leaflet. "What's the quote and who's Oscar Wilde?" Rose asked, finally looking up at them.

Sky's throat tightened as she noticed Amber's expression harden.

"He's a writer," Amber said curtly. "One of the greatest writers who ever lived."

Rose shrugged. "So, what did he write?"

The Importance of Being Earnest," Amber said.

Rose frowned. "I thought that was Shakespeare."

"No!" Amber looked horrified.

Sky started wracking her brains for some way to get Rose to leave without causing a massive scene.

"He also wrote *The Picture of Dorian Gray*," Maali said. She turned to Amber and smiled. "I googled him after you gave me the postcard."

"Oh, I love that one!" Rose exclaimed with a grin.

"You do?" Amber and Sky said at the same time, sounding equally surprised.

"Uh-huh, my dad was in it."

Amber frowned. "What do you mean, your dad was in it?"

"It's about the dude who makes a pact never to get old, right?" Rose asked. "So he has a portrait of himself painted and that gets old instead."

"That's right." Amber raised her eyebrows, looking about as shocked as Sky felt.

"My dad was in the play." Rose looked down, as if she'd suddenly thought of something sad. "He's an actor."

Sky felt a prickle of curiosity. In all of her obsessive hatred for Rose's mum, she'd totally forgotten that her dad was the actor Jason Levine.

"It was an awesome play," Rose said wistfully.

Amber smiled and Sky breathed a sigh of relief.

"So, what's this mysterious quote, then?" Rose said, picking up her leaflet.

Maali turned to her. "It's 'Yes: I am a dreamer. For a dreamer is one who can only find his way by moonlight, and his punishment is that he sees the dawn before the rest of the world.'" Maali looked at Amber. "I've read it so many times I know it off by heart."

Amber was beaming now.

"It's a really cool quote," Sky said.

"'And his punishment is that he sees the dawn before the rest of the world,'" Rose echoed, looking thoughtful. "What does that mean?"

"What do you think it means?" Amber said, watching Rose carefully.

Rose frowned. "That dreamers stay up all night? But how is that a punishment? I mean, whenever I've stayed up all night I've loved seeing the sunrise. It makes me feel lucky. Like I'm seeing something no one else is, cos they're all asleep."

"Exactly!" Amber said, nodding sagely.

"So it's not really a punishment at all," Maali said. "He was being sarcastic."

"Oh!" Rose nodded. "I like sarcasm."

"So, what do you think?" Amber looked around the table hopefully. "Are you in?"

"I am," Maali said straight away.

Sky nodded. "Me too."

They all looked at Rose.

"Why not?" Rose said casually, flicking her hair over her shoulder.

Chapter Seventeen

Maali glanced around the table at the other girls and said a quick silent thank you to Lakshmi. She was so glad she'd plucked up the courage to come. She could hardly believe she was sitting here in this café, with these girls, having just joined a secret society. It was like she'd been pulled from her boring, nothing-ever-happens life and plonked straight into a movie.

At the table across from them a skinny white guy with dreadlocks started talking loudly into his mobile phone. "I'm flying to Cuba tomorrow," he said. "We're shooting a documentary about the Havana dance scene."

Maali pinched her leg underneath the table to check she wasn't dreaming.

"So," Sky said, undoing her coat, "do you think we ought to do some kind of ice-breaker? You know, to get to know each other a little better?"

Rose yawned. "What, like one of those naff 'if you were an animal what would it be' things?"

Sky's face flushed. "No – well – yes. But not as stupid as that."

Maali couldn't quite work Sky and Rose out. Sky had brought Rose, so they had to be friends, but there was definitely tension between them.

"What, then?" Rose said, staring at Sky.

"Well, we could tell each other what we really love."

Rose frowned. "What we really love?"

"Yes. You know, like what our passions are." Sky looked at Amber hopefully.

Amber nodded. "That sounds good. And we should say what our dreams are."

"Definitely." Sky sat back in her chair.

"Can we say what we really hate, too?" Rose asked. Maali couldn't stop staring at her lips. They were so full and so red. Rose noticed and raised her eyebrows. Maali quickly looked away.

"OK. We'll each share what we really love, what we really hate and what our dreams are," Amber said, pulling a notebook and pen from her briefcase.

"Good idea," Maali said, wanting to add something to the conversation. She took the box of burfi from her bag and put it on the table. "My mum gave us these—" She broke off. What was she doing, mentioning her mum? It made her sound like such a kid.

"You told your mum about the meeting?" Amber frowned.

"What is it?" Rose said, staring at the box.

"They're sweets," Maali said. Her face felt hot enough to melt. She glanced at Amber. "I didn't tell her about the meeting. I told her I was seeing some friends to do homework."

Rose laughed. She leaned across the table, her golden curls tumbling forward, and opened the box. "What kind of sweets are they?"

"Indian," Maali said.

"I like the colours." Rose grabbed a bright green square of pistachio burfi and took a bite.

Maali looked at her anxiously.

"Wow! This is awesome!" Rose's eyes widened and she took another bite.

Amber coughed loudly and tapped the end of her pen on the table. "Right, who wants to start?"

"You should," Sky said. "This was your idea."

Maali nodded while Rose took another bite of burfi.

"OK. My name's Amber and—"

"I'm an alcoholic," Rose interrupted with a smirk. Sky and Amber frowned at her. "Sorry, go ahead." Rose reached into the box for another piece of burfi. Maali couldn't decide whether she liked Rose or not: her feelings towards her kept swaying back and forth like a pendulum.

"My name's Amber," Amber repeated, "and I live just around the corner with my dads and—"

"Your *dads*?" Rose said, arching her eyebrows.

"Yes. My two dads, Daniel and Gerald."

Maali felt her world expanding even further.

"I love vintage clothes and records, and vintage anything,

really," Amber continued, "and I hate people who think they're better than you just because they look a certain way." She glanced at Rose. Rose stared right back.

"What's your greatest dream?" Maali asked quickly.

"My greatest dream is to go to Paris to visit Oscar Wilde's grave. Oh, and to get more people reading my blog."

Amber's dreams were so interesting, Maali thought. So sophisticated. She thought of her own dream: to become confident enough to talk to a boy. It seemed so silly and dull in comparison.

"Cool dreams," Sky said.

"Thank you." Amber took a sip of her drink. "Do you want to go next?"

Sky nodded. "Sure. I'm Sky and I really love living on a houseboat—"

"You live on a boat?" Maali couldn't help interrupting.

"Yes … well, I did until today."

"What happened today?" Maali asked.

"I moved into a house," Sky muttered. "But it's only temporary."

"She moved into *my* house," Rose said with a knowing smile.

"Oh." Maali was dying to ask more, but she could tell from Sky's frown that the conversation had suddenly strayed into dangerous territory.

"She and her dad have moved into my mom's house." Rose sat back in her chair. "Her dad and my mom are screwing."

Maali realized that her mouth had dropped open. She quickly closed it and looked down.

"Yes, well, like I say, I'm sure it's only temporary," Sky said icily. "So, I love living on a boat and travelling the world and poetry, and I hate…" There was a moment's pause, and for a second Maali had the horrible feeling that Sky was going to say she hated Rose. "I hate the fact that my mum is dead."

They all fell silent. Maali instinctively reached for the box of burfi and passed it to Sky, who took a piece and smiled at her gratefully.

"I'm sorry to hear that, Sky," Amber said, her voice softer than usual. "So what's your dream?"

"To find the confidence to compete in a poetry slam." Sky took a bite from a piece of coconut burfi.

"What's a poetry slam?" Maali asked.

"It's where poets have to get up and compete against each other," Sky said.

"What, like a posh version of a rap battle?" Rose asked.

Sky nodded. Maali didn't dare ask what a rap battle was. Instead she just nodded knowingly, as if poetry slams and rap battles were an everyday part of her life – along with having two dads and living on a boat.

"I might be able to help you with that," Amber said, smiling at Sky. "I'm on the debating team for my school, so I know a bit about getting up and talking in front of a crowd."

"Thank you."

Sky and Amber turned to look at Maali.

"Do you want to go next?" Amber asked.

Maali froze. What was she going to say? She glanced down at the table and a line from the leaflet caught her eye. *Moonlight Dreamers are proud of being different*. What was the point in being here if she wasn't able to be herself? Wouldn't that defeat the whole object? She took a deep breath. "I'm Maali and I live round the corner too, on Brick Lane, above my parents' confectionery shop."

"Did your parents make these sweets?" Rose asked.

Maali nodded. "Yes, my mum did. And I love Brick Lane – oh, and Lakshmi."

Rose smiled. "Is Lakshmi your mom?"

"No. She's a goddess."

Rose's eyes widened. Maali's heart began to pound.

"A Hindu goddess, right?" Sky said.

Maali smiled at her gratefully. "Yes. She's the goddess of love, prosperity and beauty."

"Why would you love a goddess?" Rose asked, but she didn't look as if she was being spiteful – she looked genuinely interested.

"Because – because she's always there for me, whenever I have a problem or I need help."

Rose pursed her lips. "But how do you know?"

"How do I know what?"

"That she's always there? Have you ever seen her?"

"No, but I feel her." It was as if there was a giant eel

squirming around inside Maali's stomach. *Help me, Lakshmi*, she silently prayed.

"So, what do you hate?" Sky said quickly.

"Racists." The word popped out before Maali even had time to register it. It *was* what she hated, the only thing she hated.

"Anything else?" Rose asked.

"No."

"And how about your greatest dream?" Amber asked.

This was it: the moment they'd probably all laugh at her for being boring and immature and ask her to leave. "I'd like to find the confidence to talk to boys," she muttered.

"The confidence to what?" Rose asked, leaning closer. She smelled of sugar and coconut.

"To talk to boys." Maali couldn't even bring herself to look at them. They probably all had boyfriends. They probably talked to boys all day long without a care in the world. She waited for Amber to tell her she was too young and silly to be a Moonlight Dreamer.

"But what's so hard about talking to a boy?" Rose asked.

"Nothing, forget about it." Maali wanted to crawl under the table.

Sky passed the burfi back to her with a gentle smile. But Maali shook her head.

"Shall we move on?" Amber said. "Rose?"

"What? Oh, right, my turn." Rose sat cross-legged and pulled her hair back over her shoulders. "Don't worry about your dream," she said to Maali, "I've got it covered. OK, well, I'm Rose and I love New York City and motorcycles and cake."

"Is that where you're from?" Maali asked. "New York?"

"Uh-huh."

"You love cake?" Sky looked at Rose disbelievingly.

"Yes. I mean, seriously, there's just something about a cake, you know? The soft sponge. The melt-in-your-mouth frosting." Rose gazed dreamily into space for a second. A guy walked past gazing equally dreamily at Rose, but she didn't appear to notice. Maali swung back into liking Rose mode.

"And you love motorbikes?" Amber asked.

Rose nodded. "Yep. My dad has a Harley Davidson Hydra-Glide. He takes me out on it when I visit him in LA. It's awesome."

Amber nodded. "So, what are your dreams?"

Rose smiled. "To own a Harley Davidson and be a patissier – that's someone who makes cakes," she added.

"You want to make cakes?" Sky's eyes were wide. Maali wondered why she looked so shocked.

"Yes. And?"

Sky shrugged. "Nothing."

"And what about what you hate," Amber said, jotting something down in her notebook.

Rose shook her hair loose and looked straight at Sky. "I hate people who invade my privacy."

Chapter Eighteen

Amber stepped out onto the roof garden and took a deep breath of the cold night air. For the entire evening her shoulders had felt as if they'd been carved from stone. Now, finally, she could relax.

The first meeting of the Moonlight Dreamers hadn't exactly been perfect – she wasn't sure what to make of Rose, and the tension between her and Sky had been awkward – but, on the plus side, everyone had seemed really into the idea, even Rose. When Amber had suggested they exchange email addresses and arrange a date for the second meeting, they all seemed keen.

Amber looked up at the sky, searching for the moon. It was only half full now, as if someone had flung a black drape over it. She thought back to the night it was full, and how huge and bright it had been. And she remembered how she'd sat up here, gazing out over London and dreaming that there might be other people like her. Now, not even two weeks later, her dream was coming true. Hopefully.

* * *

Sky sat down on the train and hoisted her bag into her lap. Rose plonked down into the seat opposite and closed her eyes. The three men in their section of the carriage turned their gaze on Rose as if she was some kind of eye magnet. Sky felt angry at them for perving, and angry at Rose for being so – so what? For once Sky was stumped for words. So arrogant? So attention-grabbing? But Rose wasn't like her mum. She didn't seem remotely aware of the looks she got from guys, and she definitely didn't do anything to encourage them. But she had been a bitch during the meeting, with her little digs at Sky and the way she'd talked about Savannah and Liam "screwing". At least she'd been vaguely polite to Amber and Maali.

Sky sighed. She should never have brought Rose. She could tell it had pissed Amber off. This is what she hated about Rose – the way she made everything difficult. She stared across at her. Rose still had her eyes closed and a smile was playing on her lips. Or was it a smirk? Was she smirking about the Moonlight Dreamers? Did she think the whole idea was lame? Sky's tension soured into resentment. Rose was so smug. So full of herself. So—

Rose opened her eyes and raised her eyebrows as if to say *what are you looking at?* Sky glared at her, then looked away.

Rose stared at Sky angrily. What the hell was that look for? Rose had come along on her night out, hadn't she? She'd gone along with the meeting. She'd even *enjoyed* the meeting, much to her surprise. It had felt good to talk about the things she loved, and to dream about riding a Harley and being a patissier. And it had been interesting to hear what the other girls had said. They were so different from her classmates at school, who were like a bunch of factory-produced clones, all poker-straight hair and short skirts and lip gloss. Their interests were identical too – clothes and boys and money. She'd never heard a single one of them talk about loving a goddess the way that Asian chick, Maali, had. And though it bent Rose's brain to think about feeling the presence of a goddess, at least it was interesting. At least it gave her something to think about. Just like Amber and her two dads, and her dream of going to Paris to see the grave of that Oscar Wilde dude. It was only Sky who'd made her yawn, with her sappy "I love living on a boat" bullshit. "Why don't you go back there, then, you ungrateful cow?" Rose had wanted to yell.

Rose watched as Sky rummaged around her ethnic-style backpack and pulled out a book. *Right, fine, if that's the way she wants to play it.* Rose pulled out her phone. She noticed a middle-aged guy across from her gawping at her chest and flicked him the finger. Pervert. Rose typed Oscar Wilde into the search engine and clicked on a list of quotes. She smiled as she read them. He sure knew how to do sarcasm. Then she found a quote that made her want to laugh out loud. *"Fashion is a form of ugliness so intolerable that we have to alter it every six months."* Rose decided to print it out and stick it to the kitchen noticeboard as soon as she got home.

* * *

As Rose opened the front door, Sky felt a dull ache inside. She didn't even have a key for her so-called new home. And Rose hadn't said a single word to her all the way back. She'd just sat smirking at her phone. Sky felt a stab of panic. What if Rose had been slagging off the Moonlight Dreamers on social media? She imagined Rose posting a sarcastic Facebook update about them and cringed. She stepped into the hallway and heard her dad's favourite mantra CD playing in the living room. Rose slammed the front door and marched straight upstairs.

"Girls, is that you?" Liam called.

Sky crossed the hall, hoping that Savannah had gone to bed and that she and her dad would have a chance to have one of their late night chats. But Savannah was lying on one of the leather sofas in a robe, staring straight ahead. She looked different. Younger. Paler. Then Sky realized she wasn't wearing any make-up. Liam sat cross-legged on the floor in front of Savannah, like an adoring servant. Sky felt like an intruder.

"Did you have a good night?" Liam asked, leaping to his feet and coming to give Sky a hug.

"Yes, thanks."

"Where's Rose?" Savannah asked. She sounded really tired.

"I think she went straight up to bed."

Sky snuck another glance at her. Her eyes looked really puffy and bloodshot.

"Did you have a good time – together?" Liam looked at her anxiously.

"Oh yes, it was fine," Sky lied. Her mind started going into overdrive trying to work out why Savannah might have been crying. Was it because of the way Sky and Rose had stormed out earlier? Was it because she was having second thoughts about them moving in? Was it because she and Liam had had a fight?

"That's great," Liam said, perching on the sofa and taking hold of Savannah's hand.

The hope that had started chorusing inside Sky was abruptly silenced.

"I'll go to bed, then," she said quietly.

"OK, sweetheart, good night," said Liam, but he was looking at Savannah.

"Good night," Savannah said softly. "I hope you sleep well – in your new bedroom."

"Yeah, thanks." Sky headed for the hallway, her eyes stinging with tears.

LESSONS

Some things I have learned today:

- Dreams don't always work out exactly how you imagine they will
- This is OK – in fact the surprise can make them even more interesting
- Don't judge a book by its cover – or a person by their lipstick
- Lakshmi is the Hindu goddess of love, beauty and poverty (or it might be prosperity…?)
- Parents who sulk, suck!

And here are this week's Wilde words from my hero, Oscar Wilde:

"Be yourself; everyone else is already taken."

Amber

From: lakshmigirl@googlepost.com

To: wildeatheart@googlepost.com

Date: Tues 27th October 22:06

Subject: Thank you – and sorry

Hi Amber,

I just wanted to say thank you so much for organizing the

Moonlight Dreamers meeting and for inviting me! I'm sorry if my dream sounded a bit silly. I didn't mean it to. I just wanted to be truthful, and truthfully, being able to overcome my shyness and speak to boys is my greatest dream right now because I know that if I don't, then I'll never get to meet my soulmate. Anyway, I hope and pray you won't ask me to leave. I thought your dreams sounded amazing.

Maali xx

PS: I didn't tell my mum about the meeting – I promise.

From: wildeatheart@googlepost.com
To:lakshmigirl@googlepost.com
Date: Tues 27th October 22:30
Subject: Re: Thank you – and sorry

Hi Maali,

No need to apologize! Your dream is your dream. And that's fine about your mum – she makes very good sweets! It was really interesting getting to know you and finding out about your faith. I'll be in touch again soon about the next meeting…

Best wishes,

Amber

PS: Is Lakshmi the goddess of poverty?

From: lakshmigirl@googlepost.com

To: wildeatheart@googlepost.com

Date: Tues 27th October 22:34

Subject: Re: Re: Thank you – and sorry

No, Lakshmi is the goddess of prosperity – and love and beauty.

Thank you!

Maali xx

From: lakshmigirl@googlepost.com

To: halopoet@hotpost.co.uk

Date: Tues 27th October 22:41

Subject: Hello

Hi Sky,

It was so lovely to meet you this evening. I was really sorry to hear about your mum dying, though. It must be so hard for you. In the Hindu text the "Katha Upanishad", there's a quote about death which I thought you might like:

"Death is a mere illusion which appears to those who cannot grasp absolute reality. The soul is immortal, self-existent, self-luminous and never dies."

Even though your mum's body isn't here any more, her

soul is. And even if you don't believe in life after death, she will always live on in you and your memories of her and your love for her.

Maali xx

From: lakshmigirl@googlepost.com
To: roselnyc@hotpost.com
Date: Tues 27th October 22:45
Subject: Help with your dream

Hi Rose,

It was really lovely to meet you tonight. I know your dream is to be a patissier so it's not quite the same, but if you ever want to come and have a look around my parents' sweetshop and ask them questions about being confectioners, just let me know.

Maali xx

From: halopoet@hotpost.com
To: wildeatheart@googlepost.com
Date: Tues 27th October 23:37
Subject: Thank you

Hi Amber,

Thanks so much for inviting me along tonight. I really

enjoyed it. And sorry about bringing Rose along unannounced – it was a last-minute thing. Anyway, I was thinking of coming up to Brick Lane on Saturday to buy some more vintage postcards and I was wondering if you fancied going for lunch on your break – if you get a break…?

Thanks again…

Sky x

From: wildeatheart@googlepost.com

To: halopoet@hotpost.com

Date: Tues 27th October 23:37

Subject: Re: Thank you

Hi Sky,

Yes, that would be great. My lunch break is normally at 1pm. See you there.

Best wishes,

Amber

Chapter Nineteen

Amber pulled her notebook from her bag and hid it behind her textbook. She was in maths. This was usually a bad thing. A very bad thing. But they had a supply teacher who didn't look much older than them. She'd asked them to copy half a chapter from their textbooks and now she was sitting at her desk, pretending to look calm and relaxed as she read her book, but Amber could tell she was bluffing. She hadn't shifted her gaze or turned a page for at least five minutes.

Amber opened her notebook to a fresh page and wrote: MOONLIGHT DREAMERS IDEAS. Last night's meeting had been all about seeing if anyone was interested; now she had to get clear on how the proper meetings should be run. She jotted down some ideas.

More mysterious

More secretive

Meet by moonlight

But where could they meet by moonlight that wouldn't be freezing at this time of year? Amber chewed on the end of her pen. There was always the roof garden – after all, that was where it had all begun. She pictured bringing the other girls to her house. Daniel would be delighted. He was always encouraging her to invite friends over. But what about Gerald? He was bound to embarrass her in some way.

Amber heard a chair scraping on the floor behind her. She quickly covered her notebook with her folder.

"So, do you have a girlfriend?" Chloe whispered in her ear. The cloying scent of her perfume made Amber feel sick. *Don't say anything*, she told herself.

"Do you?" Chloe whispered again.

The supply teacher glanced over and looked as if she was about to say something, but then continued pretending to read her book.

"Are you gay?" Chloe said, louder this time, and a couple of their classmates started to snigger.

"You are, aren't you?" Chloe said triumphantly. "You're gay, just like your dads."

"So what if I am?" Amber snapped, her anger bubbling over.

"I knew it!" Chloe cried.

"Is everything OK?" the supply teacher called out nervously.

"Yes, miss," Chloe replied meekly. "You're such a freak," she hissed in Amber's ear before shifting back to her own table.

Amber sat motionless. Why was Chloe obsessed with sexuality? Throughout her childhood Amber hadn't even known there was such a thing as sexuality; she'd thought it was all about love. Sometimes a man loved a woman and a woman loved a man. And sometimes a woman loved a woman and a man loved a man – like Daniel and Gerald. It was no big deal. But ever since she'd started at this school, and Chloe and her friends had found out about her parents, it had become something to feel guilty about. Something to be ashamed of. And Amber hated herself for letting them get to her in this way. Oscar Wilde had had to go through far worse, and he hadn't let it get to him. He'd ended up in jail because of being gay. But that was back in the nineteenth century, when people didn't know any better. Surely things should be different now.

Suddenly a scrunched-up piece of paper landed on the table in front of her. She looked at it like it was a ticking bomb. She knew she should ignore it, but before she could stop, her hands were uncrumpling the paper and she read the scrawled note: *How do you have sex with another girl?*

A chorus of cackles rang out behind her. Amber sighed. The truth was, she wasn't even sure if she had a sexuality. The only kind of boy she ever imagined being with was tall and rakish and wore a cravat – basically a teenage Oscar Wilde. *Was there such a thing as a Victorian-writer-sexual?* As the cackling grew to a crescendo she thought of Oscar again. What would he say to Chloe and her stupid friends? How would he answer them? Like magic, one of his quotes popped into her head. *"There is no sin except stupidity."*

Amber felt a sudden burst of determination. She shouldn't be the one feeling ashamed. They should, for being so stupid. She turned round to face Chloe.

"You're a very ugly person, you know."

Chloe's glossy mouth fell open. "What?"

Amber took a deep breath. "You. You're one of the ugliest people I've ever met."

Chloe looked at her fellow OMGs. They all started shaking their heads in disbelief. "Me?" she said with a pout. "I'm not the one who has two dads and dresses like a man. I'm not the one who – who's a *lesbian*."

"No. But you're the one who's bitter and poisonous. You're the one who gets a kick out of picking on people. You're the nasty little troll."

"Is everything OK back there?" the supply teacher called again, her voice wavering slightly.

Chloe's eyes narrowed. "You're going to be really sorry you said those things."

Adrenalin was pumping through Amber's veins. "Oh, really? I don't think so." She turned back to her desk and started putting her things into her bag. "Please can I be excused, miss? I'm not feeling very well."

The teacher stood up. "Oh – I don't know. What's wrong?"

"There's a horrible smell back here. It's making me feel really sick."

"Just you wait," Chloe hissed.

Amber ignored her and headed for the door.

* * *

"So, how exactly does home-schooling work?" Savannah asked, fiddling with the drawstring on her hoodie.

Sky looked at Liam. The three of them were sitting at the breakfast bar, but only Sky and Liam were having breakfast. Savannah was drinking a glass of hot water with a slice of lemon bobbing on top. Rose had left for school already. Her only greeting had been the loud slam of the front door.

"Well, we have to stick to the curriculum now that Sky's doing her GCSEs," Liam said, taking a forkful of scrambled eggs.

"But Dad adds in loads of fun extras." Sky felt a pang of anxiety as she remembered what he'd said the day before about sending her to school.

"Wow, that's so lovely of you." Savannah smiled at Liam. She was fully made up, but Sky could see that her eyes still looked puffy. "I wish Rose's dad was that attentive."

"Where is Rose's dad?" Sky asked.

Liam frowned. "Sky, I don't think—"

"It's OK, honey," Savannah interrupted, smiling at Sky. "He's in the States, working on a movie. Which basically means he's incommunicado until they finish shooting – he won't even speak to his own daughter." She sighed. "He's a method actor."

"What does that mean?" Sky asked.

"It means he lives, sleeps and breathes his parts. Not just when he's on set, but in all of his spare time too." There was something about the way Savannah said this, a bitterness in

145

her tone, that made Sky think that Jason Levine's method acting had caused her a lot of pain in the past. "Right now he's playing the part of Saint Francis of Assisi," Savannah continued, "so he's turned his back on all earthly things, including cellphones and computers. I don't think Rose has heard from him for weeks."

Sky's feelings towards Rose softened slightly. No wonder she was so prickly all the time. It must be horrible being cut off by a parent like that.

Out in the hall, the letterbox clattered.

"That'll be the papers," Savannah said, instantly looking nervous.

"I'll get them. Don't worry." Liam put down his fork and bounded out of the kitchen.

Sky shifted awkwardly in her seat. It was the first time she'd been on her own with Savannah. She didn't have a clue what to say. She rummaged in her bag and pulled out the first thing that came to hand, a leaflet she'd grabbed in the Poetry Café advertising a poetry slam. She began studying the small print, although she'd read it so many times she could practically recite it off by heart.

"What's that?" Savannah said.

"Oh, just a leaflet." Sky's face flushed. "About a poetry slam."

"Really?"

Sky glanced at Savannah, half-expecting her to be turning away, but she looked genuinely interested. "Your dad's told me all about your poetry."

"Has he?"

"Yes. He says you're amazing."

Sky felt her anti-Savannah barrier lower very slightly.

"Are you going to be entering?" Savannah asked.

"Oh no!" Sky blushed. "Well, I'd like to, but I'm not sure I could, you know … get up in front of all those people and compete…"

Liam returned and placed the papers on the breakfast bar. Savannah looked at them anxiously.

"I'm sure you'll be great," she said, but she sounded distracted. She picked up a paper and started flicking through.

"She'll be great at what?" Liam asked.

Sky showed him the leaflet. "I'm thinking of entering this poetry slam."

"You should." Liam's face was serious. "I mean it, you really should."

"But I—"

"Bastards!" Savannah flung the paper down. "I need to call Antonio," she said, rushing from the room.

"Who's Antonio?" Sky asked.

Liam sighed. "Her manager."

They both looked down at the paper.

SAVANNAH FERNDALE CELLULITE SHAME

the headline screamed, right over a picture of Savannah in a bikini. *Has the UK's top model passed her sell-by date?* The article continued.

"That's horrible," Sky murmured.

"I know."

"Is this – is this why she was upset last night? She looked like she'd been crying."

Liam nodded and ran his hands through his hair, the way he did when he was stressed. "She knew they were going to run a story on her, and she knew it wasn't going to be good. Someone at the paper gave her manager the nod." Liam stood up. "I'd better go and see how she is."

"OK." Sky looked back at the paper. The article accused Savannah of looking "haggard" and "old", and of having had too many cosmetic procedures. *"I think it's time Ms Ferndale gave up gracefully and handed the baton to a younger, more flawless model,"* it concluded. Even though Sky wasn't exactly Savannah's greatest fan, this felt wrong. She heard the muffled sound of crying from upstairs.

Rose stared around the coffee shop blankly. In the background she could hear the monotone hum of her school friends talking – conversations they'd all had a million times before. Who fancied who. Who hated who. Who was going to get "like, so drunk" at the weekend. Yada. Yada. Yada. It was all so freakin' boring. All day Rose had had a weird sense of being disconnected from the rest of the world. In lesson after lesson she'd gone through the motions, pretending to listen, pretending to read and write. Pretending to exist. The only thing she'd wanted to think about, the only place she'd wanted to be, was in the patisserie with Francesca, eating cake and drinking chocolate and being soothed by her lilting accent and beautiful smile.

"Look, there's Matt." Rose's friend Jasmine nudged her as a group from the local boys' school walked into the café. Rose watched Matt with the same sense of detachment. If she didn't know him already, what would she think of him? She studied his shiny chestnut hair, his chiselled jaw, his tight trousers over his rugby player's legs. He was the living, breathing definition of super-cute, she was sure of it. So why did he leave her feeling so dead inside? *You know why*, her inner voice chided. But she didn't want to listen to it. Not now, anyway.

"Parker, get me a skinny hazelnut latte, bruv!" Matt yelled to his friend at the counter.

Disappointment fanned out inside Rose until she felt as if she could barely breathe. Why had she sent him that picture? It was the dumbest thing she'd ever done, and she'd done some dumb things in her time. Rose fumbled under the table for her bag. She had to go.

"Hello, babe." She looked up to see Matt standing in front of her, blocking her escape. Damn.

"Hi," she muttered, putting her bag back on the floor.

"Room on there for me?" Matt asked, nodding to the bench she was sitting on.

"Of course," Jasmine replied in a singsong voice as she shifted along to make room. She fancied Matt, Rose was sure of it.

Rose moved up, searching her brain for an excuse to leave.

Though there was loads of space, Matt sat so close, his thigh was pressing into hers.

"All day I've been looking at that picture you sent me," he whispered.

"What?" Rose's heart began thudding. "In school?"

"Yeah. It definitely made chemistry more exciting."

"But—"

"What?" Matt put his hand on her knee. It felt heavy, like a great slab of meat.

Rose took a deep breath. She didn't want him to see how stressed she was. She had to play it cool.

"Someone could have seen it."

Matt laughed. "Don't worry. They didn't." His fingers started moving up the inside of her thigh.

Rose shifted to try and get him to stop, but instead he moved his hand higher.

"Not here," she hissed in his ear.

He took his hand away. "Shall we go somewhere else, then?"

"Like where?" Rose said, trying to buy a little more time.

"I don't know. Somewhere private."

"I can't. I've got to – got to have dinner with my new step-dad."

Matt frowned at her. "What new step-dad?"

"You know, the yoga teacher." Rose didn't know why she even expected him to remember. Whenever she spoke to

Matt, he was thinking of the next thing *he* was going to say.

"Oh. Right." Matt started to smirk. "Don't think he'll be around too much longer."

"What do you mean?"

"Not if those pictures in the paper are anything to go by." He laughed and gave her leg a squeeze. "Just kidding."

Rose frowned. "What pictures?"

"Of your mum's cellulite and her facelift. They're all over the internet. Didn't you see the Ferndale Facelift hashtag on Twitter?"

Rose felt sick. "No."

Matt put his arm round her shoulder and pulled her tight. "Don't worry. It definitely isn't like mother, like daughter."

Rose pulled away. "What's that supposed to mean?"

"Well, there wasn't any cellulite on that picture you sent me."

Rose felt her hot chocolate coming back up and burning the back of her throat. "I have to go."

"Already? I only just got here."

Rose grabbed her coat and bag. "Yeah, well."

"I was only joking." Matt's face fell. "Do you want me to walk you to the station?"

"It's OK," Rose muttered, standing up.

Matt looked at her legs. She felt his hand moving up them again.

"I have to go," she said. "Can you let me out?"

"Can you let me out, what?" Matt asked with a grin.

Can you let me out, loser, echoed through Rose's mind. Then she thought of the photos he had of her on his phone.

"Can you let me out, please?" she said as sweetly as she could without actually vomiting.

Matt sighed and got to his feet. "Let me know when you're free to meet up," he said.

"Yep. Will do." Rose went to move past him, but his arms encircled her waist.

"Oy, Matthew, get a room, bro!" Parker shouted, coming over to the table with a tray of drinks.

Matt laughed. "Good idea," he whispered in Rose's ear.

Rose pulled her face into a fake smile and slipped from his grasp.

By the time Rose got back to Hampstead her body was taut with tension. A signal failure on the tube meant she'd had to spend half an hour trapped on a crowded carriage with her face in some guy's armpit. And with every automated message apologizing for the delay, her fears had amplified. What if someone saw the photos of her on Matt's phone? What had the papers said about her mom? And what kind of mood would she be in when she got home? Rose thought back to the last time a paper had run a negative story on Savannah, accusing her of having wrinkles. She'd sunk into a deep depression for a month and had so much Botox she could barely move her mouth.

Rose unlocked the front door and stepped into the hall.

Instead of hearing an ominous silence, or Savannah crying, she could hear her laughing – really loudly – in the living room. Then she heard Sky laugh. And Liam. What the hell was going on? She shut the door quietly, crept over to the living room and peered in. Savannah and Sky were walking up and down the room with books balanced on their heads.

"Keep looking ahead!" Savannah called. "Don't show any fear."

"Yeah, work that book, baby!" Liam called, and they all started cracking up laughing again.

Rose shook her head in disbelief. It was like watching a re-run of a scene from her childhood, but with Sky and Liam playing her and her dad.

"When you come to a standstill, put one hand on your hip – it makes you look like you mean business," Savannah said.

Rose watched as Sky did this and Savannah adjusted her.

Rose's throat tightened. So, the moment she'd told Savannah she had no interest in becoming a model she'd found herself a replacement. Rose's body crawled with jealousy. And to think that she'd got angry and defensive when Matt had been joking about Savannah.

Rose slunk upstairs to her bedroom and grabbed one of the pillows from her bed. The first time she punched it she felt self-conscious, but then she pummelled it again and again, pouring out all of the anger and resentment she'd been bottling up for so long. Finally, exhausted, she lay back on her bed and stared up at the ceiling. From now on she was going to do exactly what her parents did: look out for number one. She would get Matt's phone and delete that photo. Then she would leave Liam and Savannah and Sky to play happy families and get the hell out of there. And she would never, ever let anyone hurt her again.

Chapter Twenty

Amber sorted through the coat rail in Retro-a-go-go, her head bursting from a full-blown question attack. This time her questions weren't random or philosophical – they were all targeted on one subject, one person: Sky. *What should she say to Sky when she arrived? How could she keep the conversation going? Where should she suggest they go?* Amber picked up a faded denim jacket that had fallen to the floor. This having a friend business was stressful. If she could call Sky her friend… Could she call her her friend? They'd only met twice and once had been by chance, so that didn't count, did it? Aaargh! Amber shoved the coats back on the rail with such force that the whole thing toppled over.

"Everything OK, darl?" Gracie called from her bar stool behind the counter before taking a pretend puff on her 1920s cigarette holder. Gracie had given up real smoking decades ago, on the day Prince Charles married Princess Diana. Apparently, pretend-puffing on a cigaretteless holder was the only thing that kept her from starting again.

"Yes, fine, thanks," Amber called back, rebalancing the rail.

Gracie pouted her bright pink lips and blew some pretend smoke rings. "What time's your pal meeting you for lunch?"

"One o'clock." Amber flicked open her pocket watch. It was one minute to one. Her heart started to pound. This was crazy. When Sky had emailed suggesting they meet up, Amber had been really happy. And when she'd told Gracie about it earlier, she'd felt really proud. *I have a friend, just like a normal teenage girl*, she'd wanted to shout. But now... *What if she hates you, like all the other girls at school? What if you can't think of anything interesting to say? What if she decides she doesn't want to be a Moonlight Dreamer after all? What if. . .*

The bell above the door jangled. Amber carried on sorting the coats, trying to play it cool.

"Hello!"

Amber looked over her shoulder. Sky was standing by the door, grinning. She was wearing a tie-dyed dress over brightly patterned leggings, a leather jacket and Doc Martens. Her pale blonde curls were fluffed out around her shoulders like clouds of candy floss.

"Hi." Amber said brusquely. Too brusquely. She needed to be more friendly.

"You must be Amber's friend," Gracie called. "Lovely to meet you, sweetheart."

"Shall we go?" Amber said, marching over to the counter to grab her coat and bag.

"Sure. Where do you want to go?"

Amber inwardly groaned. The last thing she needed was Sky adding to her avalanche of questions.

"Take her down the Beigel Bake, darl," Gracie said, leaning back in her chair and taking an extra-large pretend inhale on her cigarette holder. "That shop's proper Brick Lane," she added to Sky. "Best salt beef in all of London. Been there since I was a nipper – not like all those new-fangled, arty-farty shops."

"OK, let's go," Amber said, heading for the door. The last thing she needed was for Gracie to go off on one of her this-place-ain't-what-it-used-to-be rants.

Outside, Brick Lane was bustling with its usual Saturday mix of tourists and hipsters.

"Do you want to get a bagel?" Amber asked, unsure what else to suggest.

"Sure. Got to have the proper Brick Lane experience." Sky grinned. "Was your boss pretending to smoke that thing in her mouth?"

"Yep. She's a little eccentric."

"Looks like lots of fun, though."

Amber nodded. Life certainly wasn't boring when Gracie was around.

When they got to the Beigel Bake they joined the end of the queue snaking out the door.

"Wow," Sky said as the queue shifted, gazing at the crates of freshly baked bagels stacked beside the counter and the silver trays in the chiller cabinets piled high with slices of salt beef and smoked salmon.

"Where would you like to go now?" Amber asked as soon as they'd ordered.

Sky shrugged. "I don't mind. Somewhere we can people-watch."

Amber relaxed a fraction. People-watching was one of her favourite pastimes, and she knew the perfect place to do it.

Amber led Sky into the courtyard at the heart of the Old Truman Brewery. Brightly painted food trucks offered everything from Venezuelan kebabs to Polish sausages. They sat down at one of the trestle tables.

"So – you want to perform in a poetry slam?" Amber cringed. She sounded like she was interviewing Sky rather than having a casual lunchtime chat.

But Sky didn't seem to notice. "Yes. I just need to pluck up the courage to do it. I've only performed once in public before."

"Really? Where?"

"At the Poetry Café. In Covent Garden."

"Wow. Well, surely if you can do it there you can do it anywhere." Amber's skin crawled with embarrassment. Now she sounded like that old Frank Sinatra song, "New York, New York"! Why couldn't she just relax?

Sky frowned. "There were only about five people there, though. And I wasn't competing against anyone else." She opened her can of Coke and took a sip. "So, how long have you been debating?"

"Since I started secondary school. I love it." Amber took a

bite of her bagel. The tang of mustard tingled on her tongue. When she was debating she never had any problem finding the right words. It was the same when she was writing – the words always flowed. It was only when she had to have a conversation that her words came out stilted and unnatural.

"What do you debate about?"

"All kinds of things. Women's rights. The environment. Politics. Once we even had a debate about whether homework should be banned. I argued that it violated the Universal Declaration of Human Rights as an act of tyranny and oppression."

Sky laughed. But it wasn't like the sneery laughs of the girls at school, it was genuine and warm. Amber felt the edges of her tension beginning to thaw. If they could just keep talking about debating for an hour she might be OK.

"So, what do your dads do?"

Amber bristled, but Sky was still looking friendly and relaxed as she took another bite of her bagel.

"Well, Daniel used to be an event manager and Gerald's an artist. Daniel gave up working when I was born to look after me and now he works part-time as Gerald's assistant."

Sky nodded. "Cool. So what kind of art does Gerald do?"

Amber couldn't believe how laid-back Sky was being about her dads. It was so refreshing. She really didn't want to get into talking about Gerald, though. He got more than enough attention. "Portraits, mainly. What about your dad? What does he do?"

Sky took a sip of her Coke. "He's a yoga teacher."

"That sounds interesting."

"Yes. It is. Or it was." Sky's face clouded over. "Until he started doing one-to-one training with celebrities."

"What do you mean?"

"Well, he used to do classes and retreats." Sky's expression lifted. "We travelled all over the world – it was awesome. But since I started doing my GCSEs he wanted me to be in one place, so now he does mainly one-to-one tuition with rich clients."

"Oh." Amber wasn't sure what to say. It was weird hearing Sky sound so bitter. "I don't like what my dad does either."

Sky looked at her hopefully. "The artist one?"

Amber nodded. "The success has really gone to his head. He's so used to everyone adoring him. Sometimes I feel like he's forgotten I even exist."

Sky sighed. "Yep. That sucks."

Amber looked across the courtyard. As conversations went, she was doing OK. It had veered a little onto the gloomy side but at least she was managing to keep Sky talking. A girl hurried past them, her head down against the cold wind. There was something familiar about the golden waves of hair spilling out from beneath her woolly hat. "Wait, isn't that...?" Amber looked at Sky.

Sky was gazing after the girl. "Rose," she said flatly.

"Shouldn't we – shall I call her over?"

"No!" Sky snapped.

"Is everything OK?"

"Yes. No. I don't know." Sky folded her empty bagel bag into tighter and tighter squares. "It's a bit awkward at the moment, what with me and my dad moving into her mum's house." Sky looked at her hopefully, like she needed Amber's support. "Anyway, I'm really enjoying just chatting to you."

Amber's eyes widened. "Really?"

Sky nodded. "Yes. So tell me more about your dream of going to Paris. And what made you like Oscar Wilde?"

Amber leaned forward, resting her elbows on the table. "Well, it all started about four years ago..." she began, and all the right words, in exactly the right order, lined themselves up in her mind.

Chapter Twenty-one

As Rose emerged from the brewery onto Brick Lane she felt a sudden jolt, like she'd just been woken from a dream. What was she doing here? This was crazy. But she felt as if she'd run out of options. Taking Maali up on her offer to visit her parents' store was the only thing she vaguely wanted to do, which showed how sad her life had become.

Rose carried on walking past a row of seedy-looking shops selling prayer mats and cheap overseas calling cards, past a small brick school which seemed so out of place in the grimy, urban surroundings, past a mosque with a huge minaret covered in mirrored tiles. Then, finally, she saw the store: Bluebird Burfi. The window was full of trays of burfi in pastel shades of every colour. Rose licked her lips and opened the door. Inside, the store was bustling with people. They were all Asian, and for the first time she could remember, Rose felt awkward and embarrassed.

"You came!" Maali rushed out from behind the counter and grabbed Rose in a hug. Rose stood there stiffly. Maali let go with a giggle. Rose's heart sank. Maali might have only been one year younger than her, but right now it seemed more like ten.

"Hello!" a woman called out from behind the counter. Rose could tell at once it was Maali's mom. They had the same sparkling brown eyes and dimples.

"Hey," Rose said, trying to look cool, as if coming to a stranger's shop to have a nose around was something she did every Saturday.

"This is Rose, Mum."

"I'm Nisha," Maali's mother said. "Welcome."

Rose nodded. "Thanks."

"Come with me, Rose. I'll show you the kitchen," Maali said, tugging her arm. She reminded Rose of an overeager puppy.

"I hear you're interested in being a patissier," Nisha said, putting some boxes of sweets in a carrier bag.

"I guess." Rose bit her bottom lip. All of this super-friendliness was making her want to clam up.

"Well, go and have a look around and feel free to ask me any questions," Nisha said. "I might not know much about making cakes, but I can tell you loads about the business side of things."

"Thanks."

Nisha's smile grew even wider. "And thank you so much for helping Maali with her maths homework. It's a great idea of the school to have mentors."

Rose frowned. "What?"

"Come on." Maali pulled on her arm, a lot harder this time.

Rose followed her through to the back of the store and into a long, narrow kitchen. Steam was spiralling from a huge metal pot on the stove. The mixture of warm cream, vanilla and coconut smelled delicious.

"I had to tell her you were my mentor at school," Maali whispered, "so she wouldn't get suspicious."

"Suspicious of what?"

Maali stared at Rose like she couldn't believe what she just said. "You're very different to my normal friends," she finally replied. "And you're obviously older. It was the only reason I could think of that you'd be hanging around with me."

Indeed, Rose thought drily. Coming here had been a huge mistake. She knew that now. She'd stay for half an hour, pretend to be interested in the shop and then get the tube to Camden. She thought of sitting in the patisserie with a pastry and a steaming mug of hot chocolate, and her stomach rumbled.

"So, did you mean it?" Maali said as she started stirring whatever was in the pan.

"Did I mean what?"

"That you'd help me with my dream?"

"With your ... oh, what, teach you how to talk to boys? Sure. Maybe some other time, though. I can't stay very long."

Maali's face fell. "How long can you stay?"

"About twenty—"

"So, Rose – it is Rose, isn't it?" Nisha said, breezing into the room.

Rose nodded.

"Would you like a cup of tea?"

"Oh, OK. Yes, please." Rose decided that she'd have some tea and leave as soon as she'd finished.

"Sweet chai or normal tea?" Maali said, turning the kettle on.

"Sweet chai, please." Rose had no idea what sweet chai was, but it sounded exotic.

Nisha gestured at her to sit down at a worn pine table at the end of the kitchen. Rose unwound her scarf, but decided against taking off her coat; she didn't want Maali to think she was staying.

"So, tell me, why is it that you want to make cakes for a living?" Nisha said, still smiling at Rose.

Rose suddenly felt vulnerable. For the past few days she'd been clinging to her dream like a life raft. Picturing a day when she was a patissier had been her only escape from the nightmare at home. What if Maali's mom told her it was a dumb idea? What if she told her it would never work? Then what would she do? What would she have to cling to?

"I love cake," Rose said lamely.

"Yes?" Nisha said, but it was more like a question, as if she wanted her to go on.

"I love the way it makes people feel." Rose frowned. Where had that come from?

"I know exactly what you mean," Nisha said.

Rose stared at her. "You do?"

"Yes. I feel the same about my confectionery and that is why I created this place – to make people feel good. To see their smiling faces when they choose their sweets."

Rose relaxed a little. "I also love the idea of creating new flavours, and new combinations of flavours."

"You're just like Maali," Nisha said. "She's always on at me to try new flavours with my burfi, aren't you, pet?"

Maali came over to the table, carrying a glass teapot filled with a honey-coloured liquid. "It gets boring making the same old flavours all the time," she said with a grin.

Her mom was smiling too. Rose tried very hard not to like them, but it was impossible. Being smiled at in stereo was wearing her down.

"I know!" Nisha cried. "Why don't you two create a new flavour for me this afternoon?"

"Seriously?" Rose said.

"Yes." Nisha turned to Maali. "Maybe you're right. Maybe we need something new."

Maali looked at Rose. "But don't you have to go soon?"

Rose took off her coat. "It's OK. I can stay awhile."

"This has been really lovely," Sky said as she and Amber made their way back up Brick Lane to Retro-a-go-go.

"It has?" Amber stared at her, her pale green eyes wide.

"Yes. Thanks so much for the voice projection techniques. They're going to be really useful."

Amber smiled shyly. "You're welcome. Glad to help. And

thank you for the advice about Paris. Asking my dads to take me for my birthday is a genius idea."

Sky smiled. "I hope they say yes."

Amber sighed. "Me too. Oh well, here we are. Better get back and let Gracie go to lunch."

"Sure. Well, see you at the next meeting, then."

"Yes. I'll let you know the venue by tomorrow at the latest."

"Cool." Sky wondered whether she should give Amber a hug but decided against it. Amber didn't really seem like a huggy kind of person. "See you then."

Sky continued walking along Brick Lane, thinking about their lunch. She thought it had gone well, considering it was only the third time they'd met. Amber was a bit guarded, but there was something about her that Sky really liked. She seemed genuine. Then Sky's thoughts turned to Rose. What had she been doing up here? Where had she been going? Sky had barely seen Rose since the Moonlight Dreamers meeting. She'd heard her, though, slamming doors and clattering plates and the *thud, thud* of basslines pounding from her bedroom.

Sky reached the turning for the train station and stopped. She thought of going back to the house in Hampstead, with its blank white walls and characterless furniture. And she thought of Savannah and Liam all wrapped up in each other and Savannah's recent drama. She turned away from the station and started heading in the opposite direction. She would go back to the boat and light some incense and make some green tea, and then she would curl up in her bunk and work on her new poem. And for one afternoon at least, she would pretend that the Savannah and Rose nightmare hadn't happened.

"Taste this. It's O.M.Genius!" Rose took a spoonful of mixture from the pot and held it out to Maali.

Maali dunked her finger in it and put it in her mouth. "This is amazing," she gasped.

After assembling every ingredient in Bluebird Burfi on every available work surface, they'd decided upon a combination of orange and cardamom. The kitchen looked like a mad scientist's laboratory, with bags of sugar and jars of spices spilling out all over.

"Do you think it could use a little cinnamon?" Rose asked, tasting the mixture again.

Maali searched for the cinnamon and handed it to Rose. Rose sprinkled some into the pot and gave it a stir. She looked so different from when she'd first arrived. Her cheeks were flushed and her hair was flecked with sugar, and she looked really, really happy.

"OK, chef, whaddaya reckon?" Rose said, holding out the spoon again.

Maali took another taste. Now it was just right. The cinnamon went perfectly with the cardamom. "You have a real gift for this, you know."

"Seriously?"

Maali nodded. "Yes. You seem to know what's going

to work before you even try it. It's like your tastebuds are psychic."

Rose threw her head back and laughed. Maali flinched. She'd been trying so hard not to appear immature and silly. She hoped she hadn't blown it.

"Psychic tastebuds!" Rose said. "I love it!"

Maali breathed a sigh of relief. This was going better than she ever could have imagined.

"So, how are you guys doing?" Nisha said, coming into the kitchen. "Oh wow! You have been busy."

"We've made orange, cinnamon and cardamom. What do you think?" Rose offered her the spoon.

As Nisha tasted it her face broke into a smile. "This is delicious. Truly. Well done, girls. I think I'm going to have to add it to the menu."

"Seriously?" Rose glowed with happiness.

Thank you, Lakshmi, Maali silently whispered, grinning from ear to ear.

Chapter Twenty-two

"Are you sure you don't mind doing this?" Maali asked as she followed Rose into the coffee shop.

"Of course not. Although I can't think why you would want to know how to talk to guys – all they ever want to talk about are sports and themselves."

Maali blushed. "It's not *all* guys, it's…"

"One guy?" Rose raised her eyebrows. "I see. OK, watch and learn, sister." She headed over to the end of the counter where a Mediterranean-looking barista was tapping some used coffee grounds into a bin. Maali watched as Rose took off her woolly hat and shook out her hair. "Hey," she said softly to the barista, pursing her bud of a mouth into a pout. Maali edged closer.

The barista turned to Rose and grinned. "Hey. What can I get you?"

"What do you recommend?"

Maali studied Rose. She'd lowered her head slightly and was gazing at the barista from beneath her long eyelashes. His grin widened, as if it were blooming beneath her gaze.

"Well, it depends what you're in the mood for." Something about the way he said it made Maali think he wasn't just talking coffee any more.

"Something really strong," Rose said. "We've been working all afternoon and I need a kick-start."

At the mention of the word "we" the barista finally flicked a glance at Maali. She lowered her gaze the way Rose had, but he'd already turned away.

"It sounds as if you need one of our new Colombian espressos," he said to Rose. "They have a really rich flavour. Almost chocolatey, with a hint of oak."

"That sounds awesome." Rose sighed. "Thank you so much!"

Maali had never heard Rose so enthused. It was as if the barista had just told her he'd give her a life-saving kidney. But he didn't look suspicious – if anything he was gazing at Rose even more adoringly.

"And your friend?" he said, still looking at Rose.

"Oh, could I have a chai latte, please? That would be awesome," Maali said, trying to mimic the same soft tone Rose had used.

"What?" The barista dragged his gaze away from Rose.

"A chai latte would be awesome," Maali said in her normal voice.

"Cool." He reached up to the shelf behind him to get some cups.

Rose winked at Maali before turning back to the barista.

"So tell me, where are you from originally?"

"I'm from Florence," he replied. "The city of love."

"I thought that was Venice," Rose said.

He shook his head. "Huh, they like to think so, but it isn't true. Are you from America?"

"Uh-huh, New York. The city that never sleeps."

"This is a good combination." The barista took a fresh scoop of grounds and put them into the coffee maker.

Rose looked at him questioningly. "What is?"

"You and me. The city of love and the city that never sleeps." He winked at Rose. Maali cringed, but to her surprise, Rose threw her head back and laughed.

"So, are you here on holiday?" the barista asked as he poured their drinks.

Rose shook her head. "No. Living here. For the moment, anyway."

Maali sighed as she tried to imagine talking to Ash so effortlessly. Rose's face hadn't flushed once. She didn't look flustered in the slightest.

The barista placed their cups on a tray. He scribbled something on the receipt and handed it to Rose. "My number," he said. "If you ever fancy meeting for a drink, Miss City That Never Sleeps."

Rose put the receipt in her coat pocket, all the while gazing at the barista from beneath her eyelashes. "Thank you," she murmured.

It wasn't until they got to a table at the far end of the café that her smile faded. She passed Maali her drink. "So, did you see what I did?"

"I think so. Speak softly and smile a lot and look at them like this." Maali lowered her gaze.

"Yes. And ask them about themselves and laugh at their crappy jokes."

Maali stared at Rose, wondering why she seemed so bitter. She was about to ask if she had a boyfriend when Rose's phone began to ring. "Sorry, won't be a minute," she said, and took the call. "Yes?... What rugby night out? But I thought we were going to the movies... OK... I'm not in a mood, that's fine. Have fun... Yep. See you." Rose terminated the call and sighed. Her face was an angry red. She put her phone down. "Men! I'm telling you, they're all completely self-obsessed."

Maali looked down. Ash hadn't seemed self-obsessed, he'd seemed really nice. She heard Rose sigh again and looked up.

"So, who is he, then?" Rose asked. "The guy you like."

"Oh, someone I met a couple of weeks ago."

"He doesn't go to your school?"

"No. He works around here." Maali cringed. The more she talked about Ash the more stupid the whole thing seemed. She'd only seen him twice and had barely spoken to him. Why was she going to all this trouble for someone she barely knew? *Because he might be your soulmate*, her inner voice gushed. Maali made a mental note to never, ever say this to Rose.

Rose's phone rang again. "What?" she answered sharply.

Maali could hear the tinny sound of a woman's voice on the other end. It sounded as if she was yelling.

"OK, no need to stress," Rose said. "I'm having coffee with a friend... No one you know... I don't know – soon... All right, no need to shout... I don't know where she is – up a tree, writing a poem?... OK, OK. I'll be back in half an hour." Rose put her phone back in her pocket. "I'm really sorry, I'm going to have to go. My mother is having a total hissy fit."

Maali nodded. "That's OK. Thank you so much for today."

Rose looked at her and her expression softened. "You're welcome. I had a great time at your mom's store. Thank you for inviting me." She put her hat on and tucked the rest of her long hair under her coat. "I guess I'll see you Tuesday, then, at the next meeting."

"Yes. Definitely."

Rose downed her tiny coffee and stood up. "Ask him about himself, laugh at his jokes and stare at him like he's going out of fashion."

Maali looked at her blankly.

"Your guy. Do all that and you'll have him eating out of your hand."

Maali smiled. "Right. Will do." She took a sip of her chai latte and watched as Rose made her way down the café. Even the way she walked screamed confidence, hips swinging loosely from side to side, her gaze focused ahead.

"See you soon, I hope, Miss New York!" the barista called after her.

"Yeah, whatever," Rose called back, and headed out the door.

Chapter Twenty-three

"So, I was wondering," Amber said as Daniel passed the gravy to Gerald. "Would it be possible for you guys to take me to Paris for my birthday?"

Daniel's face lit up. "Paris?"

"Absolutely not," Gerald said, pouring some gravy over his dinner before passing the jug to Amber.

Amber stared at him. "Why?"

Gerald gave one of his theatrical sighs, the ones that in sigh-language translated as, *Why, oh why, do you have to be so tiresome?* "I have exhibitions about to open on both sides of the Atlantic. I don't have time for any jaunts to Paris." He picked up his knife and fork and began to eat. The classical music playing on the radio built to a crescendo, perfectly mirroring Amber's growing disbelief. Surely he wasn't still sulking about that stupid Skype interview? Surely he wouldn't take it out on her on her birthday?

"But – it's my birthday."

Gerald placed his knife and fork down on his plate, slowly and deliberately. "I didn't say we wouldn't celebrate your birthday. I said I can't go on any trips anywhere for the foreseeable future."

"Perhaps we could fit in a day trip?" Daniel said. "The Eurostar only takes a couple of hours—"

"Fit in a daytrip?" Gerald gave another sigh. "Darling, I can't fit in an afternoon tea right now. You know how busy I am."

"I know, but it is Amber's sixteenth."

Gerald shook his head. "Paris isn't going to go anywhere. We can visit in the new year – after the exhibitions – oh, and the Salvador Dali Awards. Did I tell you that Sergei says I could be in with a real chance this year?" He lifted his glass of wine as if he were toasting his own brilliance and took a swig.

Hurt bubbled up inside Amber until it burned at the corners of her eyes. She'd taken it for granted that her parents would agree to her birthday request. She'd spent all afternoon in the shop dreaming of going to see Oscar Wilde's grave. She should have known Gerald would ruin it.

"Would that be OK, honey?" Daniel asked, his eyes full of concern. "If we went in springtime, once all the exhibitions are over?"

Amber's birthday was at the end of November. If they went in spring it would be an entire season too late.

"Don't worry about it," she muttered. She looked down at her dinner and the tears filling her eyes made the meat and vegetables merge into one. Damn. The last thing she wanted was to let Gerald see how hurt she was. "I think I'm going to go to my room. I'm not very hungry."

"Oh for goodness' sake!" Gerald's glass clinked against his plate as he put it down on the table.

"What?" Amber snapped.

"I didn't say we couldn't go. I said we couldn't go just now. Why do you always have to sulk when you don't get your own way?"

"*Me?*" Amber pushed her plate away and got to her feet. If she didn't leave the room in the next few seconds she was going to tip the gravy jug all over his head. "How can you tell *me* off for sulking? You've been in a sulk for the past two weeks!"

"I have not!" Gerald pushed his plate away and glared at her.

"Yes, you have, just because I wouldn't help you with that stupid Skype interview."

"OK, guys, let's calm down." Daniel grabbed Amber's hand. "Don't go to your room, honey. We can sort this out."

"There was nothing stupid about that interview," Gerald boomed. "I told you, I inspired that young man to become an artist. I was his muse. It was incredibly rude of you to refuse to help me."

"Oh, really?" Amber pulled away from Daniel and glared at Gerald. "Well, it was incredibly rude of you to miss my school debate."

She marched from the kitchen and up to her bedroom, taking the steep steps two at a time.

"Aaaaargh!" she yelled as she flung herself down on her

bed. Gerald was insufferable. How could he call her the rude one? The email notification on her phone pinged and for a moment she felt a glimmer of hope. Maybe it was from Sky or one of the other Moonlight Dreamers. But when she went to her inbox she saw it was from Dictionary.com. Amber clicked the message open and read her word of the day:

Slangwhanger: *a loud, obnoxiously offensive person*

She flung her phone down triumphantly. This wasn't mere coincidence. Even Dictionary.com knew that Gerald was vile. She vowed to call him a slangwhanger at the first opportunity. There was a knock on her bedroom door. Amber sat upright, her heart pounding. Maybe she'd have the opportunity right now.

"Honey, can I come in?" Daniel called.

Amber sank back against her pillows. "Yes, OK."

Daniel entered the room and perched on the end of her bed. "I'm so sorry," he said.

Amber felt a prickle of hope. *I can't stay another moment with that slangwhanger*, she imagined Daniel saying. *You and I are moving out. You are my biological daughter, after all.*

"You know how tense he gets before exhibitions," Daniel said. "And this time he's got two of them. But we will go to Paris. I promise."

Amber sat up a bit. "What? Just you and me? On my actual birthday?"

Daniel shook his head. "No, the three of us. Once the exhibitions are over."

"But that won't be till the spring."

"I know. But don't worry. We'll do something really fun in London on your birthday."

Amber suddenly felt exhausted by it all. She was sick of Gerald demanding his own way all the time and Daniel and her having to bend to fit around him like they were made of Plasticine.

"I hate him," she muttered.

"Amber!"

"No, I really do. It's not just tonight. It's him generally. He's so selfish." She shifted closer to Daniel and lowered her voice. "I just want you to know that if you are only staying with him because of me, it's OK. We can leave. I truly won't mind. Why would I? He's not even my dad."

Daniel looked at her, shocked. "How do—"

"It's obvious," Amber interrupted. "I mean, I look way more like you and I'm nothing like that – that slangwhanger."

Daniel's eyes widened. "That what? Amber – I—"

"It's OK. You don't need to say anything. I just wanted you to know that I know and I would be totally fine about us leaving him."

"Right." Daniel's face creased into a frown. "Right…" He took hold of her hand again. "We're both your dads, Amber."

"Yeah, yeah, whatever."

"No, really, we are. And I'm not going to leave Gerald. I love him, in spite of him being a slangwhanger, whatever that might be."

"But—"

"But nothing." Daniel gripped her hand tighter. "We're a family, sweetheart, and families have their ups and downs, but they stick together."

Amber stared at him. "No, they don't. Families break up all the time. Forty-two per cent of marriages now end in divorce. It's true. I looked it up."

"You looked it up?"

"Yes."

Daniel sighed. "Well, Gerald and I are definitely not getting divorced."

The hope inside Amber spluttered and died like a damp firework. "But why?"

"Because I love him."

"But why?"

"Because he's Gerald." Daniel sighed again. "Look, I know he can be tiring, but he can also be loads of fun, and life certainly isn't dull when he's around. And he's got a heart of gold underneath all that bluster."

Amber raised her eyebrows.

"He has. He gives away thousands to charity every year and he did set up that scholarship fund. The way I see it, his more tiring aspects are the price we pay for the good stuff."

Amber kept staring at Daniel in disbelief. What good stuff?

"Why don't you come back down and finish your dinner?"

Amber shook her head. "I'm really not hungry. But you go down. I'll be fine."

"Are you sure?"

Amber nodded.

Daniel moved closer and gave her a hug. Usually Daniel's hugs felt like the safest place in the world but not this time, not after what he'd just said. Her only escape route had just been boarded up.

When Daniel left, Amber lay down and stared at the ceiling. Great. Her pretend dad was a slangwhanger and her real dad was too nice and forgiving to see it.

One thing was becoming glaringly obvious. She was going to have to make the Moonlight Dreamers work. Her entire future happiness depended on it.

—

From: wildeatheart@googlepost.com

To:lakshmigirl@googlepost.com; halopoet@hotpost.com; roselnyc@hotpost.com

Date: Sunday 1st November 19:05

Subject: Next meeting

Dear Moonlight Dreamers,

I have found a venue for our next meeting. Meet me at the corner of Hanbury Street and Wilkes Street at 7pm on Tuesday. Dress warmly and please bring something moon-related.

Best wishes,

Amber

Chapter Twenty-four

Sky raced up Brick Lane, checking the time on her phone. It was almost ten past seven. She was late, and it was all Rose's fault. She'd assumed Rose would be coming home straight from school and they'd go to the meeting together. But Sky had waited as long as she could and there'd been no sign of her. She should have known this would happen. Rose was probably taking advantage of the fact that Liam and Savannah were away and had gone out partying with her friends.

Liam had taken Savannah to a Buddhist monastery for an overnight retreat in a bid to stop her having a complete nervous breakdown. OK, he hadn't exactly said that. He'd said it was because Savannah was "interested in finding out more about him and his life", but Sky knew the truth. Ever since the story about Savannah had broken last week she'd bounced like an emotional pinball from upset to super nice (to Sky at least) to raging. Sky had heard her yelling at Rose the night before about coming home late. "Who the hell do you think you are, treating this place like a hotel?" she'd screamed. Sky hadn't heard Rose's reply, but the whole road had probably heard her bedroom door slam.

Sky turned into Hanbury Street. A group of people was clustered around one of the doorways. "This is where Jack the Ripper murdered his first victim," she heard one of them – obviously some kind of tour guide – say. Sky shivered. The cafés and clothes shops had closed for the night, and a thin mist hung in the cold air. It was easy to picture how it had been back in the days when Jack the Ripper had prowled these streets, looking for victims. Sky looked up the road to see if there was any sign of Amber and Maali: Google Maps had said that Wilkes Street was somewhere on the left. And then she spotted them, standing beneath an old-fashioned lamp post. Amber was wearing a long men's overcoat that almost came down to her ankles. Maali was in a pretty cape-style coat with a huge pink scarf wrapped round and round her neck.

"Hey! Sorry I'm late," Sky gasped as she ran up to them.

"That's OK," Amber said briskly.

"Where's Rose?" Maali asked, looking around, slightly disappointed.

"I don't think she's coming." Sky looked at Amber apologetically. "Sorry." The truth was, she wasn't sorry at all. The meeting would be way more relaxed without Rose there.

"She is," Amber said. "She texted me earlier to say she'd be a bit late coming back from work experience."

Sky felt a weird twinge of hurt that Rose had texted Amber and not her, before reminding herself that she really didn't care.

"OK, then, let's go up," Amber said, turning onto Wilkes Street. As Sky followed her she caught her breath. The street was lined with old three-storey houses with large sash windows and tall chimney stacks. Combined with the cobbled paving and antique streetlights, it was as if they'd stepped straight onto the set of *Sherlock Holmes*. She half expected to see a horse-drawn carriage clattering around the corner through the mist.

"Up where?" Maali asked.

"To the roof." Amber stopped in front of a huge sage-green door with a brass fox's head knocker. Matching green shutters flanked each of the ground floor windows.

"Is this – your house?" Sky asked.

Amber nodded, taking a bunch of keys from her pocket. "Yep. Follow me."

The girls entered a large hallway. The floor was tiled black and white like a chessboard and the only light came from a stained-glass lamp on a small table next to the door. In the opposite corner a grandfather clock ticked loudly. Amber slung her keys on the table and gestured at Sky and Maali to follow her up a wide, winding flight of stairs. As they got to the first floor Sky could hear the murmur of men's voices from behind one of the heavy wooden doors. Amber's dads. Sky wondered what they looked like and wished one of them would come out, but Amber didn't seem in any mood to introduce them as she hurried on up another flight of stairs. When they reached the third floor she led them along the narrow passageway to a door at the end. "Yes, well, er, welcome to the roof terrace," she said and opened the door.

"This is amazing," Maali exclaimed as she stepped outside.

Sky stood in the doorway for a second, taking it all in. The roof terrace was surrounded on three sides by trellising thickly covered in ivy. The fourth wall was slightly lower and lined with huge pots full of plants.

"I thought we could have the meeting here," Amber said, walking over to the corner surrounded by the high trellis walls. She'd arranged four garden chairs in a circle around an outdoor heater. Candles in different coloured glass jars flickered beside each of the chairs. "What do you think?" Amber looked at Sky anxiously.

"I think it's perfect."

Amber's face visibly relaxed. "You do?"

Sky nodded.

"I do too," Maali said, turning full-circle to take it all in. "I think it's magical."

Amber smiled, and Sky wasn't sure if she'd ever seen anyone more transformed by a facial expression. With her square jaw and piercing green eyes Amber could look quite severe when she was serious, but when she smiled her entire face went into soft focus.

"Sit down," Amber said. "I made us some tea. Would you like—"

The sound of a clanging bell rang out from deep within the house.

"That'll be Rose," Amber said, hurrying back to the door. "Make yourselves comfortable. I'll go and let her in."

Sky sat down heavily in one of the chairs, her body suddenly static with tension.

Rose gazed up at the imposing house. It was like something out of a Victorian horror movie. No wonder Amber dressed the way she did and liked that Oscar Wilde dude – she was living in a time-warp. Rose was about to ring the bell again when the door was flung open. A tanned guy with golden hair stood holding a tea towel and smiling at her. "Yes?"

"I'm Rose. Amber's friend."

"You are?" His eyes widened in surprise. "I mean, of course. I'll just see if—"

"It's OK, I'm here." Amber came bounding downstairs. "Hi," she said, practically shoving the guy out of the way. "Come in."

Rose stepped into the hallway and looked around. The house was just as spooky and olde worlde on the inside. There was even a grandfather clock ticking in the corner.

"Who is it?" she heard another guy call from upstairs.

Amber flinched. "Come on," she said, grabbing Rose's arm. "If he says anything to you, just ignore him." As they went upstairs an older guy came out onto the landing. He had cropped white hair and was wearing an expensive-looking royal blue shirt and jeans. "Hello," he said, looking and sounding totally surprised.

"Er, hi," Rose muttered. Amber shot her a glare, but what was she supposed to do? She could hardly ignore him when he stood right in front of her.

"Aren't you going to introduce us?" the man asked Amber.

Amber shook her head. "We don't have time."

"How do you do? I'm Gerald," he said, holding his hand out.

"Rose," she said, quickly shaking it. Amber gave her another glare. Well, this was Awkward City. Still, Rose couldn't help feeling slightly relieved that she wasn't the only one having issues with a parent. The atmosphere between them was colder than the air outside.

"Come on," Amber said, leading Rose up another flight of stairs.

"It was so lovely to meet you!" Gerald called after them. He had a voice like one of those old-school British actors from the black and white movies – his words neatly clipped and polished. "Although it was over far too soon, alas!"

Rose couldn't help grinning. "Yeah, parting is such sweet sorrow and all that!" she called back. There was a moment's silence, filled only by another glare from Amber, before she heard Gerald bellow with laughter.

"Please don't encourage him," Amber hissed, leading Rose along another landing and up another flight of stairs.

"Sorry," Rose whispered. "Is he your artist dad?"

"Yes."

"And the guy who opened the door?"

"Daniel. My other dad," Amber said brusquely.

"Cool house," Rose said, quickly changing the subject.

"Thanks."

Jeez, she was hard work. Rose felt a sudden pang of doubt. Had she made a mistake coming here? Should she have just gone back to Hampstead and made the most of being home alone for once? But then she thought about being in that huge house with only her fears for company. It was better to be here and not have to think about being a total loser in the parent lottery and her so-called boyfriend playing hard to get. For about the hundredth time that day an image of her topless selfie popped into her head. She had to get hold of Matt's phone and delete it. Then he could play hard to get all he liked, she wouldn't give a crap.

"Here," Amber said, opening a door at the end of the passageway. A blast of cold air drifted down to Rose. She followed Amber out onto some kind of roof garden. The others were sitting by a heater in the corner, surrounded by flickering candlelight. Sky was looking more hippyish than ever, in a floor-length tie-dyed skirt and a fake fur coat. Maali started doing her eager puppy act, waving at her excitedly. "Hey, Rose! It's great to see you!"

Rose sighed. Why did she have to be so freakin' happy all the time? "Great to see you too, Maali." She sat down next to her, in the chair furthest from Sky, and carefully placed her bag on the floor beside her.

Amber sat down in the remaining chair. "So," she said.

The others looked at her expectantly.

"Welcome to the first proper meeting of the Moonlight Dreamers. Shall we all say the quote first to get things started?"

Rose noticed Sky glance at her. Did she think she hadn't learned it? Well, she was going to be in for a shock. Rose had had the quote as her screensaver for the past week. She knew it back to front and inside out.

"Let's stand," Amber said, getting to her feet. "It feels more…"

"Formal?" Sky said.

Amber nodded.

"Shall we hold hands?" Maali asked as they all stood up. "To, you know, make a proper circle?"

Amber looked uneasy. "Oh, I don't know."

"I think that's a great idea," Rose said, taking Maali's hand and reaching out for Amber's.

Amber and Maali smiled at her gratefully. Ha, she'd show Sky she was entitled to be here.

When they were all holding hands, Amber cleared her throat. "Shall we start by focusing on the moon?"

They looked up at the sky. It was a weird orangey black from the light pollution. Rose could make out a handful of stars, but there was no sign of the moon.

"It isn't visible at the moment because it's the dark of the moon," Amber explained, "the time right before the new moon begins to emerge. But it's still up there, looking down on us. It's always up there looking down on us."

They stood in silence for a moment. Rose wasn't sure why, but there was something strangely comforting about being reminded that the moon was always there, even when you couldn't see it.

"'Yes: I am a dreamer…'" Amber began.

"'For a dreamer is one who can only find his way by moonlight'" – the others joined in, Rose saying the words extra loudly for Sky's benefit – "'and his punishment is that he sees the dawn before the rest of the world.'"

Rose felt a shiver run up her spine. It was probably the cold. It *had* to be the cold. But it felt dangerously close to excitement.

Chapter Twenty-five

"So, did everyone manage to bring something moon-related?" Amber asked as soon as they'd sat back down. To her massive relief the others nodded, even Rose.

Maali started rummaging in her bag and brought out a small framed picture.

"Would you like to go first?" Amber asked.

"Oh. I – I don't know," Maali stammered. "OK." She held the picture up. "This is Chandra. He's the Hindu moon god." She passed the picture to Rose. "He's supposed to bring wealth and happiness, so I thought it would be auspicious – for us, I mean – to have him here. But if you don't like him I can…"

Maali fell silent as Rose passed the picture to Amber. It was of a smiley-faced man dripping with gold jewellery and sitting in a huge lotus flower carriage pulled by four white horses. Two crescent moons arced out of the side of the carriage like a pair of giant tusks. Amber wasn't sure what to say, so she nodded and passed the picture to Sky.

"I remember my dad telling me a really cool story about Chandra when I was little," Sky said, gazing at the picture.

She looked up at Maali. "You know, the one about why the moon waxes and wanes? Why don't you tell the others?"

"OK." Maali looked at them all shyly. "So, in Hindu tradition, the story is that Chandra was married to twenty-seven brides."

"What, all at the same time?" Rose asked, raising her eyebrows.

Maali nodded. "Yes. They were all different star constellations."

"Ri–i–ight," Rose said slowly.

"Then, one day, Chandra started paying way more attention to one of his brides, so the other twenty-six went to see their father, Daksha, and complained to him."

Rose nodded. "And then what happened?"

"Daksha put a curse on Chandra and made him catch consumption."

"What's consumption?" Rose asked.

"I'm not exactly sure," Maali replied. "Some kind of serious disease."

"It's what they used to call tuberculosis," Amber said.

"Right," said Maali. "So pretty soon Chandra got really sick and he started to waste away. As soon as the wives saw what was happening they regretted what they'd done and begged their father to undo his curse."

"Huh, I wouldn't have," Rose retorted.

Sky frowned. "Carry on," she said to Maali.

"Well, it was impossible to undo a curse once it had

been made, so all Daksha could do was modify it. He made Chandra shrink for two weeks, then allowed him to grow back to his full size for two weeks, then made him shrink again – and so on."

"That's why the moon waxes and wanes," Sky said. "Isn't it cool?"

"But you don't seriously believe that, right?" Rose turned to Maali and frowned. "I mean, the moon isn't a fat guy in a chariot with twenty-seven wives."

"It's a fable," Sky said curtly.

Amber sighed. She'd been hoping things would be better between Sky and Rose this week, but if anything they seemed even worse.

"It's baloney, is what it is," Rose muttered. Then she turned back to Maali. "Sorry, I don't really do religion."

Amber looked at Maali. Even though she agreed with Rose, she didn't want Maali to be upset. To her surprise, Maali was still smiling serenely. "That's fine," she said. "We can all believe whatever we want to."

Rose nodded. "It was a cool story, though."

"Thank you," Maali said.

"Shall I go next?" Amber said, eager to get the meeting back on safer footing.

The others nodded. Amber reached into her coat pocket and pulled out a moonstone. She'd found it on a gemstone stall at the market. The guy running the stall had told her he didn't have any, so when she'd found it hidden at the bottom of a box of rose quartz she'd taken it as some kind of sign. Most moonstones were mainly white, but this one glowed purple, blue and gold as well. And it was the perfect shape: round and fat, just like a full moon. "I found this moonstone the other day," she said, passing it to Sky. "I thought we could use it."

"What for?" Rose asked.

Amber shrugged. "I don't know – some kind of group talisman?"

"It's beautiful," Sky said, wrapping her hands around it. Then she passed it to Maali.

"Wow!" Maali gasped.

"Aren't gemstones supposed to have special properties?" Sky asked.

Amber nodded. "Apparently moonstones are good for bringing calm and peace." She couldn't help thinking of Sky and Rose.

"They're meant to be great for creative energy too," Rose added. "My mother went through a major feng shui phase when my dad left. We had a moonstone egg in every room of the house. Apparently you need to recharge them by the light of the moon." Rose's eyebrows were raised sceptically. Maali passed her the moonstone and her expression softened. She held it up to the candlelight. "This is really cool. I love how it changes colour."

"Me too," Maali said.

"What are we supposed to do with it?" Rose asked, still gazing at the stone.

"I was thinking we could take turns looking after it—" Amber began.

"What, like the class gerbil?" Maali said, and instantly looked embarrassed. "When I was in primary school we had a pet gerbil and we all took turns taking it home for the weekend," she muttered, looking down.

"Yes, a bit like that, but the person who takes it home for the week is the one who needs it the most," Amber said.

The others nodded.

"Kind of like a guardian moonstone?" Rose said.

"Exactly," Amber replied. "Would you like to go next?"

Rose stared at her blankly. "I'm sorry?"

"Sharing your moon-related thing."

"Oh! No, is it OK if I go last?"

Amber tried hard not to look annoyed. She still wasn't sure what to make of Rose. She seemed dangerously like Chloe and the girls at school, with her pouty lips and long hair, and the way she seemed to want everything her own way. She turned to Sky, who was rummaging through her backpack. "Sky, do you want to go, then?"

"OK, well according to Google there's this really cool ritual that people do during the time of the new moon," Sky said, pulling out a battered-looking notebook. "And as it's that time I—"

"I thought you said it was the dark of the moon," Rose interrupted.

"Yes, well, the dark of the moon happens right before the

new moon, so I'm sure it's OK," Amber said, looking at Sky anxiously. She was glaring at Rose.

"So, yes, as I was saying, apparently the new moon is a great time to manifest our dreams and desires." Sky pulled a stack of magazines from her bag.

"What's your desire?" Rose said, looking pointedly at the magazines. "To catch up on celebrity gossip?"

Sky's face darkened. "No, it isn't," she snapped. "I get enough of that living in your house."

Rose jumped to her feet. "What the hell's that supposed to mean?"

A montage of doom began playing inside Amber's head. Rose and Sky were going to kill each other – probably by pushing each other off the roof – and the Moonlight Dreamers would be over before it had even begun. And she would be left with nothing. No friends at school, no trip to Paris, no hope of achieving her dreams…

"I think you know exactly what it means," Sky said, glaring at Rose.

Do something! the voice in Amber's head cried. *Do something before it's too late!*

"Oh, really?" Rose said, taking a step towards Sky. "You think you're so clever, don't you. You think—"

"Stop!" All of them – including Amber – jumped. She hadn't meant to yell, but now that she had, they were all looking at her, mouths hanging open, and she couldn't stop.

"I don't know what the problem is between you two and I don't want to know, but, please, can you just stop? I've had the world's worst week. Everyone at my school hates me. One of my dads has made it his life's work to make my life hell and the other is too nice to stop him. And I just— I just…" Suddenly all of the anger drained from Amber's body, leaving her feeling as floppy as a rag doll. "I just want something good," she said feebly. "Something that makes me feel good about my life so that I can stop feeling like a non-person." Amber stared into her lap, mortified. Now it was definitely all over. Now they'd probably throw her off the roof before they threw each other.

Rose pulled her chair right up to hers. "I'm sorry," she said. "If it's any consolation, I think I came joint top with you in the World's Worst Week Award."

Amber glanced at her. Rose's eyes were filled with concern. "Really?" Amber could hardly believe someone as beautiful and poised and confident as Rose could have an average week, let alone a bad one.

Rose nodded. "Uh-huh. I'm sorry," she muttered. "I just want something good too."

"Me too," Sky said quietly.

Amber watched apprehensively as Rose turned to look at Sky. "Truce?" she asked.

Sky nodded. "Truce."

"Yay!" Maali exclaimed. "The moonstone is working already."

They all looked at her questioningly.

"It's brought calm and peace," she explained shyly.

"I guess it has," Rose said.

Chapter Twenty-six

"The idea is you cut out the pictures that appeal to you," Sky explained. "The ones that in some way symbolize your dreams and desires." She watched as the others started leafing through their magazines. She particularly watched Rose for any sign that she hadn't meant what she said before about the truce. But Rose was tearing out a picture already, her lips pursed in concentration. Sky was relieved. She'd felt awful when Amber got upset. And, much as she didn't like Rose, there was no way she was going to let the tension between them ruin the Moonlight Dreamers. She watched as Amber tore a picture from her magazine. What had she meant about one of her dads making her life hell? And why did no one at school like her? Amber was definitely different, but different in a really interesting and unique way. Sky couldn't understand why people wouldn't like her. As for Maali, nothing seemed to faze her.

Sky started flicking through her own magazine. There was a picture of the Eiffel Tower in the Travel section. She carefully tore it out and passed it to Amber. "I thought you might like this one – you know, for your Oscar Wilde dream."

Amber smiled, and again her entire face softened. "Thank you."

"I've got one for you," Rose said gruffly, passing Sky a picture, but barely making eye contact. Sky's throat tightened. What if it was a joke? She looked at the picture. It was of a microphone stand. What was that supposed to mean?

"It's meant to symbolize the poetry slam," Rose muttered. "I can take it back if you don't like it."

"No! I really like it," Sky said quickly. "Thank you."

Rose carried on flicking through her magazine. "Yo, Maali, I got the perfect one for you."

"What is it?"

Rose held up a picture of a huge red love heart. Sky wondered whether Rose was making fun of Maali. But Maali grabbed the picture eagerly. "Thank you."

"No problem."

How come Rose got on so well with the others? Sky kept flicking through her magazine and tore out a picture of a book to symbolize her poems. "OK, once you've got a picture for each of your dreams put them in the middle of the circle," she said. She put down her picture of a microphone stand and book. Amber put down the picture of the Eiffel Tower and a photo of a laptop.

"The laptop symbolizes my blog," she explained.

Maali put down the love heart, a picture of a dark-haired guy and a picture of a horse.

"Aha, is that *the guy*?" Rose said with a knowing grin.

Maali nodded.

"So what's the deal with the horse?" Rose said. "Is he a cowboy?"

"No!" Maali exclaimed. "He works on a farm."

"For real?" Rose asked.

Maali nodded shyly.

Sky tried really hard not to look surprised. Of all the things she could have anticipated hearing tonight, Maali having the hots for a farmer was way down at the very bottom.

Rose put a photo of a chocolate cake and a picture of a guy on a motorbike into the circle. "I couldn't find one of a Harley," she said, "so this'll have to do. I don't want the guy on it, though – just the bike."

"That's fine," Sky said. "It doesn't matter if it's not exactly like your dream, as long as it's symbolic of the dream in some way."

Rose nodded and almost appeared to smile. Their truce was definitely holding.

A breeze drifted across the roof garden, ruffling the pictures.

"Let's use the candles to hold them down." Amber took the candle by her chair and placed it over the edge of her pictures. The others followed suit.

"Shall I put Chandra down there with them?" Maali asked. "You know, for good luck."

"Sure," Sky said.

"I'll put the moonstone down too," Amber said, placing the stone next to the picture of Chandra.

"Now what do we do?" Rose looked around the circle.

The truth was, Sky wasn't sure what they were supposed to do next. On the internet it had suggested pinning the pictures onto a vision board. But they didn't have a board and, anyway, they needed to come up with something unique – something just for the Moonlight Dreamers.

"We need to focus on our photos for a moment," Sky said, "and get a really clear picture of our dreams in our minds."

Rose nodded. "And we need to bring the moon into it too, right?"

"Yes." Sky glanced at Amber for inspiration.

Amber looked thoughtful. "I think we should ask the moon to help us make our dreams come true."

"Yes, just like when I pray to Lakshmi," Maali said.

"But this definitely isn't a religious thing," Rose said.

"I know, I know." Maali smiled.

"OK, let's all look at our pictures and really imagine our dreams coming true," Sky said. She gazed down at the microphone stand. Then she closed her eyes and pictured standing at the front of a packed Poetry Café, holding the microphone as effortlessly as a pop star. *Hello, my name's Halo*, she imagined saying before performing her poem. And for a moment she was actually there: she could actually hear herself performing the poem and a ripple of applause afterwards. She opened her eyes. The others seemed to be lost in their dreams too. Sky watched as one by one they opened their eyes.

"That was amazing," Maali whispered.

"Yeah, well, I hope you and Old MacDonald didn't get too X-rated down on the farm," Rose said with a grin.

Maali giggled. "Of course not."

Amber was smiling softly. "I felt as if I was actually in Paris," she said.

"Tell me about it!" Rose exclaimed. "I could practically smell the gasoline. I dreamt I was riding to the cake shop where I worked. It was epic!" She looked at Sky. "Now what?"

"Shall we take it in turns to say something to the moon? Give thanks or something?" Amber suggested.

Sky nodded.

"Let's hold hands again," Maali said. "To, you know, link up."

Sky took hold of Maali's and Amber's hands. It didn't feel so weird this time. In fact, it felt nice. Safe.

"Why don't we take it in turns to ask the moon to help us," Sky said. She looked up into the dark night sky. "Please help me find the confidence to perform in the poetry slam." She turned to Amber.

"Please give me the patience to deal with the imbeciles at my school and my slangwhanger of a father," Amber said.

Rose looked at her. "Your what?"

"Slangwhanger," Amber said. "It means a loud, obnoxious person."

"Cool!" Rose chuckled.

Amber nodded at her. "Your turn."

Rose looked momentarily stumped, then she looked up too. "Oh – uh – please help me make my dreams come true and – uh – if you could also help out with the other issue, that would be awesome."

Sky bristled. What "other issue"? Was Rose talking about her? Rose opened her eyes and nodded at Maali.

"Dear Chandra," Maali began, "please help me make my dreams come true and help me overcome my shyness. Thank you." She closed her eyes and bowed her head.

They stood in silence for a moment.

"Now what do we do?" Rose asked.

"We should release our dreams into the cosmos," Maali said.

"And once again, in English?"

"We need to let them go, to let Chandra – the moon – do its magic."

"Yes," Sky agreed. She was sure she'd read about this somewhere: that once you'd made a wish you were supposed to let it go. "But how?"

Another breeze drifted across the roof garden.

"Easy," Rose replied, looking around. "We fold up the pictures and throw them into the wind."

"Good idea," said Amber.

Rose smiled. "Thanks."

They picked up their pictures and folded them tightly.

"Come on." Amber led them over to the wall without the trellis.

Sky looked down to the street below. It was completely obscured by the gauzy mist. It was perfect.

"Should we say something as we let them go?" Maali asked.

"The quote," Sky and Rose said together.

"Jinx," Rose muttered.

"'Yes: I am a dreamer…'" Amber chanted, throwing her dreams into the mist.

"'For a dreamer is one who can only find his way by moonlight…'" Sky said, releasing hers.

"'…and his punishment is that he sees the dawn before the rest of the world,'" Maali and Rose chanted together as they threw their dreams from the roof.

They all watched as the paper disappeared into the mist.

"Now what?" Maali said, her eyes wide and sparkling.

"Now it's my turn to share something moon-related," Rose said, looking slightly embarrassed. "I – uh – I made you some cakes."

ROSE'S RECIPE FOR MOONLIGHT DREAMER CUPCAKES

Ingredients

175g butter, at room temperature

175g caster sugar

2 teaspoons vanilla extract

3 eggs

Juice and zest of 1 lemon

200g self-raising flour

1 pinch salt

- Beat the butter, sugar and vanilla.
- Stir in the eggs, one by one.
- Then stir in the lemon juice and zest. (Don't be put off if it looks a bit gross at this point!)
- Mix the flour and salt together, then slowly add to the batter. (Don't worry about the lumps, just keep on mixing and they will eventually go.)
- Spoon the mixture into cake cases. (You will need 15–24, depending on how big you like your cakes and how much mixture ends up flying out of the bowl…)
- Bake in a pre-heated oven at 180°C (which is apparently gas mark 4) for about 15 mins.
- To test if the cake is ready, stick a cocktail stick into the middle. If it comes out clean it's done, if it's covered in gooey stuff, it isn't.

Frosting

For an awesome cream cheese frosting, mix 450g cream cheese with 125g of softened butter. Then add 1 teaspoon of vanilla extract and 250g icing sugar. (Make sure you sieve the icing sugar or you'll live to regret it!)

Chapter Twenty-seven

As Maali turned on the fairy lights around her shrine she felt weightless with joy, as if she were a giant, heart-shaped helium balloon. Tonight had been brilliant. She hadn't felt as self-conscious as before, and visualizing her dream coming true had been way more powerful than any of her daydreams about Ash – and she'd been having a lot! Plus Rose had made them the most amazing moon-inspired cupcakes. Fluffy lemon and vanilla sponge, topped with a cream cheese frosting because, as Rose had said, the moon was supposed to be made from cheese.

"Thank you, Lakshmi, for bringing the Moonlight Dreamers into my life," Maali whispered to the statuette of the goddess. "And thank you for helping Rose get her work experience."

As they'd sat eating the cakes and drinking tea from Amber's flask, Rose told them how she'd got the work experience at a French cake shop in Camden: she'd simply asked if she could help out. "You have to do stuff to make your dreams come true, right? You can't just sit around and wish," Rose had said. Maali needed to be bold, like Rose. She needed to do something. But what? She looked back at Lakshmi.

"What should I do?" she asked. She waited for inspiration, but all she could hear was the low hum of her parents talking downstairs. She said a quick prayer, then pulled her laptop from her desk and flipped it open. If Lakshmi couldn't help, then maybe Google could. *How do I talk to boys?* she typed into the search engine and hit ENTER.

Rose cracked an egg on the side of the mixing bowl and watched as the glistening yolk plopped into the cake mix like a splosh of yellow paint. It was Wednesday afternoon. Sky and her dad had gone to see an exhibition in the West End as part of her home-schooling and Savannah was in meetings with the cosmetics company she was "the face" of.

Rose wasn't sure why, but school was making her feel edgy. Her uniform felt too tight, the lessons too regimented, the noise too loud. She'd spent all morning dreaming of being alone in the kitchen baking cakes, so when the bell for lunch break rang she'd told Jasmine and the others she wasn't feeling too well and got the train home. She took the bowl into the crook of her arm the way she'd seen Francesca do it, and started to beat the egg into the mixture with a wooden spoon.

A new track began playing on her laptop. She'd picked a playlist on Spotify called *Parisian Walkways*, figuring it would help her imagine being back in the patisserie. She glanced at the title of the track. "Non, Je ne regrette rien"; No, I regret nothing. Rose started beating the mixture in time to the song. As if on cue, a shaft of pale sunlight burst through the clouds and poured into the kitchen. Even though it was pretty old and crackly, there was no denying it was a kick-ass tune. Rose started singing along. That's how she wanted to live her life – never regretting a thing. And she didn't regret a thing, apart from sending Matt that photo.

To stop herself from stressing, Rose closed her eyes and imagined she was back in the patisserie. She'd gone there on Sunday, inspired by her visit to Maali's mom's shop, and asked Francesca if she could do some work experience. Francesca had given her a breathtaking smile and grabbed her in a hug. She'd smelled of a delicious mix of vanilla and cocoa.

Rose felt a strange shivery sensation in the pit of her stomach. She quickly opened her eyes and carried on stirring. Francesca was chronically short-staffed so she'd been overjoyed at Rose's offer and told her to come in after school whenever she liked. Rose went back to the counter and tipped some flour into the mixture. Francesca didn't use scales when she baked. "Eet is all about the feeling and knowing," she'd told Rose. Rose wasn't exactly sure what she'd meant, but she had made a careful note of the consistency of the cake batter when they'd put it into the cases. She tipped in some more flour and stirred. Little puffs erupted from the bowl as the song started building to a crescendo and Rose stirred more vigorously in time. *"Non, Je ne regrette rien!"* she sang along, louder and louder as she stirred faster and faster. Everything was going to be OK. She had work experience doing something she loved, with someone she … she really liked. She and Sky were carefully choreographing their movements around the house to make sure they never met, and tonight she was seeing Matt and she would sneak his phone and delete the photo. She started dancing round the kitchen with the mixing bowl as she thought of finally being free from Matt and his wandering hands and his creepy text messages. *"Je ne regrette ri—"*

"What's going on?" Savannah's voice cut through the music like a scalpel.

Rose put the bowl on the counter and her spirits crashed back down to earth. The usually immaculate work surface was covered in splatters of cake mix and flour. She slowly turned round. Savannah was standing in the doorway, hands on hips. There were black mascara smudges under her eyes, as if she'd been crying. Shit. Something was badly wrong. Savannah was as anal about her make-up being immaculate as she was about the kitchen.

"What are you doing?" Savannah said in the tight little voice she always used right before going nuts.

"I'm baking," Rose muttered, glancing at the clock. Damn. It was only just gone two-thirty. She was well and truly busted.

"Baking?" Savannah spat the word out like it tasted bad.

"Yes." Rose felt her hackles start to rise. What the hell was her problem? Surely it wasn't a crime.

Savannah marched in and shuddered. "And what is that?" She pointed to the mess on the counter.

"It's flour, Mother."

"Flour?" Savannah's mouth fell open. They hadn't had flour in the house since she'd developed a wheat allergy right after being dropped by Victoria's Secret.

"It's OK, you don't have to eat any of them," Rose muttered.

"Any of what?"

"My cakes."

"Cakes?" Savannah looked at the bag of sugar on the counter and gulped. "You're making *cakes*?"

A new song started playing. Something bouncy and loud and very French. Rose squirmed. What had seemed fun and relaxing now seemed embarrassing and stupid under the filter of her mom's glare. Savannah marched over to the oven and switched it off. Then she snapped the laptop shut. The sudden silence threatened to swallow Rose whole. But she couldn't weaken now. She hadn't done anything wrong. Well, apart from skipping school, but Savannah hadn't even noticed that.

Savannah sighed and shook her head as she looked around the kitchen. "I want you to clean up this mess and then go to your room," she said. "I cannot deal with this right now."

"But my cakes…"

"You're not making cakes."

Rose felt her temples start to throb. "But I've made the mixture. I bought the ingredients." She gestured at the mixing bowl. "What am I supposed to do with this?"

"Throw it out. All of it. Right now. I can't believe you would do this to me."

Rose stepped back, shocked. "Do *what* to you?"

"Make cakes. Bring *that* into my house." Savannah marched over to the bag of sugar and threw it into the bin.

Rose stared at her. "Are you for real?"

Savannah slung the flour into the bin. "Don't back-chat me, Rose. After the day I've had I'm *so* not in the mood."

This was insane. Rose thought of all the things Savannah could have caught her doing and she was getting busted for baking some freaking cakes.

"I want this place cleaned and back to normal right now," Savannah said.

"Oh, really." Rose's heart was pounding so hard she could hear the thump-thump in her ears. She held the mixing bowl out in front of her, then very slowly and deliberately tipped it over. The gloopy cake mixture splattered onto the floor.

Savannah screamed and threw her hands in the air like Rose had just let loose a cage of rats.

"You'd better go get a mop then, hadn't you?" Rose said. She turned and marched from the room, tears burning her eyes.

Chapter Twenty-eight

As Maali approached the City Farm she glanced down at the index card in her hand. Lakshmi might not have been able to give her any tips on how to talk to Ash, but wikiHow had been brilliant – it had pages of advice, which she'd condensed like a set of revision notes:

- Use his name frequently
- Comment on the weather / surroundings
- Ask him for help – men love to help
- Smile and thank him
- Compliment him
- Ask interesting open-ended questions eg., if your house was on fire what would you save?
- Listen more than talk
- Ask for a pop culture recommendation
- End on a high note – like a joke (maybe dinosaur one?)

Maali stuffed the card back in her pocket. She knew it off by heart – she'd been studying it in every lesson that morning. Then she felt a flicker of doubt. What if Ash was on his lunch break too? What if they missed each other like star-crossed lovers, doomed by fate and badly timed lunch breaks never to meet? Aaargh!

Maali took a deep breath and tried to compose herself. She had to get a grip. Rose wouldn't act like this. When Rose wanted to work in a cake shop she just marched into one and asked for a job. So Maali was going to march into the farm and ask Ash for some tips on pigs. She'd decided to pretend she was researching pigs because a) she'd last seen Ash feeding some pigs, so he must know something about them, and b) there was no way she could tell him the real reason she was there.

Maali stared up at the rusty sign and gulped. *It's fine. There's nothing to fear.* Ignoring the churning in her stomach, she made her way over to the pig enclosure. He probably wouldn't even be there. He probably—

"Hello again." She felt a tap on the shoulder and spun round. Ash was standing behind her, grinning. In the pale winter sunlight his brown eyes were flecked with gold. *Oh, Lakshmi, please don't let me faint.* She quickly looked away.

"Hello – I…"

"Yes?"

What had wikiHow said? What was on the card? Her mind had gone completely blank. It was as if Ash had some spooky power over her, the power to wipe all words from her mind like a human white-board eraser. *A human white-board eraser!*

What am I doing? What am I thinking? She had to get a grip. *Say his name. Ask for help,* her inner voice yelled.

"I need your help, Ash." No! That sounded all wrong. It was way too serious, way too soon. *Talk about the weather.* "Lovely weather," she added.

Ash half-grinned, half-frowned, like he couldn't decide if she was funny or deeply troubling. "What? Oh. Yes, it's nice to see the sun. So, how can I help?"

"What?"

"You said you needed help."

"Oh. Yes. Yes, I do — Ash. I need help with pigs." *I need help with pigs. Yep, that sounds really attractive.*

"With pigs?"

"Yes. For something at school." That was better. That was slightly more sane.

Ash nodded. "Ah, I see. Of course — I'd love to help."

Maali said a silent prayer of thanks to wikiHow.

Ash did up his scuffed leather jacket and rubbed his hands against the cold. "But I'm on a half-day today. I'm just off to college."

Maali's heart sank. They were doomed!

Ash took a woollen hat from his pocket and put it on, making his cheekbones even more pronounced. "Is there any chance you could come back tomorrow afternoon?"

"Yes! Of course." Maali took a deep breath and tried not to give any hint that right now a choir of angels was singing a rousing chorus of "Hallelujah" inside her head. "What time?"

"Four?"

"That's great. Thank you so much, *Ash*."

"You're very welcome, *Maali*," Ash said, an amused twinkle in his eye. "See you later."

Maali turned and headed back out of the farm. A lone blackbird perched on top of a spindly tree gave a long, piercing squawk, but to Maali it sounded as sweet as the coo of a dove.

Rose took a gulp of her drink and felt the vodka burning a trail down her neck. The music in the club was so loud it was reverberating right through her. Usually she liked this because it helped to blur the edges between her and the music, but tonight it only added to her nerves. What had happened earlier with her mom had completely thrown her. She'd been feeling so calm when she'd been baking, almost happy, but now it was like the world had tilted slightly off its axis and nothing was quite as it should have been. Matt, for instance. He should have been all over her by now so that she'd be able to sneak her hand into his jacket pocket and fish out his phone, but instead he was standing with Jasmine and Will, swigging from his bottle of beer. Rose took another gulp of her drink and adjusted her skirt. She hated wearing skirts, especially ones this short, but it was a price worth paying if it helped get Matt's attention – if it helped get Matt's phone.

The band finished playing and, in the split second of

silence before the shouts of applause, she heard Jasmine's fake laugh ring out like a siren. She watched as Jasmine brushed a floppy lock of hair from Matt's face. No freaking way! Rose was not letting that happen until she'd deleted the photo. She strode over to them. "Hey," she murmured in Matt's ear.

"Hey." He looked at her and looked away. Shit. But then it came. The double take. He looked back at her, eyes wide. The extra make-up and low-cut top had clearly paid off. "Hey," he said again, circling her waist with his arm. Rose glanced at Jasmine and felt a stab of satisfaction at the flicker of disappointment on her face. "You look amazing," Matt said as Jasmine turned away. His breath was hot and beery on her face. Rose tried not to flinch.

"Thanks. So do you."

Matt nodded. Arrogant asshole.

The band started playing another song and a loud screech of feedback rang out round the club. Rose flinched as it pierced her eardrums.

Matt pulled her closer. "Do you want to go somewhere quieter?"

"Like where?"

"Seb's."

Matt's friend Sebastian lived just off Camden High Street, about two minutes from the club. Maybe she should go there with him. Maybe if they went back there it would be easier. She could get him to take out his phone. Then wait for him to need to use the bathroom, quickly delete the photo, make her excuses and leave. That would work, wouldn't it? Her brain felt fuggy from the heat and the noise and the vodka. She didn't like feeling like this. She liked feeling sharper and more in control.

"Why not?" she murmured in his ear.

He looked at her, surprised. "Seriously?"

She nodded, then made herself kiss him.

Matt quickly put his beer down on a nearby table. "OK. Great. I'll get his keys."

Rose took out her lipstick and quickly reapplied. She wished she could shake this unsettled feeling. She shouldn't have had so much to drink before leaving home tonight. Why did her mom have to be such a crazy-maker?

"Come on," Matt said, slinging a heavy arm around her shoulders.

"Where are you guys going?" Jasmine shouted over the music.

"Private party!" Matt yelled. Again, Rose saw the flicker of disappointment on Jasmine's face. As of tomorrow Jasmine could help herself, but right now she could go to hell. Rose gave Jasmine a forced smile and put her arm round Matt's waist.

Seb's house was at the end of a narrow residential street. Matt paused before unlocking the door and pulled Rose to him. Their teeth clashed as he kissed her hard on the mouth. She pulled away, trying not to shudder.

"What's up?" he said.

"Nothing. Let's go inside."

He nodded and fumbled with the key in the lock. Finally, he got the door open and they stumbled into a darkened hallway. Matt flicked on a light switch and led her into the living room. It was like stepping inside an Ikea catalogue, all pine floorboards and white-washed walls and furniture in every shade of taupe. Rose willed Matt to sling his jacket onto an armchair and go to the bathroom. But instead he headed straight over to a drinks cabinet in the corner. "Whisky?" he asked, waving a bottle in the air.

"Sure." Rose wracked her brains trying to think of some way to get his phone. It was like sifting through treacle. "Hey, have you seen that thing on Facebook?"

Matt sloshed some whisky into a couple of glasses. "About your mum?"

Rose's heart skipped a beat. "No. What about my mom?"

"Getting dropped by that cosmetics firm." Matt brought the drinks over to the sofa and sat down.

So that's why Savannah had been in such a rage. She'd lost the contract. Her *major* contract.

"Come and sit down," Matt said, holding her drink out to her.

Rose perched beside him and took the glass. She couldn't think about Savannah now, she needed to get the photo. "No, I meant the video that everyone's talking about on Facebook. The one about the – the kitten. Do you have your phone? I can show it to you."

Matt looked at her and laughed. "There's only one thing I want you to show me," he said, his voice slurry from drink, "and it's not on Facebook." He took a swig from his glass, then shifted up close to her. As he moved in to kiss her Rose blocked her mouth with her glass. She took a slug of whisky and almost wretched. It was vile. But it was better than kissing him. Anything was better than kissing him.

"We don't have much time, you know," he said, leaning forwards to put his drink on the floor. "Seb will be back soon." He took hold of her hand. "I can't believe I've finally got you alone. I was beginning to think you were just a tease."

Rose took another mouthful of the vile drink. How could she get hold of his phone? Her head began to pound. Matt took her glass and put it down on the floor. "You drive me crazy," he whispered, right in her face.

"I — I need to use the bathroom," she said. His face clouded over. "Before, you know..." His expression lifted.

"Sure. It's down the hall, last door on the right."

Rose stumbled out into the hallway. She looked longingly at the front door. She could leave right now, but then she'd never get the photo, so she turned and headed for the bathroom. It was like walking on a ship. With every step the floor seemed to lurch and roll away from her. Rose staggered into the bathroom and over to the sink. She. Had. To. Sober. Up. She splashed some cold water on her face, then looked in the mirror. Her reflection was out of focus, as if the mirror were covered in steam. Rose sat on the edge of the bath and took a deep breath and then another. Finally, when she was feeling slightly more together, she made her way back to the living room. Matt was standing, his jacket flung on the floor. "I need to go now too," he said. "Back in a sec."

Through her vodka-haze Rose felt a sharp stab of relief. Heart pounding, she crouched on the floor and fumbled in his jacket pocket for the phone. What if he'd taken it with him? What if he'd put it in his jeans pocket? But he hadn't. It was there. She typed in the passcode. He'd told it to her one time when he'd asked her to take a photo of him playing rugby. She clicked on his text messages and started scrolling through, but her message wasn't there. Why wasn't it there? He must have moved the picture. He must have saved it to his phone. She opened the pictures folder and started flicking through selfie after selfie of Matt. In his rugby kit. In the mirror. On the beach. On the ski slope. Where the hell was the picture of her?

"What are you doing?" Matt stood in the doorway, glaring down at her. She wasn't sure if he was swaying or the whole room was.

"I was just…"

"What?"

She stumbled to her feet. "I was just going to show you that video on Facebook."

"On my phone?"

"Yes. I left mine at home."

They stared at each other for a second. Matt carried on frowning. He didn't believe her. Shit. Rose took hold of his hands and pulled him towards her. Something else flickered in his eyes and his frown softened. "Come here," she whispered.

And then he was up against her, holding her so tight she could barely breathe, his mouth sucking on hers like a leech.

He wouldn't let her come up for air and she felt as if she was falling, falling down into darkness. Rose staggered backwards towards the couch. "I need to sit down." Matt nodded. His eyes were glazed and he was panting like he'd just run a race. She blinked and gasped for breath. And then she heard something clink: a belt buckle. He was undoing his belt and walking towards her. "No, I…" Her words felt like fluffy balls of cotton wool clogging up her mouth. "I don't…"

"Rose," he whispered, pushing her back on the couch. She heard him panting in her ear. It was so loud it was like he'd crawled inside her head.

"I can't, I…" She started pushing back against him.

"What?" he said, pulling the strap of her top down over her shoulder.

"I can't do this," she said.

"Don't be silly," he said. And then his mouth was crushing down on hers, bringing with it the sour taste of stale beer. The weight of his whole body was pressing down on her now. She tried to push him off, but his arms were pinning hers. She tried to kick out, but her legs were pinned down too. He was so heavy. It was like being trapped beneath a boulder. Fear ricocheted through her body and bile burned at the back of her throat. She couldn't move. She couldn't escape. Then he let go of one of her arms and started fumbling with her skirt. She brought her hand up into his face and pushed it away. "I said no!" she yelled.

He slammed her arm back down. "Are you serious?" His face was right in hers now, angry and flushed. "What the hell is wrong with you? You send me those photos. You come back here with me and then you don't want to do it."

"I want the photo," Rose gasped. "I want it back. Where is it?"

Matt raised himself up slightly and stared at her. "Is that why you were looking at my phone?"

Rose looked away. "I want you to delete it."

He started to laugh. A horrible sneery laugh. "Oh, yeah. And what's it worth?" he slurred.

"What do you mean?"

He narrowed his eyes. "What are you going to do to get it back?"

Something took hold of Rose, cutting through her drunkenness and fear. She wriggled and slammed her knee up between his legs. Matt let out a horrible high-pitched wail and keeled over to the side. Rose shoved him off her and stumbled to her feet. She staggered to the door, then glanced over her shoulder to make sure he wasn't coming after her. Matt was hunched up on the sofa.

"Come – back—" he gasped, pulling himself upright.

Rose turned and ran.

Chapter Twenty-nine

Sky lay on her bed, gazing out at the tree silhouetted against the glow from a nearby streetlight. She'd recently started talking to the tree in her mind. There was something so calming and wise about it. Something so solid. And she didn't exactly have loads of other options on the conversation front at the moment – her dad was engrossed in Savannah, who seemed to be lurching from crisis to crisis, and Rose was clearly avoiding her at all costs.

"I've entered the poetry slam," she said to the tree. It bobbed its branches as if to say "Well done". Or was it "You've what?!" Sky frowned. Was she crazy to enter a poetry slam so soon? Was she going to make a total fool of herself? Although she hated to admit it, what Rose had said at the Moonlight Dreamers meeting about asking for work experience in the cake shop had been her main motivation. Sitting around and dreaming was good up to a point, but then you had to do something. "Do you think it's too soon?" she asked the tree. This time its branches swayed from side to side, as if to say, "No, not at all."

She heard Savannah and Liam coming upstairs on their way to bed, but they were talking too quietly for her to make out what they were saying. They were too caught up in Savannah's latest drama to realize that Rose had snuck out earlier this evening and still wasn't home. Before Liam had got together with Savannah, Sky had had no interest in celebrities or their lives, but now she'd developed a kind of morbid fascination with what was happening to Savannah. Every day this week there'd been a new story in the papers and online about her age. Today Sky and Liam had got home from a trip to an art exhibition to find her sitting in the kitchen, flicking manically through Facebook and Twitter to see what people were saying about her.

Sky thought of the houseboat lying empty on the canal and felt hollow inside. Life had been so much simpler when they'd lived there, just her and her dad, the boat and the water. Now they'd got stuck in the middle of a horrible web of gossip and hatefulness. She looked down at her notebook, lying open on her poem-in-progress. Writing was the only way she had of making sense of it all. She didn't know how Rose dealt with it. No wonder she hid away in her room most of the time.

Sky heard footsteps on the path outside and looked down. Under the streetlight Rose fumbled in her bag for her key. She looked terrible. Her hair was all over the place and her face was shiny, like it was wet – but it wasn't raining. Sky burrowed back under her duvet and lay staring up at the ceiling. Had Rose been crying? She heard the click of Rose's key in the lock and the door shutting very quietly.

Sky lay motionless as she listened to the gentle creak of Rose's footsteps on the stairs, then outside her door. Was Rose about to knock? Was she about to come in? She heard a muffled sound, like a cough, then the footsteps faded away. Sky rolled over and closed her eyes.

Rose half-opened one eye and looked at the clock. It was six-fifteen. Forty-five minutes since she'd finally fallen asleep. She'd been hoping that sleep would make what happened last night seem better, but it didn't. It was a million times worse. Plus her head felt as if a marching band had taken up residence and her mouth was as dry as sandpaper. She pulled herself upright and staggered into the en-suite bathroom. When she'd got home last night she'd crawled into bed without undressing. Now, she wanted to tear off her clothes and set fire to them, to get rid of all trace of Matt – all trace of what had happened. She undressed and looked in the mirror. There was a dark grey stain on her shoulder. She rubbed at it and winced. A bruise. She looked down at her legs. They were bruised too, where Matt's knees had pinned her down. Her stomach lurched up into her ribcage at the memory. She spun round and retched into the toilet.

Afterwards, Rose stood in the shower, the water pounding her skin like hundreds of tiny darts. But no matter how hot she made it and how hard she scrubbed at her body, she couldn't remove the feeling of dread. She hadn't got the photo back and now she never would. *What if Matt uses it against me to get his own back? What if he shows it to his friends? What if he puts it on Facebook?*

She turned off the shower and wrapped a towel around herself, then raced back into her bedroom to check her phone. No messages. She checked Facebook. No notifications. She did a quick search for Matt's page. He hadn't updated it since he'd checked into the gig last night. She took a deep breath. Matt wouldn't do anything like that. He was probably just as shaken up as she was. They'd both been so drunk.

She went downstairs to grab some coffee before the others got up – hopefully it would make her feel a bit more human. But when she got to the kitchen she found Sky already there, pacing up and down, muttering to herself. Great, that's all she needed, Hippy-Chick going gaga. Rose was about to sneak back upstairs when Sky turned and saw her. Her face flushed bright red.

"Oh – I was just – rehearsing – my poem. I'm entering a poetry slam – tomorrow night."

Rose pulled her robe tighter and looked at the floor. She didn't want Sky to see her face. She felt as if what happened last night was written all over it. "Go ahead. I was going to get some coffee."

"Here." Sky grabbed the cafetière and offered it to her. "I just made some."

"Thanks." Still avoiding eye contact, Rose took the jug and poured herself a cup.

"Are you… Are you OK?" Sky asked cautiously.

Rose froze. "Yeah. Why shouldn't I be?"

"No reason. I just…"

Rose needed to get back to her bedroom, where she could keep the events of last night safely locked away inside her. "I'm great. Good luck."

"With what?"

"The poetry slam." Rose turned and hurried back upstairs.

Amber groaned and rolled onto her side. But no matter how she lay, it felt as if a giant claw had reached inside her and was twisting her stomach slowly and painfully. *Why do periods have to hurt so much? Why do we have to get them in the first place?* Of course, she knew the biological reason, but why did they have to start when you were a teenager? She wasn't planning on having kids for at least another twenty years. She wasn't really planning on having kids full stop. So why did her body have to start releasing eggs when they just weren't needed and the whole thing was so damn painful? She shifted in her bed. She needed pain relief, and she needed it now. *What did women and girls do before painkillers were invented? How did they cope?* She also needed a letter excusing her from PE. PE was bad enough when she was feeling OK, but having a giant claw inside you was in no way conducive to running about like a lunatic. She hauled herself up and pulled on her dressing gown. Daniel would write her a note.

He was always really understanding about "women's issues". And he'd been extra nice to her since their conversation the other night.

Amber slowly made her way downstairs to the kitchen. A note in Daniel's handwriting lay on the table beside a plate of croissants.

Happy Thursday, sweetie!

I've gone swimming. Help yourself to the croissants. Have a great day!

D x

Amber stared in disbelief. Have a great day? Was he kidding? If she didn't get a note for PE this was going to be the very worst day ever. Various options flicked through her head. She could ask Gerald for a note. But Gerald's exhibition was looming, which meant he was locked away in his studio, painting 24/7. And it wasn't as if they were getting on well. She'd barely seen him since their argument. If she went to him now he was bound to say no and she didn't want to give him that satisfaction. She went to the cupboard where Daniel kept the painkillers. She was just going to have to tough it out. What was the worst that could happen?

Miss Savage stood in the middle of the changing room, hands on hips. "OK, girls, today we're playing hockey." A collective groan rumbled around the room, echoing in Amber's head.

The painkillers were wearing off and she could feel a dull ache returning.

"I need you to get into two teams," Miss Savage continued. "Chloe and Darcy, can you be captains, please, and take it in turns to pick?"

Great, Amber thought, now she'd have the added humiliation of being the one left till last, like battered goods in a supermarket.

"Yes, miss," Chloe trilled.

Amber glanced at her. It was unlike Chloe to be so enthusiastic in PE. But Chloe had been surprisingly good-natured since their run-in. Maybe Amber's standing up to her had made her back off. Daniel was always saying that bullies were just big cowards at heart. Maybe he was right.

"I'll have Amber," Chloe said, smiling sweetly.

Amber stared. This never happened. She was never, ever picked first in PE. She was always in the bottom two – with a bifocal-wearing girl called Sonal. Something was up. The pain in her stomach intensified

"Come on, then," Chloe said, gesturing at Amber to come and sit on the bench next to her. Amber numbly moved over, entering the cloying cloud of Chloe's perfume. Why had Chloe picked her before any of her fellow OMGs? It didn't make sense.

"I want Amber playing up front with me," Chloe said once the teams had been picked and they were assembled on the playing field. Surprise rippled around the team. There was no way she should be up front. She was one of the slowest runners in the class. Normally she was tucked away on the subs bench or in defence. Was Chloe trying to humiliate her? Was that what this was about? Well, if it was, it would be no different to any other PE lesson. All she had to do was suck it up for forty minutes and then it would all be over for another week. She gripped her hockey stick and went to join Chloe at the centre of the pitch. It was one of those bleak winter days when the entire world seemed shaded in grey. Her fingers were already numb with cold. *Come on, you can do this*, she told herself. *You're a Moonlight Dreamer.* She smiled. Who cared if she looked stupid on the hockey pitch? It wasn't as if she ever wanted to play hockey again once she left school, and she couldn't care less what Chloe and her friends thought of her. Miss Savage blew a sharp burst on her whistle. Chloe looked at Amber and smirked. Yep, it was definitely a smirk. *Oh, whatever*, Amber thought with a sigh as the game began.

The first few minutes weren't that bad. The other team had most of the play, so Amber and Chloe had to hang back, waiting for the ball to be passed to them. Or in Amber's case, praying that it wouldn't be. She looked over at the wall of leafless trees lining the playing field. Their silhouettes looked so beautiful against the grey sky, so intricate and—

"Amber!" Chloe screeched.

Amber turned to see the ball sailing out from a cluster of players at the far goal, straight towards her. She gripped her hockey stick tighter and braced herself. She felt a contraction in her abdomen, so sharp it made her eyes water. Her nearest opponent was racing down the wing towards her, cheeks flushed bright red. Amber focused on the ball, managed to control it with her stick and hit it over to Chloe. Somehow the ball actually went in the right direction. Chloe controlled it and started descending on the goal. She had a clear run. Amber felt something hot between her legs and hoped that her super-absorbent towel was as super-absorbent as the advert claimed. "Shoot!" one of their teammates yelled from behind them. But at the very last minute, Chloe turned and hit the ball back across the pitch, to a few yards in front of Amber.

What the hell? Amber lurched forwards trying to reach the ball. She felt more blood seeping from her, hot and wet. The other team's defenders were descending upon her. Why had Chloe passed to her when she had a clear shot on goal? Amber reached the ball and prepared to hit. But just as she raised her stick something struck the back of her legs. And then she was on the ground. Mud squelched and splattered in her face. She felt another stab of pain as someone kicked her, hard and swift in the small of her back. She looked up to see Chloe's best friend, Tanya, sprinting off after the other team. So this was Chloe's plan. It wasn't just to make her look stupid, it was to hurt her at every opportunity.

"Get up!" Chloe screeched at her. "You idiot, you just cost us a goal."

"Amber, are you OK?" Miss Savage called, running over.

Amber rolled onto her side. Her entire body throbbed with pain.

Miss Savage blew her whistle. The other team let out groans of frustration.

"Are you OK?" Miss Savage asked again as she crouched down.

Amber made herself nod even though her legs were stinging so much she thought she might be sick. She couldn't let Chloe beat her.

Miss Savage turned to Chloe. "Why did you pass to Amber? You had a clear run on goal."

Chloe wiped a spot of mud from her knee. "I wanted to give her a chance, miss. Amber never gets to play up front."

Miss Savage's frown softened. "Oh, I see. Well, that's very kind of you, Chloe. Come on then, Amber, up you get."

"Are you OK, Amber?" Chloe asked, fake sincerity dripping like syrup from every word.

Amber sat up. She felt another contraction. She looked down and saw a dark red stain on her white shorts.

"Ewww!" Chloe gasped. "Is that…? Oh my God, that's, like, so gross!"

Shame burned through Amber.

"Miss, miss!" Chloe called after Miss Savage, who was walking back up the pitch. "Amber's had an accident."

Everyone stopped and stared.

"What kind of accident?" Miss Savage called back.

"Er, like a personal accident," Chloe yelled at the top of

her voice. Amber imagined classes all over the school putting down their pens to listen.

"Oh my God, has she wet herself?" Tanya called out, equally loudly.

Amber hugged herself and hunched over. She wanted to run away. She wanted to run away and never come back. But that would mean running past them and then they'd all see.

Miss Savage came striding back. "What's happened, Amber?"

"It's her period, miss," Chloe said loudly, staring at Amber's shorts.

Amber looked pleadingly at Miss Savage. *Please save me.* Miss Savage glanced down at her. "Ah, I see." She pulled off her tracksuit top and handed it to Amber. "Tie this round you," she said briskly. "Then go back to the changing rooms and have a shower."

Amber nodded, unable to say anything in case she sobbed. She tied the top around her waist, fingers clumsy and numb with cold.

Miss Savage patted her on the back. "Don't worry," she said. "Happens to all of us."

Amber trudged back across the playing fields, the wind biting into her face. She knew Miss Savage had been trying to comfort her, but what she'd said wasn't true. It didn't happen to "all of us". It only happened to people like Amber. And now Chloe had been given a bonus prize. Not only had she had the satisfaction of seeing Amber humiliated and hurt, but she'd got enough ammunition to make her campaign global.

By lunchtime what had happened would be all round the school and Amber's status would go from "bit of a freak" to "total outcast".

Chapter Thirty

Rose walked out of the tube onto Camden High Street and switched on her phone. Everything was going to be OK. Going to the patisserie instead of school was the best decision she could have made. She'd told Francesca her school was closed for a teacher training day. Francesca had been delighted to see her, as her assistant had just called in sick. A few hours of washing dishes and clearing tables had been the perfect distraction. Francesca had chatted away about her life in France and how she'd always dreamed of coming to London to open a cake shop. She'd looked so pretty in her gingham dress and matching bandana, and so happy as she'd talked. And this had filled Rose with hope. If Francesca had been able to do it, then surely so could she.

The alert on Rose's phone went off, then again, and again. She took the phone from her pocket and looked at the screen, heartbeat quickening. Two missed calls and four new messages. One was from Jasmine and three were from Savannah. *Crap!* She opened Jasmine's first.

OMG! Xxx

What was that supposed to mean? Was it because she wasn't in school? But why all the drama? Rose's mouth went dry. Did she know what had happened at Sebastian's last night? But how could she? Matt was hardly going to tell her. She clicked open Savannah's messages.

CALL ME!

Where are you?!

I don't know where you are or what you're playing at but you need to come home immediately.

Rose leaned against the side of the bridge. Down below, Camden market was in full swing. What had happened? It couldn't be anything to do with Matt, she told herself as she hurried to the station. It had to be school. They must have rung Savannah to find out why she wasn't in today. And that had to be why Jasmine was texting too. Didn't it?

On the train home Rose tried to convince herself that it was OK. She'd get yelled at, but then Savannah would forget all about it like she always did because she'd be too caught up in her own dramas. She ran up the street towards the house, preparing her excuses. *I wasn't feeling too good so I went to study in the library instead.* And she could always play the *Sky doesn't have to go to school* card if things got really bad.

"There she is," she heard a guy shout. She looked up and saw a group of men with cameras standing further up the road, right outside the house. Paps. Rose sighed. Clearly Savannah being dropped by the cosmetics company was major news. She adopted her anti-pap pose, coat collar up, head down, and marched towards the house.

"Here, Rose, give us a smile."

"Nice pic, Rose. Is it true you're going into modelling?"

"Should do, body like that."

The men started to snigger.

Rose stopped and stared at them and there was a flurry of shutters going off and lights flashing. She blinked hard and turned away. Why were they after her picture? What was going on? Rose sprinted up the path. Just as she got to the front door it was flung open and Savannah grabbed her arm and pulled her into the house.

"What have you done?" she said, slamming the door behind her. Liam was next to her, grim-faced. He placed his hand on Savannah's shoulder. "Stay calm, honey."

"Stay calm?" Savannah yelled. "Stay calm?!" She turned to Rose. "Were you trying to get back at me? Is that it? Were you trying to hurt me?"

"What are you talking about?" Did Savannah know she'd been going to the patisserie? Is that what this was about? Had Sky told her?

"I just don't know what the hell is going on with you any more," Savannah yelled.

Rose sighed. This was ridiculous. "It's only a cake shop."

Savannah looked at her blankly. "What's only a cake shop?"

"The patisserie. I'm sorry I skipped school, but seriously, there are way worse places I could have been."

Savannah stared at her. "You've been in a cake shop?"

"Yes. I'm doing some work experience there. It's what I really want to do."

"Oh my God." Savannah turned to Liam, speechless with shock.

Liam smiled gently. "She's not talking about where you've been, Rose. She's talking about the photo."

"The photo?" Rose felt her legs buckle. She leaned against the wall to steady herself.

"How could you?" Savannah said, grabbing her shoulders. A memory of Matt flashed into Rose's mind. His hands pinning her shoulders to the couch, his sour beer-breath in her face.

"Get off me!" Rose yelled, pushing her away. She looked at Liam, desperate for reassurance that something far beyond her very worst nightmare wasn't about to come true. "What are you talking about?"

"The photo you posted on Instagram," he said softly.

"What photo?" Every cell in her body quivered.

"What photo?" Savannah shrieked. "You know what

photo. The topless photo. The topless photo that *Showbiz Now* have told the entire world about."

Rose couldn't move. She couldn't breathe.

"Are you OK?" Liam asked. He took hold of Rose's arm.

Rose nodded, even though she was so far from OK she wasn't sure she'd ever find her way back again.

They all jumped at the sound of a key in the lock. The door swung open and Sky bounded into the hall, holding two bags of shopping.

"Oh, hello," she said. "Did you guys know there are some photographers outside?"

"Yes. We've called the police, so hopefully they'll get moved along soon," Liam said.

"Oh. Right." Sky looked at Rose.

"You need to delete the picture immediately," Savannah said, but her voice was softer this time. "*Showbiz Now* have linked to your Instagram page."

Rose nodded and stumbled towards the stairs.

"What picture?" Sky asked.

Rose raced up the stairs before she could hear Liam's reply. She took her phone from her pocket with trembling fingers. Matt couldn't have. He wouldn't have. He didn't have access to her Instagram for starters – or did he? Dread coursed through her body as she remembered the day they'd gone on the London Eye together. She'd left her phone at home and used his to take a really cool shot of Big Ben. She'd got him to log into her account before she took it. She clicked onto her Instagram and stared numbly at the screen. The pouting, topless photo of her stared back.

Sky poured herself a glass of water, her mind racing. What was going on? When she'd got home to find the photographers hovering outside the house she'd assumed it was to do with Savannah and all the recent stories about her, but why was Rose so upset? And why was Savannah so upset with her? She took her glass of water and went out into the hall. She could hear the murmur of Liam and Savannah talking in Savannah's study. She crept over and pressed her ear to the door.

"We need to find out the truth," she heard Liam say.

"I know the truth," Savannah snapped. "She's doing this to get back at me. And now the press are here it will be all over the internet by the end of the day."

What would be all over the internet? Sky turned and headed upstairs. Maybe she could find out online? She went into her room and over to the window. A motorbike was pulling up down below. A guy got off and took a camera from his backpack. Great, another one. She looked back up at the tree, its branches bobbing and swaying. She thought of all the people it must have seen over the years it had been there. All the things it must have witnessed. What, she wondered, would it be making of what was going on below it right now? A pack of humans armed with cameras, holding a house hostage.

She sighed and sat down on her bed and booted up her laptop. As she typed Rose's name into the search engine she felt a pang of guilt. Wasn't it sneaky and wrong to spy on Rose like this? But how else was she going to find out what had happened? Rose was hardly going to tell her. She hit ENTER. There at the top of the list was a post entitled: **SAVANNAH JUNIOR'S SEXY SELFIE**. It had gone up today. Sky's stomach flipped. She clicked open the link and there was a picture of Rose – topless, with a **CENSORED** sticker superimposed over her breasts – pouting at the camera. Sky looked away. She should shut the laptop. She should turn it off and wipe what she'd seen from her mind. But she couldn't. She had too many questions. How had they got that picture? Why had Rose taken it? Had she sent it to them? Sky looked back at the screen and scrolled down.

It looks like Savannah Ferndale has a new contender to her crown – her own daughter! In a week that Ferndale will definitely want to see the back of – losing her contract with Infinity Cosmetics and #FerndaleFacelift trending on Twitter – her daughter, Rose Levine, has come storming on to the scene in the sensational selfie above. Having avoided the celebrity spotlight thus far, sixteen-year-old Rose, daughter of Ferndale and actor Jason Levine, posted this photo last night on her

Instagram account. *Showbiz Now* says: it's time to give in gracefully, Savannah, and make way for a younger model.

Sky glanced at the comments.

Like mother, like daughter – what a pair of sluts.

Phwoar, yes please! ;)

Just what we need, another great role model for our teen girls. Her mother should be ashamed, allowing her to post photos like this online!

Sky snapped her laptop shut. What had Rose done? And why had she done it? If it had been to get back at Savannah, surely it was going to backfire. Rose didn't seem to like the limelight – in fact, she seemed to hate it. Why would she do something that would bring this much attention to herself? None of it made sense.

Chapter Thirty-one

Maali walked into the farm, running through all the reasons why what she was about to do wasn't crazy or stalkerish, but bold and empowering. She was sick of living in a daydream. She needed something to actually happen. If she wanted to meet her soulmate one day, she had to overcome her fear of talking to boys.

A gust of icy wind swept through the farmyard, biting right through her clothes into her skin. Why couldn't it have been sunny, like yesterday? Ash was hardly going to want to stand around talking about pigs while he fought off hypothermia. She walked over to the pig enclosure. There was no sign of anyone, not even the pig. He had to be curled up warm inside his sty. Maali made her way to the stables. Maybe Ash was mucking out the horses. A bearded man came out of the stables, holding a broom.

"Can I help you?" he asked.

"I — er — I'm looking for Ash," Maali said.

"I think he's on his break," the man said, looking at his watch. "Check the café," he added, nodding towards a converted barn on the other side of the yard.

"Thank you." Maali was unsure of what to do. What if Ash was with other members of staff? What would she say then? Surely they'd see through her stupid pig project. Surely Ash would see through it. But she was here, and she couldn't exactly leave now that the guy had told her where Ash was. Maali walked over to the café and peered in the window. Ash was sitting at a table in the far corner on his own, reading a book. Joy blazed through Maali like a shooting star. He liked reading. She had to go in. If she walked away now she'd always regret it, always be plagued by what-ifs. Just like Juliet would have been over Romeo – if she hadn't killed herself. Bad example. Maali cleared her throat and walked in. A large woman with a smiley face was wiping down a table. "Hello, love, what can I get you?" she asked.

"Oh, I'm, er, here to see him." Maali nodded in Ash's direction.

"Are you, now?" The woman nodded as if she knew something Maali didn't. "Ashley, you have a visitor!" she called.

Ash looked up from his book. As soon as he saw Maali he smiled, and instantly she felt at ease. He looked genuinely pleased to see her. She wasn't crazy. This was OK.

"Can I get you a drink?" the woman said. "Or is this a flying visit?"

"Oh – I don't know."

"Get a hot chocolate!" Ash called over. "They're awesome."

Maali breathed another sigh of relief. He wanted her

to stay long enough for a drink.

"I'll have another one too, please, Mum."

Maali inwardly groaned. This never happened in romantic movies. In romantic movies, when the girl and guy were first getting to know each other, the guy's mum wasn't hovering around in the background, holding a dishcloth. She made herself smile and nodded at Ash's mum, then made her way over to him. "Hello, Ash."

His eyes twinkled in the fairy lights strung around the walls of the café. "Hello, Maali. Take a seat."

She'd been rehearsing her opening line all day at school, but his mum's presence had completely thrown her. "So, about pigs…" she stammered.

Ash laughed. "What, no small talk first?"

"Sorry, I…"

Ash pushed his book away and leaned in towards her. He was wearing a hoodie with a faded picture of an eagle on the front and he had a small silver hoop in the top of his left ear. She hadn't noticed that before. She hadn't been this close to him before. A strange heat rose up inside Maali, thawing her frozen limbs.

"Do you want whipped cream and marshmallows on top?" Ash's mum called across the café.

"You have to have whipped cream and marshmallows on top," Ash said. "If you don't, it's like getting a burger without a bun or a—"

"House without a roof?" Maali suggested.

"Yes!" Ash grinned at her, causing a supernova of joy to explode inside her chest.

"Yes, please!" Maali called to his mum. She quickly wracked her brains for some small talk. "Do your family own this farm then?"

Ash shook his head. "No, the council own it. My mum's worked in the café since I was little, though, so it kind of feels like I've grown up here. I just work here part-time while I'm in sixth form."

"You're in sixth form?"

"Yes, first year. How about you?"

"Oh. Year Ten. I'm one of the oldest in my year. I'm fifteen already," she said quickly, then regretted it.

"Oh. Right. Well, I'm one of the youngest in my year. I'm not seventeen until July." Ash grinned at her again.

Even though he was two years above her in school, right now, technically he was only one year older than her. She fought to stop herself grinning and looked down at his book. "You're reading *The Lord of the Rings*."

Ash nodded. "Have you read it?"

"Yes. I love it."

"Me too." Ash picked up the book and showed her a dog-eared page near the end. "I've only got this much left." He looked around the café as if to make sure no one was listening. "This is going to sound weird, but I've started reading it really slowly because I don't want it to end."

"That's what I do!" Maali exclaimed. "The first time I read

Harry Potter, I actually started rationing my pages once I'd gone over two hundred. Well, I tried to, but it was just too good!"

Ash laughed. "Yep. That's why I'm glad you're here. Now I've got a little bit longer before the book ends."

Maali grinned.

"That's not the only reason I'm glad you're here," Ash said quickly.

Maali stared at him, her heart pounding. "What do you mean?"

Ash looked embarrassed. "Well, that sounded a bit rude. I am pleased to see you again." He laughed. "You're not just a *Lord of the Rings* lengthener."

Maali giggled. She wasn't just a *Lord of the Rings* lengthener. It was quite possibly the most romantic thing anyone had ever said to her.

"So, what is it you want to know about pigs, then?"

"Oh – I – I've got some questions." Maali fumbled in her bag for the questions she'd hastily scribbled down in her French class.

"What subject's it for?" Ash asked.

"English."

"English?" He laughed. "What are you studying, Pig Lit?"

"No." Maali's cheeks began to burn. Could he tell she was lying? "I'm writing a story for Creative Writing – about a pig farmer." Why, oh why, had she chosen pigs? Who wrote stories about pig farmers? Horses would have been way more believable.

"A story about a pig farmer?" Ash echoed, his eyebrows furrowing.

"Yes, I – I didn't choose it. We were given a title."

"And yours was 'The Pig Farmer'?"

"Uh, no, it was – uh, 'Bringing Home the Bacon'. It made me think of a pig farmer."

Ash tilted his head to one side. "A pig farmer who brings home a pig?"

Panic sent words stumbling from Maali's mouth. "Yes. No. I don't know. I haven't really worked out the plot yet. I thought I'd find out some more about pigs first and see if that inspired me."

Ash nodded, bemused.

"Here you go." Ash's mum plonked down two enormous hot chocolates covered in swirls of whipped cream, dotted with marshmallows and dusted with powdered chocolate.

"Thank you." Maali grabbed her cup, grateful for the distraction.

"Cheers, Mum," Ash said, raising his cup.

"You're welcome," his mum replied, picking up an empty cup from the table. "So, what are you pair up to?"

Maali kept her eyes glued to her drink.

"We're having an important meeting about pigs," Ash said.

"Pigs?" Her eyebrows shot up.

Maali's cheeks began to burn. This would never, *ever* happen in the movies.

Chapter Thirty-two

Back when Rose's parents were "civilians" and they still did normal things like talk to each other, they loved to reminisce about the day she was born. Her dad had become obsessed with the machine attached to Savannah's stomach, monitoring her contractions. Apparently the graph would register a few seconds before the contraction hit and her dad would say helpful things like, "ooh, there's a big one coming" or "this one's off the scale".

Rose was reminded of this now as she lay on her bed listening to the sounds coming from downstairs. Every time she heard Savannah yell or a door slam she knew that another website had got hold of the photo and some new piece of crap had hit the fan. Rose had deleted the Instagram picture as soon as she'd gotten over her shock, but it was too late by then. People had already taken screenshots of it and the story was going viral.

She heard the sound of a plate clattering in the kitchen and opened her laptop and refreshed her Twitter feed. Another tabloid was running the story, this time with the headline **ALL HAIL THE NEW FERNDALE**. Then she saw something that made her blood freeze. Her name was in the box on the left of the screen. She was trending: one place below Madonna, who'd apparently had some kind of costume malfunction onstage, and two places above #FerndaleFacelift.

Rose clicked on her name and her feed filled with comments and pictures. She scrolled through them numbly. This was too big, too surreal. It was as if her brain didn't have the gigabytes needed to process what had happened. Maybe it hadn't happened. She felt a tiny glimmer of hope. Maybe she was still asleep. She pinched her arm. No, she was still there, on the bed, watching as the whole world talked about a topless photo of her. Rose pinched her arm harder. She wanted to make it bruise. She wanted to hurt herself so badly that the pain would block out the enormity of what had happened. The notification "23 new results" popped up at the top of her feed. Twenty-three more complete strangers feeding on the story like vultures on a corpse. Unable to stop herself, she refreshed the feed.

@glasshouse: What a tart

@mummybrown_22: Her mother should be ashamed of herself #SavannahLoser #FerndaleFacelift

@armylad27: Sexy bitch

Rose shoved the laptop away. Her body was burning up, but her skin felt clammy and cold. She thought of people looking at that picture of her; other women judging her, creepy guys getting off on her, and she wanted to puke. Then she thought of people she knew seeing the picture and it was even worse. OK, so all of the websites were covering her chest with superimposed **CENSORED** signs, but it was still blatantly obvious that she was topless. And that stupid pout... Rose crawled under her duvet and dug her nails into her arms. She thought of everyone at school looking at it. She thought of Liam. She burrowed further down into the bed, trying to hide from the thoughts. But she couldn't escape them – they were spreading like mould. She thought of her dad in America having breakfast with his girlfriend, shaking their heads in disgust as Rose pouted up at them from the *New York Times*. She dug into her arms, harder.

"Stupid, stupid, stupid," she hissed. She'd ruined everything. What if Francesca saw the photo? What would she think of her? And the Moonlight Dreamers? She thought of Maali, and her sweet smile finally fading as she saw the picture. And for the first time in what felt like years, Rose cried. Everything was over. No one would want to know her now. No one.

"Rose?"

At first she thought she'd imagined Sky's voice. But then it came again, louder and closer. So close she had to be right next to the bed.

"Rose?"

"Go away," she muttered from under the duvet, frozen rigid by embarrassment and shame.

She felt something against her legs. Sky had sat down on the bed. *Crap!*

"I said, leave me alone."

"No."

What the hell? Rose pulled the duvet down just enough to peer over it. "What do you want?"

"I want to help you."

Oh, great, this was just what she needed – Sky doing some holier than thou routine.

Rose held the duvet tightly under her chin. "I don't need your help."

"Oh, really?" Sky stared back at her defiantly. "So you want to have an evening being debriefed by that slimy toad-man Antonio, do you?"

Rose shifted up slightly, her heart pounding. "Antonio's coming here?"

Sky nodded. "They're planning a mother and daughter interview with *Hello* magazine for…" she made a pair of air quotes with her fingers … "'damage limitation purposes'."

Rose sat upright. "Shit!"

"Exactly. I'm here to help you escape. So for once in your life could you just get over yourself and stop acting like I'm the enemy?" Sky looked her straight in the eye. "I'm not, you know."

Rose gulped. Her guilt multiplied. Why had she been such a bitch to Sky? And why was Sky being so nice? She didn't deserve this.

"Come on, let's go." Sky tugged on the duvet. "Your mum's just asked my dad to give her a guided meditation to help her relax. We can sneak out the back while they're getting their *om* on."

Rose nodded and threw back the duvet.

Sky looked at her shoulders and gasped. "What happened to you? How did you get those bruises?"

"Long story," Rose muttered, grabbing a jumper from the floor and pulling it over her head. "Where are we going?"

"Somewhere those photographers can't get to you," Sky replied. "Somewhere sane. Somewhere a million miles from here."

Amber opened the front door and walked into the hallway. As soon as she heard the soothing *tick-tock* of the grandfather clock she wanted to cry. She'd managed to keep it together all day at school, building a force field of Oscar Wilde quotes around herself to keep out the whispers and the pointing and the stares, but now that she was finally home all she wanted to do was collapse in a heap on her bed and never get up again.

"Amber, honey." Daniel appeared on the landing. "How was your day?"

Oh, you know, pretty disastrous – as in nuclear disastrous,

Amber felt like saying. Instead she somehow forced herself to smile. "All right," she muttered through gritted teeth.

"That's great," Daniel said. "Is it OK if we just have a quick chat?"

Amber wished she could go and hibernate for the rest of the winter and possibly the rest of her life. But she didn't want Daniel to know there was anything wrong because there was no way she wanted to have to tell him and relive the agony all over again. "OK," she muttered as she slowly climbed the stairs.

When she got to the kitchen she was shocked to see Gerald sitting at the table, staring solemnly into space. She'd assumed when Daniel said "we", he'd meant just the two of them. It was almost unheard of for Gerald to emerge from his studio so close to an exhibition.

"Is everything all right?" she asked, sitting down opposite Gerald.

"Yes, yes, everything's fine," Daniel said, sitting next to her. "We'd just like to chat to you about what you and I talked about the other night in your room."

Amber froze. Which part of what they'd talked about? Had Daniel told Gerald that she knew he wasn't her real dad? Had Daniel told him that Amber had begged him to leave and take her with him? Is that why he was looking so serious?

Gerald cleared his throat.

Amber took a deep breath and clenched her fists beneath

the table. What if Daniel had had second thoughts? What if he did want to leave? Maybe he hadn't been swimming this morning after all. Maybe he'd been out looking for a new property for them to move into. Hope started bubbling up inside her.

"As you know," Gerald began, still looking into space rather than at her, "Daniel and I decided long ago that the identity of your biological father should not be an issue in this family. We decided that, although it was obviously only humanly possible for one of us to be your biological parent, we would always be equally, and indeed legally, your fathers."

Amber held her breath. She could sense a "but" coming — a big and hopefully life-changing "but".

"But it's come to my attention," Gerald continued, "that you have been drawing your own conclusions in this matter."

"I felt I had to tell him about our conversation the other night," Daniel said gently, placing his hand on her arm. "It made me realize that we may have been a little selfish, not talking to you about this."

"I wouldn't call it selfish," Gerald said with a frown. "I'd call it loving."

Daniel nodded. "Yes, but we can't blame her for wanting to know." He looked at Amber and smiled. She noticed his eyes were glassy. Why was he crying? Was he about to leave Gerald? Was her dream about to come true? *Oh, please, please, please,* she silently begged. It would make all of the humiliation and hurt at school pale into insignificance if it meant that she would finally be free of Gerald. And if she and Daniel moved out maybe she could start again at another school…

Gerald sighed. "No. I don't suppose we can blame you." He finally looked at Amber. "You have to know that we both love you equally. We have both brought you up. We are both your fathers in every other way."

Amber nodded. Just say it, please say it.

Gerald swallowed. She'd never seen him look so uneasy. But it had to be hard, telling her that he wasn't actually her real dad.

"I am your biological father," Gerald said quietly.

"But you know I love you just as much," Daniel added quickly. "And this doesn't change a thing."

Amber couldn't move. This couldn't be happening. Gerald couldn't have just said that. Maybe they were lying to her. Maybe they'd panicked after what she said to Daniel and they were lying to make her not want to leave Gerald. "But – but you can't be," she stammered.

"What do you mean?" Gerald stared at her.

"You can't be." A giant sob was welling inside of her. "I'm nothing like you. I'm like Daniel. I even have the same eyes."

The sob reached the back of her throat. She looked at Daniel desperately. "Are you making this up so that I don't want to leave him?"

Daniel shook his head. A tear rolled down his face. "No."

"What do you mean, so that you don't want to leave me?" Gerald said, looking from Daniel to Amber and back again.

"You can't be my dad." The sob burst from her mouth. "You can't be. It doesn't make sense."

Daniel put his arm around her shoulder. "Honey, it doesn't make any difference. We're both your dads. We both love you—"

"Well, I'm sorry to be the bearer of such awful news!" Gerald said, his face flushing.

"Don't, darling," Daniel said, shaking his head at Gerald.

"But look at her," Gerald said. "It's as if she's just been told the world's ending."

Amber stumbled to her feet. Selfish slangwhanger Gerald was her dad.

"Don't go," Daniel said, looking up at her imploringly.

"I need to be on my own. Please." Tears were pouring down her face now.

"Why are you so upset?" Gerald said. "I don't understand."

Amber looked at him and for the first time ever, she couldn't find any words.

Chapter Thirty-three

Maali drained the last of her hot chocolate. The way she was feeling reminded her of that children's nursery rhyme about little girls being made of sugar and spice and all things nice. Her entire body, from the tips of her toes to the top of her head, felt filled with a sugary, hot chocolatey happiness. Her conversation with Ash could not have gone better. In the hour she'd been in the café they'd barely mentioned pigs. And she hadn't needed to refer to her notes from wikiHow at all. Instead they'd talked about all the things they loved – books, movies, food, places. Ash had asked her loads about herself too. He'd even asked to see some of her photos when she told him that photography was her passion.

"Oh crap, look at the time," he said now, glancing at the clock. "I haven't helped you at all with the pig stuff."

"That's OK," Maali said, and she held her breath. Would he ask to see her again? *Please, please, please*, she silently prayed.

"We'll have to—"

"Hey, babe."

Maali jumped at the sound of a girl's voice.

Ash stood up, smiling. "Hey. How was your day?"

"Oh, you know, same old, same old."

Maali looked up to see a beautiful girl with a heart-shaped face and long, silky blonde hair standing by their table.

"Maali, this is Sage," Ash said. "Sage, this is Maali. I've just been helping her with a school project."

Sage looked at Maali frostily. "Oh. Right."

"Sit down." Ash pulled out a chair.

Maali tried hard to stop the procession of anxious thoughts marching into her mind. Sage might just be a friend from college. She might be one of those girls who calls everyone babe. She might be glaring at Maali because she glared at everyone. Maali pushed her empty cup away.

"Well, I'd better get going," she said in a singsong, I'm-totally-happy-because-I've-got-nothing-at-all-to-be-stressed-about voice.

"But what about the pig stuff?" Ash said, looking concerned.

"Oh, that's OK. I need to get home now. I can find out whatever else I need on the internet."

"Are you sure?"

Maali could feel Sage's eyes boring into her. "Yes. Yes. It's fine." She got to her feet. "Thank you so much for your time."

Ash stood up too and grinned. "Thank *you*. And not just for being a *Lord of the Rings* lengthener."

Maali felt a small bubble of hope but it was burst by a

pointed cough from Sage. "Well, I'll be off, then."

Ash nodded. "OK. Hopefully see you again soon?"

He said it like a question, but Maali couldn't answer it in front of Sage so she walked away.

When she got to the door, she stopped and glanced over her shoulder. What she saw made her heart splinter with disappointment. Ash was leaning down over Sage and kissing her gently on the mouth.

Sky unlocked the padlock on the door of the boat. When she'd seen what was happening to Rose and heard her crying, she'd been determined to get her out of the house. Rose might hate her guts but, like it or not, they had both ended up becoming Moonlight Dreamers and surely that meant something. Surely that meant they were supposed to look out for each other. But Rose was used to gleaming Hampstead houses with marble worktops and polished floors. What would she make of the houseboat, with its chipped paintwork and well-worn furnishings? It was definitely shabby without the chic.

Rose had barely said a word on the tube. She'd sat with her hat pulled down low and her scarf up high, and her eyes shut tight. Even when Sky had led her down to the towpath she had numbly followed in silence. As Sky opened the door, a waft of musty cold air hit her. "It'll be a lot cosier once I get a fire going," she said, gesturing at Rose to follow her down the narrow steps into the kitchen. Sky grabbed a box of matches from the shelf above the sink and lit a couple of candles. "Come through," she said, leading her into the living area. She didn't dare to look at Rose's face.

"Is this where you and your dad lived?" Rose asked. Her voice was so flat and lifeless it was impossible for Sky to gauge what she made of it.

"Yes." Sky opened the wood-burning stove and lit some kindling. She waited for Rose to make some snide remark or demand to go back home.

"Is it OK to sit down?" Rose asked. She was standing in the middle of the boat, fiddling nervously with the zip on her leather jacket.

Sky smiled at her. "Of course. Go ahead."

Rose sat down on the sofa-bench. Her eyes darted around, taking in the woven wall hangings, the multicoloured cushions, Liam's woodcarvings and the stacks of books. Sky held her breath.

"This is awesome," Rose said quietly.

Sky wasn't sure what she'd heard. Had Rose said awesome or awful? "What?"

"This is awesome. The boat." She looked down. "I can see why you didn't want to leave."

"Really?" Sky sat cross-legged on the floor.

"Yes. It's really cool. It reminds me of the caravan we stayed in on holiday once when I was little."

"You went on a caravan holiday?" Sky couldn't disguise her surprise.

Rose nodded. "Yes. Before my parents became … assholes."

They both laughed.

Rose grabbed one of the cushions from the bench and hugged it. "It's really snug."

Sky nodded. It was as if someone had taken a giant eraser and rubbed out all of Rose's colour and spark. "Would you like a cup of tea?"

Rose nodded. Sky went back into the kitchen and placed the old copper kettle on the stove.

"I didn't do it, you know," Rose said quietly from the doorway.

Sky jumped and turned to face her. "Didn't do what?"

"I didn't post that photo on Instagram. Someone else did."

"Oh. OK." Sky wasn't sure what to say.

"You don't believe me, do you?" Rose stared at her, a glimmer of her old defensive self in her eyes.

"I do. Who did it, then?"

"This guy."

"What guy? Sorry, you don't have to tell me." Sky took a couple of mugs from the cupboard and placed them on the tiny work surface.

"A guy who was supposed to be my boyfriend." Rose laughed bitterly.

"But why?" Sky stared at her.

"Because I wouldn't give him what he wanted." Rose bit her bottom lip and turned away.

"What did he—?" Sky stared at Rose. Then she remembered the bruises on Rose's shoulders and her face shiny with tears under the lamplight last night. "Rose, did he...?"

"I don't want to talk about it," Rose said. Her voice was small, like a frightened child's.

"That's OK."

"I don't want to talk about any of it," Rose said, her voice even higher. "I just want it all to go away."

"You don't have to talk about it. We can just stay here and drink tea and – and" – Sky searched her brain for something she and Rose could do on the boat, with no TV and no Wi-Fi – "and read."

"Read?" Rose raised an eyebrow.

"Yes. If you like. Or we could talk about something else."

"Why are you doing this?" Rose asked as Sky turned back to make the tea. "Why are you being so nice to me when I've been such a bitch?"

Sky put the kettle down. "Because I hated seeing what was happening to you. Because you're a Moonlight Dreamer. And because I have a sneaking suspicion that you might not actually be as much of a bitch as you make out."

Rose let out a weird half-laugh, half-cry. "Thank you," she whispered.

Maali flung herself on her bed. She felt so stupid. Of course someone like Ash had a girlfriend; a girlfriend as perfect as Sage. What had she been thinking, going to the farm like that and pretending to be interested in pigs?

"What's wrong with me, Lakshmi?" she wailed, picturing Ash and Sage laughing about her and Ash saying, "She's just some dumb school kid," as Sage flicked her silky hair. "I was just humouring her." Then she imagined Ash's mum joining them at the table and the three of them roaring with laughter at her stupidity. It was as if the night she first met Ash the full moon had cast some kind of spell on her, turning her into a lovestruck fool. How could she have thought he might be interested in her? How could she have thought he might have been her soulmate? "Aaaargh!" Maali rolled over and pummelled her pillow, as if she could somehow release the shame that was pouring into her. Then, in desperation, she went and knelt in front of her shrine.

Her eyes rested on a quote from the Hindu text *The Bhagavad Gita*:

"Perform all thy actions with mind concentrated on the Divine, renouncing attachment and looking upon success and failure with an equal eye."

She'd copied out the quote and put it on her shrine about a month ago when she had a physics test, but now it seemed even more relevant.

"I'm sorry, Lakshmi," she whispered. "I shouldn't have got so attached. Please help me to let go."

Maali closed her eyes and focused on her breathing: in

through her nose and out through her mouth. Very slowly her body relaxed and she became filled with the most beautiful sense of peace.

Rose gazed into the flickering fire and snuggled deeper into the cushions. It was weird. This crazy houseboat was so different from everything she was used to, it was as if Sky had spirited her away to another world: a magical world where selfies and the internet and Twitter and paparazzi didn't exist. A bird squawked, and in the distance she could hear the soft sound of water cascading through the lock gates. It was so soothing. She wanted to stay cocooned in this magical boat world for ever. She looked at Sky, lying on her stomach on the floor, reading by the firelight. This would have been a normal night in for her and her dad before they'd moved to Hampstead – all cosy and safe. Sky glanced up from her book as if she'd heard Rose's thoughts.

"Are you OK?" she asked.

Rose nodded.

"Everything will look fresh as a daisy in the morning," Sky said and she smiled. "That's what my mum used to say whenever I was sad about something."

Rose shifted onto her side. "How old were you when your mum … when she died?"

"Eleven." Sky's smile faded.

"You must really miss her."

"Yeah. I do. She was my best friend."

"What was she like?"

Sky started playing with the pendant around her neck. "She was lovely. She … she made everything so much fun. She was always inventing stories about things – even the dullest things. She made everything an adventure."

Rose hugged one of the cushions to her. "How do you mean?"

"Well, if we had to go food shopping, she'd invent characters for each of us to play, and we'd have to buy the kind of food that they would like. So one time, we pretended to be fairies and bought nothing but fairy cakes and iced gems and these pink marshmallows covered in glitter. And another time we were mad professors, so we had to buy the craziest food we could find." Sky laughed. "We ended up making pumpkin bolognese for tea. I don't think my dad was too impressed with that one!" Sky looked down into her lap and sighed. "I miss her so much. I try not to, but it's impossible."

Rose frowned. "Why? Why would you try not to miss her?"

"It's been five years."

Rose shook her head. "There's nothing wrong with missing her. It shows how much you love her."

Sky looked back at the fire. "Do you – do you miss your dad?"

Rose nodded. "He stayed in America when he and my mom broke up. I'm supposed to go see him in school vacations, when he's not filming. Sometimes I feel like my parents love their jobs way more than they love me." Rose cringed. She sounded pathetic. Sky's mom had died, for chrissakes. She'd probably give anything to have her alive and living in America. She must think that Rose was being a total brat. But Sky was nodding. Rose felt something inside her soften. Suddenly she wanted nothing more than to tell Sky everything. Maybe Sky would try and hug her again; this time she would let her. This time she would—

There was creaking from the other end of the boat. "What was that?"

Sky scrambled to her feet. "Someone's trying to open the door. Wait there."

Rose panicked. Was it the paps? Had they followed them here? She sat frozen, listening and waiting. She heard Sky call out, "Who's there?"

"Only me," she heard Liam reply. He walked into the living area. There was no sign of Savannah.

"Where's my mom?" Rose asked.

"Back at the house." Liam turned to Sky. "We've been going out of our minds worrying about you. Why didn't you tell us where you were going?"

"Right, like you'd have let us come here," Sky said sharply.

Liam looked hurt. He ran his hand through his hair. "What were you thinking?"

"What was I thinking? Are you serious? I was thinking that someone had to do something to protect Rose."

Rose felt a burst of gratitude.

"What are you talking about?" Liam said. "Savannah and I can take care of Rose."

"You're kidding. Neither of you even bothered to ask Rose what happened. She didn't post that photo on Instagram. Someone else did." Sky turned away, her face flushed bright pink.

"Is that true?" Liam asked Rose. Rose nodded. "I still need to take you back home. Your mam will be—"

"No!" Sky yelled. "This is my home and I'm staying here tonight – and so is Rose. How can you want us to go back there with the press hanging around outside? Please, Dad. Let us stay here tonight. Let things calm down a bit. Things will look better in the morning."

Liam closed his eyes and took a deep breath. "OK," he said. "But I'm staying here too. There's no way I'm leaving you here on your own."

Sky nodded and suddenly she was in her dad's arms and they were hugging. Rose watched in disbelief. How could they go from shouting to hugging so easily? Where were the slamming doors and moody silences that came in between?

Liam held out his hand. "Group hug," he said, beckoning her over.

Rose stepped between them. As Liam and Sky wrapped their arms around her it took every fibre in her body not to dissolve into a pool of tears.

Chapter Thirty-four

Why is it, Amber thought as she rolled herself up in her duvet, *that when something really bad happens, everything else goes wrong too?* Her life was over at school. Gerald was her biological dad, and now she couldn't find a single Oscar Wilde quote to fit her mood. This had never happened before. She flicked through the pages of her quotations book.

"I never put off till tomorrow what I can possibly do – the day after."

Usually this quote made her laugh, but not today. Nothing would make her laugh today. The only vaguely good thing that had happened was that Daniel had let her have the day off sick. She'd told him it was because of her period – and it was, even though the pain was gone. News of what happened in PE had torn through school and she couldn't bear another second of people sniggering and staring.

Daniel had sent her back to bed with a mug of ginger tea. His guilt and concern had been obvious. Amber felt a sharp stab of despair. When she came to him with problems did he inwardly sigh and think, *she isn't even my daughter*? If he and Gerald ever did split up, he might never want to see her again. And then a question that Amber hadn't allowed herself to think for a very long time crept into the corner of her mind. She flicked through her quotation book. She couldn't think it. She mustn't. Her eyes scoured the quotes.

"All women become like their mothers. That is their tragedy. No man does and that is his."

She dropped her book on the bed, staring at it in shock. Now there was no way she could avoid the question. Not now that Oscar had raised it. Amber sat up straight and took a deep breath. *If Gerald was her father, who was her mother?* The question mushroomed until it seemed to fill the entire room.

Outside the boat a goose honked loudly, wrenching Sky from her sleep. Slowly, the events of the previous day trickled into her mind. The paparazzi outside the house, the photo of Rose. Rose. Sky looked across at the other bunk. Rose was sitting up, peering out of the porthole.

"Hey," Sky said softly.

"Hey." Rose turned and gave her a weak smile. The goose honked again.

Sky propped herself up on her elbow. "How did you sleep?"

"Really well," Rose said, looking surprised. "You know, considering."

Sky sat up and wrapped her blanket round her shoulders. She could hear the clatter of cutlery in the kitchen. Liam must be making breakfast. She felt a twinge of sorrow. It was so nice to wake up on the boat again. If only they didn't have to go back to that house.

"I'm dreading going back home," Rose said quietly.

"Yes, I bet."

Rose looked out of the porthole again. "When I'm here I can pretend nothing's happened."

"Hey, girls, are you awake?" Liam called.

"Yes," Sky called back. She turned to Rose. "Don't worry. You've got me."

"Thank you."

Liam knocked on the door. "Can I come in?"

"Sure," Sky replied.

Liam stepped into the cabin, holding a tray. "Breakfast is served."

Sky was relieved: Liam seemed back to his cheery self. He placed the tray on the floor. On it were two steaming mugs of tea and a plate of buttered toast. Sky's stomach growled. She was starving. Rose clearly was too – she'd already grabbed a piece of toast. "Thanks," she muttered, nodding to Liam.

"You're welcome." Liam sat down on the end of Sky's bunk. "Now here's the plan. You pair are going to be staying here for the time being."

Sky stared at him. "What?"

"For real?" Rose's eyes lit up.

Liam nodded. "Yes – just until everything calms down."

"But what about my mom?" Rose asked.

"Your mam is on the case with her lawyers," Liam replied. "I told her that you didn't post the photo so she's threatening lawsuits to newspapers left, right and centre. Don't worry, we're going to take care of you. Both of you."

Sky felt light-headed with relief. Liam was still her same old dad. Savannah hadn't changed him. She heard a weird noise from across the cabin. At first she thought Rose was laughing, but when she looked she saw she was bent forward, shoulders quivering.

"Thank you," Rose gasped between sobs.

Sky and Liam went and sat on either side of her.

"I know that right now it seems like the end of the world," Liam said softly. "But it isn't. Those gobshites will get bored soon and they'll find some other poor sod to hound. Until then, I want you to sit tight."

As Maali walked up Brick Lane on the way to school she felt so much older and wiser than she had just the day before. She might not have a boyfriend but she'd finally had a proper conversation with a boy and had her heart broken – all in one day. She gave a worldly sigh – at least, in the movie of her life that's how it would have been scripted. Ash's heart belonged to another; it was exactly like Romeo and Juliet – apart from the fact that Romeo didn't actually have another girlfriend and his heart only ever belonged to Juliet. But it was just as tragic, and for some strange reason that almost felt good. What had happened hadn't been at all what she'd been dreaming of, but at least something had happened with a boy and that had to be better than nothing. Didn't it? Maali took a deep breath. *Please, Lakshmi, help me to believe this.*

Then she saw something that made her stop dead still: Rose – or at least a picture of Rose – on the front cover of one of the newspapers outside the corner shop. Maali stared in disbelief. The paper had superimposed little **CENSORED** signs over parts of the photo, but it was obvious that Rose was topless. But what…? And why…? Maali scanned the headline: ***FOXY FERNDALE JUNIOR***. She took a copy of the paper from the stand and started to read. Rose was the daughter of Savannah Ferndale and Jason Levine. Maali's heart skipped a beat. When Rose had said her dad was an actor, she hadn't realized he was one of the most famous actors in the world. And her mum was one of the most famous models.

According to the newspaper article, Rose was desperate to follow in her mum's footsteps and had posted the photo of herself on Instagram. Maali frowned. It didn't make sense. Why hadn't Rose mentioned that in the Moonlight Dreamers meeting? Why had she said she wanted to be a patissier? Why had she started work experience in a cake shop if she wanted to be a model? And why had she come to look around Maali's parents' shop? Maali put the paper back on the stand, her stomach churning. Something wasn't right – not right at all.

Rose sat on the small deck at the back of the boat and looked down into the glimmering water. Even though it was cold out, the sun was shining and the sky was a clear, forget-me-not blue. Sky's mom was right; Rose might still be feeling taut with tension but at least everything looked fresh, and that was definitely comforting. She watched as a brightly painted boat chugged past. Its roof was covered with potted plants and stacks of logs.

"Morning!" the guy steering the boat called out with a grin.

Rose froze. Did he recognize her? Had he seen the picture? But the guy was already looking away, down the canal.

"Morning," she called back softly. She leaned back in her chair. Sky and Liam had gone to Hampstead – Liam to see how Savannah was getting on with the legal side of things and Sky to get them both some clean clothes.

Rose stuffed her hands into her coat pockets and thought about Liam. She'd seen another side to him in the last twenty-four hours. Perhaps he wasn't quite the new-age wimp she'd thought. In fact, she was actually starting to like him. And she was really starting to like Sky. Rose thought back to last night – how Sky hadn't pried, and how she'd believed Rose and got angry at Liam in her defence. The tension inside her began to ease. Maybe it wouldn't be so bad after all. Maybe things didn't just look as fresh as a daisy. Maybe they actually were. Should she go online and check? Things might have calmed down. The photo might already be yesterday's news and she could put her mind at rest. She pulled out her phone and nervously turned it on.

"Look, Mummy, a duck!" she heard a child cry, and glanced up to see a family walking towards her along the towpath. The dad was pushing a pram and the mom was running after a toddler who, in turn, was waddling after a duck.

"Quack, quack!" the kid called to the duck, before dissolving into a fit of giggles.

Rose smiled. Then she felt her phone vibrate, again and again. The palms of her hands went clammy as she looked at the screen. She had three missed calls from Savannah and two new texts. One from Savannah and one from Matt. Her heart plummeted. She opened Savannah's first:

Liam told me the truth about what happened. Hope you're ok. Call me. Love you. xoxo

Then, fingers trembling, she opened Matt's.

I'm sorry. Can we talk?

He was *sorry*? Before she could even think about replying her email notification went off. She clicked on her inbox. There were over one hundred new emails. She scrolled down. Most of them were Twitter notifications: people she *didn't know* mentioning her in tweets. She clicked one open.

Gill June @junechild6
SLUT!!! @roselevine

Rose pressed delete. She saw a Facebook notification. One of the girls in her class had tagged her in a post. Classy! Not! she'd written, under a link to a newspaper story on Rose. Her comment had got twenty-seven likes.

Rose went back to her emails. She saw the name of a newspaper in her inbox. Then another. And another. The subject lines were *Press Inquiry, Possible Interview, Feature Piece*. She clicked on one of them.

Dear Rose,

I'm writing an article about you and your mother for *Lady and Home* magazine and I was wondering if it would be possible to have a chat with you.

All best,
Felicity Barker-Brown

Anxiety scurried through Rose's body like an army of ants. People weren't just writing tweets and comments about her, they were writing whole articles – people who didn't know her and didn't even know the truth. Things hadn't got better at all. They'd got worse. A lot worse.

"Hello, lady!" the little kid called up to her from the towpath.

Rose stared at him blankly. What was she going to do? She'd spent years trying to avoid Savannah's spotlight. Now it was beaming straight down on her. Everyone would recognize her and think they knew her – the way they did with her parents – and she'd never be able to have a normal life. She pictured trying to help Francesca in the patisserie and people coming in to point and stare. "There she is – the slutty daughter of Savannah Ferndale," they'd say before ordering their cakes. "I'm afraid I'm going to have to let you go," she imagined Francesca telling her, disappointment written all over her beautiful face.

"Hello, lady!" the little kid called again.

Rose blinked. His mom was with him now, and they were both staring up at her. Oh God, did the mom recognize her?

Rose jumped to her feet and leapt down the stairs into the boat, slamming the door behind her. What if the woman told the press that she'd spotted her on the boat? What if they found her here? Then where would she go? What would she do? *OK, get a grip*, she told herself, leaning against a kitchen cupboard. *You have to do something. But what?*

And then it came to her. She pulled out drawers until she found the cutlery. She rummaged through the knives and forks until she found what she was looking for. But would they be sharp enough? Rose didn't care. She grabbed the scissors and headed for the bathroom.

From: lakshmigirl@googlepost.com

To: roselnyc@hotpost.com

Date: Fri 6th November 13:05

Subject: Are you OK?

Dear Rose,

I hope you're OK. I saw your picture in the paper this morning and I was worried. The things they were saying – it didn't sound like you. I mean, if it is true then that's fine, obviously, but if it's not then I hope you're all right. Do call me if you need to chat.

Lots of love,

Maali xxx

PS: I saw "the farmer" yesterday. It didn't go how I had dreamed, but at least I've had my first proper conversation with a boy. So that's something. I guess…

---

wildeatheart.tumblr.com

BULLYING: WHY?

Why, in a world that produced wordsmiths like William Shakespeare and Oscar Wilde, would you waste your words on spite?

Why, when words can be crafted into beautiful things, like "The curves of your lips rewrite history" and "Journeys end in lovers meeting", would you twist your words into cruel weapons?

Why, when you could be trawling through a vintage fair for hidden treasure, would you rather be hunting for your next prey?

Why, when you could be eating creamy French cheese, satiny Swiss chocolate or grapes ripened by the Italian sun, would you rather spew your poison?

Why, in a world where one in nine people are starving, where millions of children are denied an education, where 774 million people cannot read and write, would you waste your anger on those who don't deserve it?

Why, when you can make someone's day with a smile or kind deed, would you ruin it with a sneer?

Why, when you are made from the dust of exploded stars, would you act as if you've been carved from ice?

Why, in a world where there is love, would you ever choose hate?

Amber

Chapter Thirty-five

Sky followed Liam into the hall and slammed the door behind her. The clamouring of photographers faded into the background. The police had cleared them off last night, but this morning a new pack arrived.

"Bunch of scumbags," Liam muttered under his breath.

The house was deathly silent. Then the study door flew open and Savannah rushed out, followed closely by Antonio, his tan glowing almost orange against his pale pink jumper.

"Where is she?" Savannah cried, looking from Sky to Liam. "Where's Rose?"

"It's OK, she's still on the boat," Liam said, placing a hand on Savannah's shoulder.

Savannah brushed him off. Her face was puffy and her eyes were bloodshot. She stared at Liam wildly. "You've left her alone?"

"Only for an hour or so. We've just come to get some clean clothes." Liam turned back to Sky. "Do you want to go and get some stuff together?"

Sky nodded and headed towards the stairs.

"But I don't understand!" Savannah cried. "Why didn't you bring her back?"

"I think it's best to keep her out of the spotlight for a few days – away from yer men outside," Liam said gently.

"We need her back here to do an interview," Antonio said, keying something into his phone.

"Oh, do you now?"

Sky froze on the landing at Liam's tone. He never, ever lost his temper, but occasionally, when he was very pissed off, he would be ultra-sarcastic.

"Yes," Antonio said. "I need her to set the record straight."

"*You* need?" Liam said, again his voice icy cool.

"Yes. I need to do some urgent damage limitation," Antonio muttered, still tapping away on his phone.

"Will you take a listen to yourself?" Liam said. "What about what Rose needs?"

Antonio gave a dramatic sigh. "For God's sake, you stupid man, it's all over the internet. We need to make it go away."

Every cell in Sky's body went on high alert. She peered down over the banister. Liam's face had flushed crimson.

"And how is this anything to do with you?" he asked, staring at Antonio.

"I'm Savannah's manager," Antonio said patiently, putting his phone in his pocket. "If it's hurting her career it has everything to do with me."

Liam took a step towards him. "Tell me, when you were little and all the other kids were dreaming of being footballers or astronauts, did you dream of one day being a parasite?"

Antonio frowned. "What?"

"Well, that's exactly what you are, isn't it? Getting rich off somebody else's talent. Not giving a shit about how much pain they might be in or that you might be causing."

"I'm sorry, but I really don't have to listen to this."

"No, you're right, you don't." Liam spun round behind Antonio and got him in an arm lock. "Rose won't be doing any interviews."

"This is assault!" Antonio cried out.

"No, actually, this is not assault," Liam said, frogmarching Antonio to the door. "This is throwing out the crap. But if you want to know what an assault feels like, I'm sure it can be arranged."

"Savannah!" Antonio shrieked. "You can't let him do this to me."

"You should be ashamed of yourself," Liam continued. "Always pushing her to do more work, lose more weight, have more surgery, just so you can get fat off her back."

"Savannah!" Antonio cried again.

Sky peered over the banister to see what Savannah was doing. Surely she was going to go nuts. But Savannah was leaning against the wall, head in hands.

Liam opened the door and shoved Antonio outside. "Go on, join the rest of the parasites. Why don't you be the star of the picture for once?" Sky heard the whirr of camera shutters before Liam slammed the door shut. He rubbed his hands as if he were getting rid of every last trace of Antonio. Then he took a deep breath.

"I'm sorry," he said to Savannah softly. "I'm just trying to look out for you and Rose."

"I don't know what to do," Savannah sobbed. "What should I do?"

Liam held her hands. "Just be her mam," he said softly. "She needs you. And you need her. What you pair have got as mother and daughter – that's real. It counts. All that other nonsense" – he gestured to the door – "it's not real. And it's killing you." Liam walked across the hallway. "I'll see how Sky's getting on. And I promise I'll bring Rose back on Monday. Please let her have a bit of time and space to get over what's happened."

"No," Savannah said.

Then Sky heard Savannah start to cry again.

"I want you to take me with you."

Rose stared in the mirror, unsure whether her reflection made her want to laugh or cry. Strangely, the urge to laugh seemed to be winning. At first she'd cut her hair shoulder-length, but then she'd kept on going. It had felt great to cut away at her hair, and such a release from all the tension that she didn't want to stop. Now she was rocking a jagged crop that at worst could be labelled "demented" and at best "prison inmate chic". The sink was full of her golden locks. The inch or so of hair left on her head was dark brown. She looked like a completely new person. She leaned closer to the mirror. This new person looked nothing like the pouting girl in the photo. She looked edgy and serious. Rose stepped back. She felt lighter – physically and emotionally.

She heard Liam's and Sky's voices, quickly scooped the hair out of the sink and went to meet them.

"Hey," she said as she saw Sky coming down the narrow passageway towards her.

"Your hair!" Sky gasped.

"Yeah, I felt like having a makeover," Rose said as breezily as she could. "I was going for the—" She stopped abruptly. Her heart felt like it stopped beating. Liam was coming down the passageway. Behind him was Savannah. The hair Rose was holding drifted to the floor.

"Rose, honey – what have you done?" Savannah cried, pushing past Liam and Sky.

Rose waited for the "How could you?" and the "What were you thinking?" But instead Savannah's eyes filled with tears.

"I'm sorry," she whispered.

Rose looked at Sky and raised her eyebrows.

Sky nodded. "It's OK," she mouthed.

"I'm so sorry," Savannah said again.

Rose's eyes filled with tears too. Every inch of her felt exhausted.

"I tell you what," Liam said. "Why don't you two go down into Sky's cabin and have a chat, and I'll make us all some tea."

Once they were in the cabin Rose sat down on the bunk she'd slept in the previous night. Savannah perched on the edge of Sky's bunk and looked around. Rose tensed. She'd better not say anything snooty.

"This is nice," Savannah said, picking up one of the patchwork cushions on Sky's bed. "It reminds me of the caravan we stayed in when you were little."

"That's exactly what I said!" Rose exclaimed. They looked at each other for a moment. Rose wished more than anything in the world that they could rewind time and be back in that caravan right now. Just her and her mom and dad. Before her parents got too famous to think straight. Before everything went wrong. She looked down. "Do you ever – do you ever wish you weren't famous?" She flushed. What a dumb question. Savannah loved being the centre of attention.

Rose glanced at her mother. She looked different. Like an older, faded version of herself.

"Lately, yes," Savannah replied.

Rose felt a stab of guilt. "I didn't put that photo on Instagram, Mom, I swear."

"I know you didn't, and I'm so sorry I didn't realize it from the start. But I wasn't talking about that." She sat back on the bunk. "Liam said something today, and although I didn't want to hear it, I can't get it out of my head because I think it might be true."

Rose leaned forward. It was ages since her mom had opened up to her like this. It felt weird, but kind of nice. "What was it?"

"Antonio wanted you to come back for an interview. For

my career. And Liam said, 'What about what Rose needs?' He was right." Savannah sighed. "Being famous is like being a kid at your own birthday party, every single day. Everyone's giving you all the gifts and all the attention. But eventually it has to be somebody else's birthday, and then no one wants to make a fuss of you any more. And it hurts…"

"Is that how you feel?"

Savannah nodded. "And when your dad left, it was like the party had ended. It hurt so bad. And then the press started turning on me…"

"It's OK, Mom." Rose crossed the cabin and sat down next to her.

Savannah shook her head. "No, it's not OK. It's not OK at all. I've been taking it out on you, when you're the last person I should have taken it out on. I'm so sorry. Look at what's happened to you. That photo and" – she put a hand up to touch Rose's ragged hair – "your beautiful hair."

"I kind of like it like this," Rose said.

Savannah put her hand up and stroked Rose's head. "It is pretty fierce," she said with a little laugh.

Rose nuzzled her head against Savannah's hand. It was so long since her mother had touched her, since they'd hugged or kissed or snuggled up together. As if reading her mind, Savannah shifted so that their legs were pressing against each other.

"New start?" she asked quietly.

Rose nodded. "New start."

"Who put that photo on Instagram, Rose? Who did that to you?"

Rose gulped. She didn't want to talk about it. She didn't even want to think about it.

"Was it that boy you've been seeing?"

Rose nodded and swallowed hard. "I wish I'd never sent it to him, Mom. I only did it because ... well, I was in a stupid mood. And then he got mad at me because I wouldn't ... I wouldn't..."

Savannah's eyes widened. "Because you wouldn't sleep with him?"

Rose nodded.

Savannah leapt to her feet and paced up and down the narrow cabin. "That little ass-wipe!"

"Seriously, Mom, it's OK."

"OK?" Savannah stopped pacing and stared at her. "Oh no, honey, it is not OK." She came to a standstill in front of Rose and stared down at her. "He needs a punch in the mouth. Oh, I am so mad right now. Where does he live?"

"Mom!"

"What?"

"You are not going round to Matt's to punch him. I can handle it."

Savannah sat down next to her. "But you shouldn't have to. You shouldn't have to handle this on your own."

"I'm not on my own. I've got you guys." Rose looked at Savannah cautiously. "Haven't I?"

Savannah took hold of Rose's hand and linked their fingers together. "Of course."

They sat in silence for a moment. Liam's laugh rang out from the other end of the boat.

"He's a lovely guy, you know," Savannah said. "He's really helping me see things more clearly."

Rose nodded. "Yeah. I guess he's not too bad – for a hippy yoga teacher."

They both laughed. And Rose felt the faintest glimmer of hope that there might be a way back to their old closeness after all.

From: halopoet@hotpost.com

To: wildeatheart@googlepost.com;

lakshmigirl@googlepost.com

Date: Fri 6th November 16:05

Subject: Poetry Slam – TONIGHT!!!

Hi guys,

I know this is really short notice, but I've entered a poetry slam, and it's tonight, and I'd love it if you could come. Maybe we could have an impromptu Moonlight Dreamers meeting too? It's at the Poetry Library on the Southbank (I've attached a link for directions) and it starts at 8 pm. It would be so great to see you there.

Love,

Sky xx

Chapter Thirty-six

"Are you sure you want to do this?" Sky asked Rose as a train drew into the platform. "I'd be more than happy to go back to the boat with you."

Rose looked at her from under the peak of her cap. "Oh, no, you don't," she said.

"What?"

"Try and wriggle out of the poetry slam."

"I'm not," Sky lied. The truth was, she was terrified, and with every second that ticked by, that terror was growing like a ... like a... She was so terrified she couldn't even think of a metaphor to describe it. "I just don't want to drag you out after all that's happened. I'd totally understand if you'd prefer to spend a night in."

Rose arched her eyebrows. "Are you kidding me? Playing dysfunctional families on the boat with our parents? No thanks!" The train juddered to a halt and the doors slid open. "I'd much rather be cheering you on. And anyway, who's going to recognize me now?"

Sky smiled, but she wondered if Rose was really as happy

about her hair as she made out. She was certainly putting on a very brave face. They got on the train and sat down.

"Are you nervous?" Rose asked.

Sky shrugged. "No… Yes. I'm terrified."

Rose shifted sideways in her seat to look at her. "Don't be. Your poems are awesome."

"How do you know?"

"Because — well, you're pretty awesome." Rose grinned. "It's funny to think how much I used to hate you."

Sky laughed. "Thanks!"

"Sorry, I didn't mean…"

Sky shrugged. "It's OK — I hated you too."

Rose pulled an expression of faux shock. "Really? But you're a peace-loving hippy; you're not supposed to hate anyone."

Sky nodded. "Yep, that's how bad it was." They both grinned. Sky lowered her voice. "So, is everything OK with your mum now?"

Rose nodded. "I guess so. Your dad seems to have worked a miracle."

Sky smiled. "Yeah, my dad's pretty good on the miracle front. Did Savannah tell you what he did to Antonio?"

"Yes, I would have given anything to have seen that. I hate that man, he's such a phoney." Rose's smile faded. "Do you think things will ever get back to normal?"

"Of course," Sky said, hoping with every fibre of her body that she was right.

* * *

As Amber stepped onto Hungerford Bridge she felt the slightest prickle of something resembling hope. To her right, the Houses of Parliament shone gold against the night sky, like a palace from a gothic fairy tale. Across the river, the London Eye was lit up silvery blue as if coated in frost.

"It's so beautiful," Maali gasped, turning a full 360 degrees to take it all in.

Amber nodded and watched as Maali pulled a camera from her bag.

"Doesn't being here make you feel as if anything is possible?" Maali said, pressing up against the railings to take a picture of Westminster.

"I suppose so." Amber watched as Maali sprang from one position to the next taking photos. It was a relief to see her looking happy again. All the way up on the train she'd seemed so different: quieter, and not smiling. Was she making Maali that way? Maybe she was such a loser that she even made Maali sad.

Amber joined Maali by the railings. Further along the bridge a busker was performing. She could just make out the strains of a Bob Dylan song above the chatter of people walking by.

"What do you do if your dream doesn't come true?" Maali asked suddenly. "How do you move on?"

Amber took a breath. What *did* you do? This was a question she'd been unable to answer for the past couple of days. "Find another dream, I guess," she muttered as visions of Paris and Daniel went swirling down a giant plughole in her mind.

"But what if...?" Maali looked into the distance.

"What?"

"Never mind." Maali put her camera back in her bag. "Come on. We don't want to be late."

The Poetry Library was on the fifth floor of the Royal Festival Hall. As the lift door opened Maali said a quick prayer to Lakshmi: *Please let Rose be here and please let her be OK*. The library was packed. Maali scanned the chairs for Sky and Rose.

"Hello, everybody," a woman dressed head to toe in black said into a microphone.

Maali and Amber hastily sat down at the back.

"There's Sky," Amber said, pointing to the front. There was no sign of Rose.

Sky's stomach had been doing a very good impression of a pancake being flipped. Now it morphed into a washing machine drum on spin cycle.

"Welcome to the November slam," the host continued.

She looked so confident. How was she so confident when there were so many people?

"We've got some great poets lined up for you tonight. Some old favourites and some brand new to the Poetry Library."

The woman gazed out into the audience. "To anyone new to poetry slams, here's how it works. We start with twelve poets performing one poem each. Our four judges will award them points on the content and performance. The top six will go through to the second round and perform a different poem. The top three from that round will go through to the final."

Sky looked at the microphone standing centre stage, ready and waiting for the poets. When she'd visualized her dream at the Moonlight Dreamers meeting it had seemed so easy, but now... Now she could imagine how a prisoner on death row felt.

"You OK?" Rose whispered in her ear.

Sky nodded. What if she forgot the words? What were the words? Oh my God, she couldn't even remember the title. Her mind had turned into a giant fog.

"And first up..."

Please don't let it be me, Sky silently pleaded.

"First up, we have someone making her debut at a Poetry Library slam, so please give her a nice warm welcome – Halo!"

Sky got to her feet amid scattered applause.

"Is that you?" Rose hissed.

Sky nodded. Somehow, her feet were still working and somehow, they carried her up onto the stage. Then she was standing behind the microphone, in front of the crowd, just like in her visualization.

"Hi. I'm Halo." Sky's voice squeaked. She cleared her throat. "And my poem's called 'Awaken Your Sleeping Beauty'." She took a deep breath and closed her eyes. Maybe if she pretended she was back in her bedroom performing the poem to the tree it wouldn't be so scary.

"Beauty doesn't come trimmed and plucked and nipped and tucked," she began. Her mouth had suddenly gone so dry she could barely get the words out. "Beauty flows wild and raw with the pure power of oceans. Beauty – er – beauty revels in its imperfections." Sky focused hard, trying not to lose her place. It was only when she was more than halfway through that she thought about the audience. She had to open her eyes. She was being marked on her performance as well as the poem. Sky forced them open, blinking at the brightness of the spotlight.

"Beauty blows..." Sky's mind went blank. What did beauty blow? She gazed out blankly into the crowd and saw one of the judges shaking his head. Her face flushed. What would happen if she just left the stage right now, mid-line, mid-poem? Surely it would be less painful for everyone? But then she spotted some movement at the back of the audience. Maali! She was standing up and waving something. Amber was sitting next to her. Sky felt a jolt of determination. She wasn't going to run off stage. She was a Moonlight Dreamer. She took a deep breath and suddenly the words came.

"Beauty blows heart-shaped smoke-rings in Pretty's face and says, 'Come back when you've lived a little.'" There was a murmur of something from the audience and it didn't feel hostile, so Sky carried on. "Beauty isn't skin-deep, it's bone-deep, heart-deep, soul-deep." Sky heard someone give a whoop and saw Rose grinning up at her.

AWAKEN YOUR SLEEPING BEAUTY
BY SKY CASSIDY

Beauty doesn't come trimmed and plucked and
    nipped and tucked
Beauty flows wild and raw with the pure power of
    oceans
Beauty revels in its imperfections.
Beauty isn't created with an airbrush or Photoshop –
    that's its soulless second cousin, Perfection.
Beauty beats and vibrates and pulses and glows
It lights up rooms and transforms lives
It lives in laughter lines and freckles and scars
Beauty revels in its imperfections.
Beauty is woven into our emotional wounds
As golden threads of wisdom
And sings aloud in acts of compassion.
Beauty blows heart-shaped smoke-rings in Pretty's
    face
And says, "Come back when you've lived a little."
Beauty isn't skin-deep
It's bone-deep
Heart-deep
Soul-deep,
Only put to sleep
When we prick our finger on fear.
Beauty can't be bought or made.

It can only be awoken
Through laughter, and living, and love.
Through being *you*
And being true.

Chapter Thirty-seven

"You were great," Amber said, patting Sky on the back and instantly thinking *oh-crap-that's-such-a-Gerald-thing-to-do*. She was having a lot of these moments lately and it was making her skin crawl.

"No, I wasn't." Sky laughed. "I was awful. What was it the second judge said? I need to open my eyes and learn how to breathe."

"Pompous idiot," Rose muttered, glaring over at the judges. "I wanted to sock him one when he said that."

Amber stared at Rose curiously. Maali had told her that there was a photo of Rose in a newspaper that morning, but when Amber said that she hadn't seen it, Maali had quickly changed the subject. She wondered if it had anything to do with Rose's bizarre haircut. Whatever it was, it was a relief to see her being nice to Sky for once.

"Why don't we go someplace else?" Rose said. "Unless you want to hang out here and see the second round."

Sky shook her head. "I think I'm all poetry slammed out."

"You should have gone through to the next round," Maali

said. "You were great once you got going."

"Yeah, once I saw you," Sky replied with a smile.

"Did you see what I was waving?" Maali pulled the moonstone from her coat pocket. "It must have worked its magic again."

"Is that what it was?" Sky laughed. "Well, it definitely helped. Come on, let's go."

They walked to the lift. It was great to be back with the Moonlight Dreamers. For the first time since Amber's entire world collapsed she could feel herself being pulled from the rubble.

"Hey, you guys, take a look at this." Rose headed over to a door in the corner. It led onto a balcony overlooking the river. It was deserted.

"Shall we?" Rose said, opening the door slightly.

"Are we allowed?" Maali asked.

"Are we *allowed*?" Rose echoed. "We're the Moonlight Dreamers. We don't need to be allowed."

Amber felt a mixture of hope and pride. She'd been so traumatized by what had happened that week that she'd forgotten the reason she set up the Moonlight Dreamers in the first place.

They walked over to the edge of the balcony. Way below them, the Thames glittered and hummed with life.

"What a great place for a Moonlight Dreamers meeting," Sky exclaimed.

"Absolutely," Amber said.

Maali pulled out her camera and took a picture of the river. "It's so romantic," she sighed.

Rose pulled up the collar of her coat against the cold. "It sure is nice to see you all again," she said quietly.

"Are you OK?" Maali asked. "I've been worried about you. Did you get my email?"

Rose shook her head. "I'm sorry. I haven't been checking my mail. I've been avoiding the internet, to be honest."

"That's OK. I understand." Maali gave her a hug.

Amber sighed. Why couldn't she be as tactile as Maali? Why did she find it so difficult to be affectionate or say just the right thing? *Because you're that slangwhanger's daughter*, her inner voice said.

Rose cleared her throat. Amber was struck by how different she looked. It wasn't just the haircut, although that was most definitely different – there was something else. She seemed more serious. More grown-up, despite the fact that she wasn't wearing a scrap of make-up.

"I didn't post it, you know," Rose said. "The topless photo – on my Instagram. Someone else did."

Amber stared at her in shock. *Topless photo?*

Maali gasped. "Who?"

Rose shook her head and frowned. "It doesn't matter."

"Yes, it does!" Maali exclaimed. "How could someone do that to you? Why would they do that to you? It's horrible."

Rose's eyes suddenly filled with tears. "Can you please stop being so damn nice? It's killing me!"

"Are you sure you don't want to talk about it?" Sky asked softly. "It might help."

Rose hesitated. "It was a guy I'd been seeing," she muttered. "I don't know why I sent him the picture. Well, I do know — I was pissed off and wasn't thinking straight. But as soon as I sent it I regretted it and tried to get it back."

"But why did he put it on your Instagram?" Amber asked, trying to process everything she was hearing.

"To hurt me," Rose said, huddling deeper into her coat. "Now, can we please talk about something else?"

Amber had thought that having the whole school talk about her being on her period was bad enough but this was something else. No wonder Rose looked so pale and drawn. Amber took a deep breath. "Well, if it's any consolation, I've been competing with you again for the Worst Week Ever award."

Rose looked at her. "Seriously?"

Amber nodded, painfully aware that all eyes were on her. But if telling them what had happened made Rose feel any better, it would be worth it. "You know how I told you that one of my dads was making my life hell?"

Rose nodded.

"Well, I found out this week that he's actually my biological dad."

They all stared at her blankly.

"My dads never told me which one of them was my biological dad — they said it didn't matter," Amber explained.

"But it does matter. I mean, it's who I am. And for all these years I've thought that it had to be Daniel – the nice one – but it isn't. It's Gerald."

Rose looked at her. "The slangbanger?"

"Slangwhanger. Yes."

Rose sighed. "Man, that sucks."

Amber felt vindicated. It did suck, and it felt great to hear someone else say it.

"But the other guy, Daniel, he's brought you up since, like, for ever, right?" Rose asked.

Amber nodded.

"And you still love him just the same, right?"

"Of course." Amber bristled. She really hoped Rose wasn't going to come out with one of the lines Daniel had been saying on repeat for the past couple of days about love being all that mattered.

"Yeah, still sucks."

Sky and Maali nodded.

Maali placed her hand on Amber's arm and gave it a gentle squeeze. "You're still you, though. That will never change."

"Yes," Sky said with a smile, as though Amber being Amber was a very good thing, not a total and utter loser thing.

"And you're pretty damn awesome," Rose said.

Amber felt a giant gulp building in the back of her throat. How could they say these things? How could they not see what a loser she was, the way her entire school did? Tears started burning in the corners of her eyes and she looked away.

"Are you OK?" Sky said.

Amber nodded, but the tears kept coming. All the pain and sadness of the past few days was finally spilling over.

"Please don't cry," Maali said. "It will get better, honestly. Things are always passing."

"What do you mean?" Rose asked.

"Like that boat." They followed Maali's gaze to a ferry gliding along the Thames, all lit up and full of people dancing. "Sometimes it feels as if things will last for ever," Maali said softly, "especially the bad times. But they never do, because all things are just passing by, just passing through life."

Amber watched as the boat disappeared from view beneath the bridge. "But what if they don't pass quickly enough?" she said, thinking of the years she still had left at school.

"The way you feel about your dads will change," Sky said. "It will get better. I never thought I'd get over my mum dying, and I won't, but it's definitely getting easier."

"No, you don't understand. At school..." Amber broke off. What was she doing? If she told the other Moonlight Dreamers what had happened at school there'd be no escaping the shame.

"What's happened?" Sky asked, her expression full of concern.

Amber shook her head. "It doesn't matter."

"Hey, what happened to the rule about Moonlight Dreamers

telling each other everything?" Rose said with a grin.

"That isn't a rule," Amber said.

Rose frowned. "Well, it should be. Seriously. Tell us what happened. Maybe we can help."

"I doubt it," she said, looking down at her feet. "There's this girl at my school" – she leaned on the balcony wall for support – "and, for whatever reason, she and her friends hate me and they want everyone else to hate me too."

"But why?" Maali looked genuinely surprised. It made Amber well up again. She forced herself to carry on.

"It started because I have two dads. And now it's all about how I must be gay too."

"What's wrong with being gay?" Rose said.

"Nothing. Obviously," Amber replied. "Well, not to us at least, but to this girl and her friends – they just hate anyone who's in any way different. They go on and on about the way I look and the clothes I wear. They say I look like a freak."

"I think you look great," Rose said softly.

Amber forced herself to smile. "Thank you. Anyway, on Wednesday … on Wednesday in PE…" She looked down at the river, wishing she was on one of the boats gliding further and further out to sea.

"What happened?" Sky asked gently.

"We were playing hockey…" Amber could hardly believe she was about to tell them; that the shame she'd been carrying around like a dirty secret was finally coming out. "I had my period and…" She could hear Chloe's voice again, screeching

308

across the playing field. "Some blood got on … my shorts … and now the whole school knows." Amber turned away, unable to say any more.

"Oh, man!" Rose gave her a hug. "You're right. You and I – joint winners of Worst Week Ever – for the second week running. We've gotta be breaking all the records."

"Periods suck," Maali said, with a sympathetic grin.

"Did you know that our periods are controlled by the moon?" Sky said.

"Get out of town!" Rose laughed.

"It's true," Sky said. "That's why most women have them every twenty-eight days. It's something to do with the moon's gravitational pull – the same way it controls the tides."

The moon was a beautiful silver crescent suspended over St Paul's Cathedral. Amber thought of it pulling the river below them back and forth into the ocean. She thought of those same mysterious powers reaching deep inside her and some of her heaviness lifted. Maybe periods weren't something to be dreaded after all. Maybe they were something magical. Maybe they made her even more of a Moonlight Dreamer.

"If that's true, then it's pretty cool," Rose said. She looked at Amber. "There are a lot of idiot girls in my school too. You should see what they've been saying about me lately. But you know what? Who gives a crap? If the only way they can get their kicks is by hurting others, why should we care?" Her face lit up as if she'd just worked out something really important.

Amber nodded. "Thanks, everyone. Seriously. You've been a real help."

They gazed at the river in silence.

"I haven't had the greatest week either," Maali said finally. "I mean, obviously it hasn't been as bad as yours, Rose and Amber, but—"

"Not you too!" Rose interrupted. "What happened?"

Maali hesitated, then said, "I plucked up the courage to talk to the guy I like – *liked*."

"The farmer?" Rose asked.

"He's not a farmer, he works on a farm."

"And the difference is?"

Maali sighed. "He has a girlfriend – called Sage."

Rose raised her eyebrows. "What, Sage as in sage and onion?"

Maali nodded.

"I'm really sorry," Sky said, placing her hand on Maali's arm.

"Yes. Bad luck," Amber added, patting her on the back.

"Well, you know, any guy who dates a girl called Sage has to be a bit of a schmuck," Rose said.

Maali gave a weak smile. "Do you think?"

"For sure! What are they gonna call their kids? Oregano and Thyme?"

The others laughed, even Maali.

"It's really weird," she said. "Before I came here tonight I felt so down. Now I feel great again."

"Me too," said Amber.

"Me three," said Rose.

"Me four," said Sky.

"So what do we do now?" Maali asked.

They looked at Amber and she felt a glow of pride. They still thought of her as the leader. They still trusted her. "I think we need to reboot," she said. "We've all had a difficult few days, but we mustn't let that get us off track. We need to remember exactly why we're here. Why we're Moonlight Dreamers."

"Hell, yeah!" Rose said. "And can we add a new rule?"

"What, about telling each other everything?" Amber said.

"As well as that. Can we add that Moonlight Dreamers never give up?"

"Yes!" Maali and Sky both exclaimed.

Amber pulled one of the flyers from the first meeting out of her briefcase. "OK, so the rules are as follows: The Moonlight Dreamers is a secret society. We start every meeting with the Oscar Wilde quote, which is our motto and must never be forgotten. We must always support one another in the pursuit of our dreams. We're proud of being different. And we have to tell one another everything and never give up." As she wrote the two new rules down, she felt a shiver of excitement. Daniel might not be her real dad and she might not have any friends at school, but she still had her fellow Moonlight Dreamers. And she still had her dreams. And she was never, ever going to give up on any of them.

MOONLIGHT DREAMERS ~ THE RULES

1. *The Moonlight Dreamers is a secret society – members must never speak a word of its existence, or what happens at the meetings, to others.*

2. *Meetings will begin with members reciting the "moonlight" quote from Oscar Wilde.*

3. *This quote is the Moonlight Dreamers' motto and must be memorized by members – and NEVER forgotten.*

4. *All members must vow to support the other Moonlight Dreamers in the pursuit of their dreams – always.*

5. *Moonlight Dreamers are proud of being different. Being the same as everyone else is a crime against originality; the human equivalent of magnolia paint.*

6. *Moonlight Dreamers tell one another everything – even the bad stuff. Especially the bad stuff.*

7. *Moonlight Dreamers never, ever give up.*

Chapter Thirty-eight

As Sky opened the door on the boat she was hit by a waft of incense and wood smoke. Her wave of happiness quickly curdled into sorrow. The boat smelled lived-in again, like home again, but for how long? Coming back had been wonderful, but it would make returning to Hampstead even harder.

"Jeez, I'm tired," Rose said, coming down the steps behind her. She was as pale as a ghost in the lamplight.

"I'm not surprised. It's been quite a week."

Rose nodded. "Sure has. I – er – I don't know what I would have done without you these past couple of days. And thanks so much for taking me to the Moonlight Dreamers. It's the first time I've – well, it's the first time I've felt like I belong someplace in a long time." She looked at Sky anxiously. "I do belong there, right?"

Sky smiled at her. "Of course you do."

They heard the creak of footsteps in the passageway and Liam entered the kitchen, stooping in the low doorway.

"Hey, girls. Did you have a good night?" He looked at Sky. "How did the poetry slam go?"

Sky shook her head. "Don't ask!"

"She was awesome," Rose said.

"Yeah, apart from not opening my eyes or breathing," Sky said with a laugh. She turned to Liam. "It was terrifying."

"But you did it?"

Sky nodded.

Liam put his arm round her shoulders and pulled her close. "That's my girl."

Sky rested her head on his shoulder and breathed in the comforting scent of patchouli oil.

"I think I'll go to bed," Rose said. "I'm exhausted."

"Your mam's the same," Liam said. "She went to bed hours ago." He put his hand on Rose's shoulder. "How are you doing now?"

"OK," Rose said. "Thanks to Sky." She gave her a grateful smile. "I'll see you in the morning."

"Yes. Sleep well."

When Rose had gone, Liam put the kettle on. "Fancy a camomile tea?"

Sky couldn't think of anything she'd rather do than have a cup of tea with her dad – just the two of them.

Liam put teabags in a couple of mugs and turned back to Sky. "How are you doing?" His voice was soft and serious.

"OK."

"No, how are you really doing?"

Sky looked down at the floor. "OK."

"I'm so sorry," Liam said softly.

Sky looked at him. "What for?"

"Bringing all of this into your life. I don't know what I was thinking, moving in there so soon." He shook his head.

Sky stared at him. Was he saying he'd made a mistake? Did he regret moving in with Savannah? If he'd said this a week ago she would have felt triumphant, but now she only felt sad. It was horrible seeing her dad so deflated. He was usually so happy. So strong.

The kettle started to whistle. "Savannah and I had a long chat tonight while you girls were out and we've decided that you and I should move back in here."

"Really?" This was so far from what Sky was expecting to hear, so beyond her wildest dreams, that she didn't know what to say.

"Yes. I don't want you being a part of that world. It's too…"

"Crazy?" Sky offered.

Liam nodded. "That's the polite way of putting it."

"But what about you and Savannah?" *What about me and Rose?* she thought.

Liam started pouring water into the mugs. "Savannah has to make some important decisions about her life, and I think it's best if she's on her own while she's making them. We still care about each other – a lot – but…" He put the kettle down. "I thought I could help her. I thought us all being together as a family would give her the stability she needed, but…"

"You did help her," Sky said as she walked up behind him

315

and put her hand on his shoulder. "And you've really helped Rose."

"Really?" Liam turned to face her.

"Of course. Letting her stay here is probably the only thing that's kept her sane."

Liam forced a smile. "I promise I won't let you down again."

"You haven't."

"Yes, I have. And your mam." Liam glanced at the pendant around Sky's neck. "She'd be going crazy seeing the mess I got you into. I'm so sorry."

Sky shook her head. "It's fine. Seriously. Sometimes things don't work out the way you want, but it's OK because something else good happens instead."

Liam smiled. "Since when did you get so wise?"

"Since you taught me," Sky replied.

Liam put his arms round her and pulled her in for a hug. And slowly, slowly, all of the tension and resentment of the past couple of weeks began to melt away. Their life together had been thrown up into the air, but now the pieces were falling back into place. Their new life would be different, but it would be richer and stronger. Because she was stronger. And so was their love.

Amber quietly let herself into her house and began to walk up the edges of the stairs. If she walked up the middle, the wooden floorboards made horror-film–style creaks, which seemed to get louder the later it was.

"Hello."

Amber jumped at the sound of Gerald's voice. He was sitting in the dark on the top step.

"Hello," she muttered, taking a deep breath to try and get her heart rate back down to normal. "What – what are you doing?"

"Waiting for you," he replied. "Where have you been?"

"Out with friends." Amber felt a tingle of joy at being able to say it and really mean it.

"What friends?"

"It doesn't matter." Amber started walking up the stairs towards him. Why wasn't he locked away in his studio? Why was he waiting for her? "Where's Daniel?"

"Gone to see that god-awful *Phantom of the Opera* with his brother." Gerald shuddered. He was not a fan of musical theatre. He called it "music for your soul to die to".

"I've been worried about you."

"Really? Why? It's not that late." Maybe it was the half-light of the hallway, but he looked older. His wrinkles seemed more pronounced and there were heavy bags under his eyes.

"I don't mean the time, I mean..." Gerald broke off and looked away.

"What?" Amber's heart rate began to quicken again.

"What you said, the other night. Can we – could we just sit for a moment – and talk?" He gestured for her to sit next to him.

"OK." Amber didn't know what to make of this turn

of events, but she was still so happy from the Moonlight Dreamers meeting that she felt strong enough to endure one of Gerald's lectures. She sat down and clutched her briefcase.

"I – er – I think I owe you an apology."

"Oh? What for?" Amber held her breath, not daring to look at him. Was this a trick? Gerald never apologized. Not ever.

"I'm not exactly sure."

Of course. She knew what was going on here. Daniel had told Gerald to apologize. It was so typical that he didn't even see what he'd done wrong.

"I mean, I try my hardest to be a good father, I really do, but clearly that hasn't been good enough."

Amber could see exactly where this conversation was going. Instead of an apology, it would be yet another speech about how wonderful Gerald was. Well, she could do without it. There was no way she was going to let him ruin her good mood – it had taken her long enough to find it. She started getting to her feet.

"No, please. Don't go!" Gerald cried, grabbing her hand. There was something weird about his voice. Something wavering. He sounded like he was going to cry.

Amber sat down again and stared into the darkened hallway. The ticking of the grandfather clock echoed as if counting every long, drawn-out second of awkwardness.

"I was very upset to see you react the way you did when

I told you that I was your biological father," Gerald said. "Is it really so horrific?"

"It's not horrific," Amber said, continuing to avoid his gaze. "It was just a real shock."

"But why?" Gerald asked.

"Well, because you don't…" Amber tailed off.

"I don't what?"

"You don't seem at all interested in me."

"That's not true!" Gerald cried. "I'm always asking Daniel about you."

"But why?" Amber turned to him, her heart pounding with a mixture of anger and fear. "Why not ask *me*?"

"Well, because you're both so…" Gerald hesitated. "Sometimes I feel as if you and Daniel are so close there's no room for me."

"But you're always busy with your work."

"But my work is…" Gerald put his hands together as if in prayer, the way he always did when he had an important point to make. "Are you passionate about anything?"

Amber nodded.

"Would you like to tell me what?"

"Oscar Wilde."

"Really?" Gerald's face lit up. "He was my hero when I was your age."

"Seriously?" Amber felt a weird sensation in her stomach. She'd strayed into the previously uncharted territory of having something in common with Gerald.

"So, when you're reading Oscar Wilde, do you ever lose track of time?"

Amber nodded. She'd lost entire days immersed in his books and plays.

"Well, that's what it's like for me when I'm painting. I lose all sense of time and place. I know it makes me difficult to live with, but it doesn't mean…" He cleared his throat. "It doesn't mean I don't love you," he said gruffly.

"Really?" Amber whispered, still barely able to believe what she was hearing.

"I love you very much," Gerald said. "The day you came into the world was the happiest of my life."

Amber stared at him. "Honestly?"

He looked sad. "You have no idea how much it pains me to see your surprise and disbelief at this fact." He sighed. "You might be familiar with this quote." He leaned forward slightly. "'Children begin by loving their parents; as they grow older they judge them; sometimes they forgive them.'"

Amber nodded. "Oscar Wilde."

"Yes. Well, I would like it very much if you would be the rare exception to that quote and find it in your heart to forgive me, Amber."

Amber swallowed hard to try to maintain her composure. "I'd like that very much too," she muttered.

"You would?" Gerald smiled broadly and suddenly he looked years younger.

"Yes."

Gerald patted Amber on the back and coughed. "That's wonderful!"

They sat in silence for a moment, but this time it didn't feel awkward.

"Ger – er – Dad," Amber said.

"Yes?"

"I've been thinking."

"Yes?"

"Well, all this stuff about you being my biological dad." Amber took a deep breath. "It's made me want to know more about my biological mum. I mean, I know she was a surrogate and I know it would probably be really hard to track her down, but – I – I'd just like to…" She tailed off, hoping that what she'd said wouldn't make Gerald upset.

But to her relief, he simply said, "You'd like to know more about who you came from?"

"Yes!" Amber looked at him hopefully.

"Wait here." Gerald grabbed hold of the wrought iron banister and hauled himself up. "I'll be back in a tick."

As Gerald disappeared into his studio Amber sat in the darkness, barely able to believe her luck. Gerald and Daniel had never really talked about her biological mum, other than to say that they'd used a surrogacy agency in the States. And ever since she'd seen a documentary about surrogacy when she was about twelve she'd been too wary to ask any more. All the women in the programme had seemed slightly hard and scary.

Amber heard the stairs creak behind her and Gerald sat back down. "Here you are," he said, handing her a faded sketchbook. She opened it nervously. On the first page was a pencil sketch of a heavily pregnant woman in side profile, leaning against a wall.

"I did them while we were at the hospital waiting for you to arrive," Gerald said quietly.

Amber turned the page. There was another sketch of the woman, face-on this time, with one hand resting lightly on top of her stomach. Amber swallowed hard. She and the woman had exactly the same square jaw. The woman was gazing off into the distance and looked kind of sad. Amber turned to the next page. On it was a picture of a baby, swaddled tightly in a blanket. Gerald had doodled the word *LOVE* underneath it so many times that the letters all overlapped.

"She was a very nice young woman," Gerald said. "She'd been through some tough times, and having you for Daniel and me, well, it helped her turn her life around."

Amber felt a bittersweet mixture of sadness and happiness. Sadness for the thin woman in the sketch who'd needed to sell her baby, to sell *Amber*, to make her life better, but such happiness that she'd ended up with Daniel and Gerald.

"Are you OK?" Gerald asked.

Amber nodded and held out the pad.

"No, no," he said, shaking his head. "Please keep it. And if there's – if there's anything else you'd like to know, about any of it, please ask."

"OK," Amber whispered.

"And before I forget," Gerald continued, "to try and make amends for being so tardy in the parenting department, I would like to take you to Paris for your birthday."

Amber's eyes widened. "What, on my actual birthday?"

"Yes."

"But what about your exhibition?"

Gerald smiled. "I'm sure one day away from my paint-brushes won't hurt."

How was it possible that this was happening? First the Moonlight Dreamers meeting and now all this. It was as if her brain didn't have the capacity to process so much joy. "Thank you," she sobbed.

"Oh dear. Don't cry. Let me…" Gerald fumbled in his pocket and pulled out a handkerchief. "There, there," he said, dabbing awkwardly at her face.

Downstairs they heard Daniel step into the hallway, humming the theme tune from *Phantom* under his breath.

"What the hell?" he exclaimed when he saw them sitting at the top of the stairs. "What are you doing?" He climbed the steps two at a time. "Is everything OK?"

"I think so," Gerald said, looking at Amber anxiously.

Amber nodded and wiped her eyes. "Everything's great," she said.

"We've just been sorting some things out," Gerald explained.

Daniel raised his eyebrows. "What things?"

"Amber's birthday trip to Paris."

"On my actual birthday," Amber added.

Daniel broke into a grin. "That's great." He opened his arms and pulled them both into a hug. And as Daniel and Gerald's arms wrapped around Amber, she felt all the empty places inside her slowly filling with love.

From: roselnyc@hotpost.com

To: wildeatheart@googlepost.com

Date: Saturday 7th November 14:17

Subject: An idea…

Hey Amber,

Hope you're OK.

I think I might have figured out a way to help you make your dream come true. Not the one about Paris – I'm afraid that's a bit out of my price range :-) – but I think I can help you get more readers for your blog. Let me know if you want to find out more.

Rose xoxo

From: wildeatheart@googlepost.com

To: roselnyc@hotpost.com

Date: Saturday 7th November 14:27

Subject: Re: An idea…

Dear Rose,

That would be wonderful! Do tell me more.

I hope things are getting better for you now. I found a quote from Oscar Wilde that I thought you might like:

"There is only one thing in the world worse than being talked about, and that is not being talked about."

I'm not sure if you would agree with that right now, though!

I look forward to hearing from you.

Best wishes,

Amber

Chapter Thirty-nine

Rose looked at her reflection in the mirror. Her heart was pounding so hard it felt like her ribcage might crack. *Don't do this,* her inner voice pleaded, *it's insane.* Rose took a deep breath and stood up straight. Yesterday she'd gone to a hairdressers on a backstreet in East London and asked them to tidy up her hair and dye it jet black. She ran her hand over the short crop. It was weird to think that her initial reason for cutting her hair had been to disguise herself, because this look actually felt far more like the real her: fierce and strong and never a quitter. "Moonlight Dreamers never give up," she whispered to her reflection.

Outside the changing room toilets a whistle blew and a cheer rang out from the crowd. Rose's stomach lurched. *There's still time. You can still leave. You don't have to do this.* But if she didn't do it she'd always feel bad about herself and she'd never be able to sing that kick-ass French song "Non, Je ne regrette rien" again. Hands trembling, Rose opened the door.

Outside, the sky was a blank, unforgiving sheet of white and an icy wind whipped across the rugby pitch. Rose could see the players making their way over to the changing rooms, their faces and legs raw from the cold. Muted applause rippled through the small crowd as the players walked past. Rose's heart was pounding so hard now she could barely hear herself think. She couldn't do this. She had to leave. Then she remembered the moonstone. Maali had given it to her on their way home from the Poetry Library. "I think you really need it this time," she'd whispered with a smile.

Rose put her hand into her coat pocket and wrapped her fingers around the cool stone. She *could* do this. She was a Moonlight Dreamer.

Out of the corner of her eye she saw a girl running towards the rugby players, holding her phone up to take a picture. Jasmine! What the hell? Rose swallowed hard as she registered this turn of events. Was Jasmine here to watch Matt? Was she taking photos of Matt? Had she got her claws into him already?

Jasmine and the players were just a few metres away now. She didn't have time to figure out what was going on; she had to stay focused. Her eyes searched the players for Matt. There he was, towards the back of the pack. And there was Jasmine, running alongside him, smiling and giggling at something he was saying. Rose clenched the moonstone and started walking towards them.

"Can I have a word?" she called, her voice trembling slightly. *Get a grip*, she scolded herself.

Matt looked at her – blankly at first, and then she saw a

flicker of recognition and his jaw dropped open in shock. "Rose?" he gasped, staring at her hair.

"OMG!" Jasmine cried. "Rose, is that you? What have you done to your hair?"

"It was time for a makeover," Rose replied drily, keeping her gaze fixed on Matt. His floppy hair was slick with sweat. He brushed it from his face and looked away. He was out of breath from the game. "What are you...? Why are you here?" he panted.

"Oh, I think you can probably guess," Rose said curtly.

"Could we – can we go somewhere more private?" Matt said, taking hold of her arm.

"Don't touch me!" Rose yelled, shaking him off.

Matt looked horrified. "I'm sorry – honestly, Rose." He looked her straight in the eye. "I'm so sorry. I didn't mean..." He looked down and started scuffing the toe of his boot into the mud.

"You didn't mean what?" Rose stared at him.

Matt looked at her imploringly. "Can we go somewhere private? Please?"

Rose glared at him. "Are you kidding? After what happened the last time you asked me that?"

"What's going on, guys?" Jasmine looked from Rose to Matt and back again.

"Why don't you tell her?" Rose challenged him. He looked away.

"I – uh—"

"*What?*" Jasmine asked, looking stressed.

"Do we really have to do this here?" Matt pleaded.

Rose nodded. "Yup."

Matt sighed. "I posted that photo on her Instagram," he muttered to Jasmine.

"*What?* But you said…" Jasmine turned to Rose. "He said…"

"I was drunk. I – I wasn't thinking straight," Matt stammered. "Please, Rose, I didn't mean to, I—"

"You *didn't mean to*?" Rose was furious. "What, you *accidentally* logged into my account and posted that picture there? Just like you accidentally pinned me to the sofa and…" Rose broke off, feeling suddenly close to tears. She'd thought that confronting Matt like this and seeing him squirm would make her feel better, but it didn't. It was making her feel sick to her stomach.

"What's going on?" Jasmine asked, her voice high and wobbly.

"Don't worry about it," Rose muttered. She turned and started to walk away. No way was she going to let Matt see her cry.

"Rose!" Matt called after her. She kept walking.

"Rose, please!" She heard him running up behind her. "Please, can I just talk to you alone for a second?"

She turned to face him. He looked so different. All of his cockiness had disappeared – along with his fake Cockney accent. He looked frightened as he shifted from foot to foot. It made her feel better. Stronger.

"What?" she said with a piercing look.

"I didn't mean—"

"Oh please, not again!" Rose started to turn away.

"I didn't mean for things to get so heavy," he said. "I didn't think … I didn't … I'm sorry." She heard a tremor in his voice and turned back to see tears in his eyes. "I'm so sorry I hurt you."

She swallowed hard to stop herself from crying. "So why did you do it?" she said, her voice barely more than a whisper.

"I was angry. I was drunk. I wasn't thinking straight. I didn't think anyone would see it apart from our friends."

"I'm not talking about the photo. Why did you…" Rose couldn't bring herself to say it. "Why didn't you listen to me when I said no?"

Matt looked at the ground. "I'm not used to people saying no to me." It would have sounded like the most arrogant line in the world if he hadn't been so upset. "Why didn't you like me, Rose? Why didn't you fancy me?"

Rose sighed. "Not everything's about you, you know. No means no, no matter how much you're used to getting your own way."

Matt wiped his eyes with the back of his hand, leaving a muddy streak across his face. "I would never have – I mean, I'm not a – I'm not a rapist," he whispered. "I promise, I would never have done that to you – or anyone. I would have stopped. Seriously, Rose, you have to believe me."

Rose stared at him. "I don't *have* to do anything," she said.

His face fell. "I do forgive you, though," she added. "My mom's shrink reckons that not forgiving someone is like drinking poison and hoping the other person will die. And there's no way I'm drinking poison for you."

Matt looked at her confused. "So can we still – are we still friends?"

Rose laughed and started heading for the gate. "I don't think so," she called over her shoulder. "I have all the friends I need."

INTERVIEW WITH ROSE LEVINE

Today I have a special guest at Wilde at Heart: my friend, Rose Levine. Many of you will have read about Rose recently, online or in the papers, and many of you will have seen a certain photo of Rose. In our interview – the only interview she is giving on the subject – Rose sets the record straight.

AMBER: Welcome to Wilde at Heart, Rose. First of all, can I ask you why you've decided to do this interview?

ROSE: Sure. I was sick of seeing so much crap written about me by people who don't even know me and don't have a clue about what really happened.

AMBER: What would you like to say to those people?

ROSE: Here are the facts: I took that photo to send to my then-boyfriend. It was supposed to be private and I regretted doing it almost as soon as I'd sent it. But that's irrelevant, really, because even if I hadn't regretted it, it was only ever meant to be private, between me and him.

AMBER: So how did it get on your Instagram account?

ROSE: My ex-boyfriend put it there.

AMBER: Why would he do something like that?

ROSE: I'd rather not go into that. The fact is, he did it and he's apologized. End of story.

AMBER: How did it feel when the photo went viral?

ROSE: I wanted to die. For real. It felt like the whole world was looking at me and I was trapped under their magnifying glass. And it wasn't just that they were looking, they were judging me too – even though they didn't know the full story. Even though they didn't know me. It was like they didn't want to know. All they wanted to do was get high on gossip and hate. They've been doing it to my mom for years.

AMBER: Didn't your parents being famous at least prepare you in some way for what happened?

ROSE: Nothing can prepare you for that kind of scrutiny. And anyway, I've always tried really hard to stay out of the spotlight. I hate all that fame BS. I think the celebrity world is full of fakes and phoneys and I don't want any part of it.

AMBER: Some people will still probably say that it was your own fault for taking that photo in the first place. What do you have to say to them?

ROSE: When I take my clothes off, I have a naked body. Deal with it. Seriously, at first, when it all happened, I actually started agreeing with what those people were saying. I felt dirty and ashamed, but then I realized how messed up that was. I reckon if a spaceship full of aliens were to land on planet Earth right now they'd think they'd landed in the universe's psych ward. It's so messed up. Why are we so afraid of naked bodies? We all have one. It's nothing to feel bad about. And what I hate the most is that women have people in the media constantly telling us that we should look as sexy as possible, but if we actually do, we're called sluts. I've had adults sending me messages calling me a slut. They should be ashamed of themselves. What gives them the right to judge me? What gives them the right to hound my mom, just because she's getting older? It doesn't make any sense. We're all naked underneath our clothes and we're all getting older. Every single day. GET. OVER. IT. And then get a life – one that doesn't involve wrecking somebody else's.

AMBER: Thank you! So what do you want to do next?

ROSE: I'm going to get on with my life – out of the spotlight. I've never had any desire to be a model, so maybe *Showbiz Now* would like to apologize for printing all those lies about me? I'm about way more than just my body.

AMBER: And finally, what is your favourite Oscar Wilde quote?

ROSE: "Be yourself; everyone else is already taken."

Thanks so much, Rose, for being my very first guest on Wilde at Heart.

If you've enjoyed Rose's interview, you might also like a recent post I wrote called: Bullying: Why? You can read it right *here*.

Amber

Chapter Forty

As Amber walked through the gates of Père Lachaise Cemetery behind Daniel and Gerald, she pinched the back of her hand. She had to make sure that she wasn't dreaming – this felt way too good to be true. But here she was, in Paris, beneath a porcelain white sky, about to see Oscar Wilde's grave.

"Wow! This place is like a town for dead people!" Rose exclaimed. "The tombs are just like streets of little houses."

Amber grinned, and corrected herself. Here she was, in Paris, about to see Oscar Wilde's grave, *with the Moonlight Dreamers.*

There was a grassy island right in front of them, with narrow cobbled roads leading off in three directions. Each of the roads was lined with tombs of all shapes and sizes. Rose was right: it did look like a miniature, if slightly surreal, town.

"It's beautiful," Maali gasped, rushing off to take a photo of a nearby tomb adorned with the crumbling statue of an angel.

"And so peaceful," Sky said in a hushed voice, turning full circle to take it all in.

"OK, ladies," Gerald said. "I'm under strict instructions from my daughter to let you visit Oscar Wilde's grave alone." He gave Amber a knowing smile. She felt sparks of happiness inside her. "So," Gerald continued, "Daniel and I are going to visit Modigliani's grave – he's a famous Italian painter who's buried here. My work is often likened to his, actually, especially my portraits." Amber inwardly groaned. "Anyway, you have maps," he said, thankfully cutting his self-congratulatory diversion short. "We'll meet you back here in an hour. Don't get abducted, or anything."

"We'll try not to," Rose said.

Daniel grinned. "Just give us a call if you get lost. This place can be a bit of a rabbit warren." He pointed up the road straight in front of them. "You need to head up that way for about five minutes, then turn right."

"Thank you," Amber said as her dads started to walk off in the opposite direction, arms linked. She felt another burst of happiness.

"Your dads are so cool," Rose said. "Even the slangbanger. You have to admit he's pretty funny."

Amber nodded. In the weird parallel universe she'd been living in since she and Gerald had had the chat on the stairs, he did seem funny. He also seemed a lot kinder. When she'd asked him if he would pay for her friends to come to Paris too, he'd agreed immediately. He'd even convinced Maali's mum to let her come, charming her with offers of artwork for her shop and buying several kilos of her burfi.

As they started walking up the cobbled road Rose fell into step with Amber. "Did you see what happened to your blog post?"

Amber nodded. She'd published her interview with Rose a week ago and as soon as Rose tweeted the link to it the visitor stats to Wilde at Heart had gone crazy. She looked at Rose anxiously. "Are people being all right about it? To you, I mean?"

"Yeah, people are being really cool. But I wasn't talking about that. I was talking about your bullying post."

Amber felt a shiver run up her spine. "What about it?"

"Loads of people are sharing it and they're all saying what a great writer you are."

Amber carried on walking, her body one giant firework display of happiness.

Maali crouched down beside the grave and zoomed into the bunch of withered roses that lay across the inscription. There was something very powerful about their faded beauty. Death intertwined with death. She took a picture and stepped backwards – straight into someone.

"Oh, sorry!" she exclaimed.

A young guy with shiny black hair and dark eyes smiled back at her. "English?" he said.

Maali nodded, her face reverting to its default *see-a-boy-*

catch-on-fire setting. *"Oui,"* she said, instantly causing her face to flush even hotter.

"It is fine," the boy said, in a strong French accent.

Maali's heart sprang a pair of fluttering butterfly wings. The French accent was so cute – and *so* romantic.

"This grave – it belongs to my great-great-grandmother," he said.

"Oh. I'm so sorry!" Maali said. "I shouldn't have taken a photo. It was just that the flowers are so beautiful."

The boy looked at them and frowned. "Really? I think they are – what is the word? Sad. They have been here too long."

Maali shook her head. "I think that makes them more interesting."

The boy tilted his head to one side as if he wasn't sure what to make of this strange English girl and her love of dead flowers.

Why could she never do or say something normal when it came to boys? "Nice weather," she muttered lamely.

The boy looked up. "Hmm, I think it might snow." Then he leaned down and gently pulled a withered rose from the bunch. "Here," he said. "For you."

"Oh no – I couldn't," Maali said. "They're your great-great-grandmother's."

"She would want you to have one," he said.

Maali took the flower. "Thank you. I mean, *merci.*"

"You are welcome. It was nice to meet with you." The boy turned back to the grave.

"Yes. You too." Maali hurried back to the cobbled road. The other Moonlight Dreamers were waiting for her.

"Did you just steal that from a grave?" Rose asked, staring at the flower.

"No! A guy gave it to me." Maali felt her face flushing again.

"Oh, really?" Rose linked arms with her. "So, I guess the tips I gave you must be working if you're even getting lucky in a graveyard!"

Maali giggled and shook her head, but inside she felt a glimmer of hope. After things had gone so wrong with Ash she'd become convinced that she'd never meet her soulmate. But this was how it happened. This was how love started, every day, in every village and town and city all over the world. Chance meetings. Stolen glances and random exchanges. "*Oh, Maali,*" she imagined the French guy exclaiming to her over a bouquet of roses. "*Je t'adore!*"

Sky was having trouble taking in all the tombs as she followed the others along the road. There were so many, and they were all so different, and so *interesting*, that she didn't know where to look first. It was weird, because ever since she'd lost her mum she'd studiously avoided anything to do with death. And cemeteries had as much to do with death as you could get. When Amber emailed them to say that her dads had agreed to pay for them to come on a day trip to Paris, and that they'd be going to see Oscar Wilde's grave, Sky's first instinct had been to say no. But now that she was here, surrounded by death, carved and sculpted into stone, it didn't feel scary at all. In fact, it felt peaceful.

A robin swooped down and perched on the arm of a statue. It cocked its head and whistled. Sky smiled. Then she thought of the email Maali had sent her after the first Moonlight Dreamers meeting. What if Hindus were right? What if death wasn't the end? What if it was just people's bodies that died, and their souls lived on? She felt something shifting deep within her, as if the shard of pain that had been piercing her heart was finally dislodging. The robin chirped again, then flew off. Sky watched it, feeling lighter with every second.

Rose leaned against a tree and smiled as Maali took yet another photo of yet another grave. Even though she still thought all of that religion stuff was for chumps, Rose couldn't shake the overwhelming sensation of wanting to thank the universe, or whatever the hell it was that had caused the chain of events that led to her ending up right there, in that moment. The events of the past couple of months had been hellish, for sure, but she could see now that it had all been worth it.

Everything she hated had been sloughed away from her life. She no longer had to see Matt and Jasmine and all the phoneys from school – Liam had been home-schooling her with Sky for the past few weeks, and in January she was starting at a new school in Islington. Her mom had sacked Antonio and was seriously thinking about quitting modelling. She'd also been seeing a new therapist, who was getting her to work on her "rejection issues", *and* she'd agreed to Rose having a Saturday job in the patisserie. She'd even eaten one of the red velvet cupcakes Rose had made last week, including the frosting. Afterwards, Rose had heard her working out like crazy on the exercise bike, but it was a start. And she was going to be spending the Christmas break in New York with her dad.

But best of all, by doing the interview for Amber's blog, Rose had finally managed to rid herself of the curse of the photo. As soon as Amber published the interview Rose had felt a huge weight lifting. She'd had her say. It didn't matter what other people thought any more, she'd stood up for herself and she could hold her head high. And now here she was, in Paris, with the first real friends she'd had for years, and she was so, so grateful.

She followed Maali on to the next grave. "It says here that this person was a famous singer," Maali said, studying her map of the cemetery.

Rose glanced down at the gravestone. It was shiny dark granite, with a small statue of Christ on the cross laid out across it. **FAMILLE GASSION-PIAF** was engraved in gold letters at the base. Piaf. Rose frowned. Where had she heard that name before? And then it dawned on her. Edith Piaf, Francesca's favourite, the singer of "Non, Je ne regrette rien". Rose looked up at the sky. In spite of everything that had happened and all the pain she'd been through, she still didn't regret a thing.

Amber turned into the side road and every muscle in her body tightened. This was it. She was finally going to meet her hero – or see his grave, at least. She'd looked it up online many times. She recognized the huge grey structure as soon as she saw it, and a shiver ran up her spine. The others were still quite a long way behind her. Amber hurried on.

A solid block of grey stone with a flying sphinx carved into it, the tomb wasn't the most beautiful in the cemetery by a long shot, but Amber didn't care. Oscar Wilde was actually buried there. The man who'd saved her life with his words over and over and over again was just a few feet away from her. A Perspex screen had been erected around the bottom of the grave. Gerald had told her this was because fans would come from all over the world to write messages and plant lipstick kisses on the tomb. The grey stone was still covered in kisses in every shade from frosty pink to scarlet, as was the screen. The inscription on the base of the stone read simply: OSCAR WILDE. Beneath that, on a square of black slate, there was a quote from his poem *The Ballad of Reading Gaol*:

> *And alien tears will fill for him*
> *Pity's long-broken urn,*

For his mourners will be outcast men,
And outcasts always mourn.

A couple of small bouquets of flowers had been thrown over the screen and were lying on the base of the grave. Amber fumbled in her pocket and pulled out the letter she'd written late last night. She hadn't known then if she'd be able to leave it on the grave, but the Perspex screen filled her with confidence. No one would be able to read it once she threw it over: it would be between just her and Oscar. She stood on tiptoe and quickly pushed the letter over. It floated down and landed on the base of the tomb. She pictured Oscar lying beneath, somehow able to read her words. She really hoped he could.

"Is that it?" she heard Sky call.

Amber turned and saw the others heading towards her. She was too emotional to speak.

"Whoa – it's so different from all the others," Rose said. "I love it."

Amber felt a strange burst of pride.

They all stood in a line, looking up at the huge winged sphinx.

"Isn't it weird to think that the person who inspired the Moonlight Dreamers is under there?" Rose said.

Amber nodded. It was weird and magnificent.

"Well, his body is…" Sky said, looking at Maali. "I think his soul might be up here, with us."

Maybe that was the best thing about being a writer, Amber

thought. *Your spirit lived on for ever in your words.*

A breeze drifted by, causing Amber's letter to dance.

"It's snowing!" Maali cried.

Sure enough, a huge snowflake floated past Amber's face and landed on the sleeve of her coat.

Rose nudged her. "Come on, then."

Amber frowned. "What?"

"We can't come all this way to see the inspiration for the Moonlight Dreamers and not say the quote." Rose grabbed hold of Amber's and Sky's hands. Maali took hold of Amber's other hand. The four girls stood in a row and looked up at the tomb. Snowflakes swirled like feathers in the cold air. Rose and Maali squeezed Amber's hands at exactly the same time and she felt a surge of warmth rush through her. She thought of Oscar Wilde sitting at a lamplit desk on a winter's day over a hundred years ago, and she pictured him writing the words that would end up tumbling like snowflakes through time to land inside each of the Moonlight Dreamers and change their lives for ever.

"'Yes: I am a dreamer,'" she began, and she was sure that in the stillness of the cemetery she could hear a man's voice, deep and resonant, echoing hers.

Dear Oscar,

I just want to thank you so much for all you have done for me. I know you went through some terrible times in your life and I can't even begin to imagine what it must have been like to have been sent to jail just because of your sexuality, but if it's any consolation, your words have made such a difference to me.

Your writing was there for me at the very lowest points in my life. You made me feel that it was OK to be different – that it was something to be proud of, even. And because of you I've found other kindred spirits and I'm not alone any more.

I only wish that you could have found your fellow Moonlight Dreamers while you were still alive.

With love and deepest admiration,

Amber

ACKNOWLEDGEMENTS

Firstly, a HUGE thank you to all the team at Walker Books for making me feel so welcome. In true Moonlight Dreamers' style, being published by you is a dream come true for me. Editor extraordinaire Mara Bergman, Gill Evans, Ed Ripley, Emily Damesick, Jo Humphreys-Davies, Sean Moss, David McDougall and everyone else at Walker who has shown such overwhelming enthusiasm for this book – thank you.

Merci beaucoup also to Marie Hermet and Celine Vial at Flammarion for encouraging me to think outside the box and dream big as a writer. It's a pleasure to work with you and to have my books published in France.

I've been fortunate enough to have been guided throughout my writing career by the loveliest literary-guardian-angel agents. Massive thank you to Judy Chilcote, Erzsi Deak and Jane Willis.

Pursuing our dreams can sometimes be a scary business and we all need our own band of Moonlight Dreamers to support us through the bad times and celebrate with us during the good. I'm indebted to the following people for being there for me through thick and thin: Sara Starbuck, Tina McKenzie, Linda Lloyd, Jeanette Smith, Angela Woodward and Jenny Davies. And of course, my family: Jack Phillips, Michael "Love & Simplicity" Curham, Anne, Bea, Alice, Luke, Katie, Dan and John and my American family, the awesome Delaney clan (next dream: to live Stateside with y'all, writing books fuelled by vanilla coffee and Brownie Brittle).

Much gratitude also to my Facebook family for all the laughs and the likes and the shares. Special thanks to my old Nower Hill chums, my writing workshop buddies and my fellow yogi dancers.

Thank you from the bottom of my heart to the book bloggers and readers who've been so supportive of my work. And to all the young people I've met in my workshops – talking to you and learning all about your hopes and challenges inspired me to write this book. I hope it helps you dare to dream. You have so much to offer the world and the world has so much to offer you – never forget it.

Thank you to Oscar Wilde for providing us with so much wit and wisdom – and for the quote that planted the seed for this book.

And finally, thank YOU for reading *The Moonlight Dreamers*. I hope it's encouraged you to live and dream boldly.

Siobhan Curham is an award-winning author and life coach. Her books for young adults are: *Dear Dylan* (winner of the Young Minds Book Award), *Finding Cherokee Brown*, *Shipwrecked*, *Dark of the Moon* and *True Face*. She loves helping other people achieve their writing dreams through her writing consultancy, Dare to Dream, and she was editorial consultant on Zoe Sugg's international bestseller *Girl Online*. You can find Siobhan online at:

www.siobhancurham.co.uk
Twitter: @SiobhanCurham
Facebook: Siobhan Curham Author

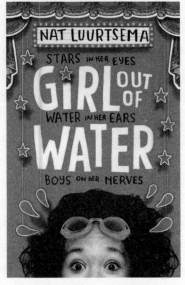

NAT LUURTSEMA

STARS IN HER EYES

GIRL OUT OF

WATER IN HER EARS

WATER

BOYS ON HER NERVES

I am **LOU BROWN**:

SOCIAL OUTCAST,

PRECOCIOUS FAILURE,

5'11" and *STILL GROWING*.

I was on the FAST TRACK
to OLYMPIC SUPER-STARDOM.

Now I'm TRAINING boys
too *COOL* to talk to me.

IN a sport I've just MADE UP.

In a FISH TANK.

My LIFE has GONE WEIRD very Quickly.

#girloutofwater   @natluurtsema